Significant Others

by

Marilyn Baron

This is a work of fiction. Names, characters, places, and incidents are either the product of the author's imagination or are used fictitiously, and any resemblance to actual persons living or dead, business establishments, events, or locales, is entirely coincidental.

Significant Others

Contact Information: info@thewildrosepress.com

Cover Art by *Kim Mendoza*

The Wild Rose Press, Inc.
PO Box 708
Adams Basin, NY 14410-0708
Visit us at www.thewildrosepress.com

Publishing History
First Mainstream Edition, 2013
Print ISBN 978-1-62830-110-6
Digital ISBN 978-1-62830-111-3

Published in the United States of America

Mom still hasn't come to grips with my father's death. Otherwise she wouldn't choose to stay in a two-bedroom condo in Boca when she has a spacious home in Atlanta, one she hasn't stepped foot in since my dad passed away. So I've given her a deadline. I am determined to bring her home by Christmas. But she hardly needs an artificial deadline when a real one is looming. The generous offer she's received from billionaire investor Hammond Reddekker to acquire the family business is set to expire on Christmas Day. No one, not even one of the richest men in the country, is going to swallow up my father's company. So it's up to me to stop the sale and bring my mother back home to Atlanta, where she belongs.

Praise for Marilyn Baron

First Place, Suspense Romance category, 2010 Ignite the Flame Contest of the Central Ohio Fiction Writers chapter of Romance Writers of America;
Finalist, Single Title category, 2005 Georgia Romance Writers Unpublished Maggie Award for Excellence;
First Place, Paranormal/Fantasy category, 2012 Georgia Romance Writers Unpublished Maggie Award for Excellence.

~*~

"Baron offers a bit of everything...There's humor, infidelity, murder, mayhem, and a neatly drawn conclusion." ~*RT Book Reviews (4.5 Stars)*

"Expertly handled relationship...page-turning journey... riveting read." ~*Anna K.*

"Wonderfully witty writing...sharp characterization and...brilliant dialogue...humorous asides and...the quite fantastic twist at the end...left me with a real lump in my throat...highly recommended. Worth more than 5 stars if that were possible." ~*Andrew Kirby*

"Ms. Baron's portrayal of her heroine's thoughts, feelings and actions was spot-on. Five stars! Highly recommended!" ~*Pam Asberry*

"[*UNDER THE MOON GATE*] is a surefire blockbuster…a treasure trove of mystery and intrigue. It sparkles with romance…I couldn't recommend this more." ~*Andrew Kirby*

~*~

Previous Releases with TWRP

UNDER THE MOON GATE

DESTINY: A BERMUDA LOVE STORY

SIXTH SENSE

Dedication

I would like to dedicate this book to my mother,
Lorraine Meyers,
who lives in a retirement community in South Florida
much like Millennium Gardens.
And to my father,
George Meyers,
who was her significant other for 63 years.
Thanks, Dad, for your bomber missions,
which I've incorporated into this story.
And to my wonderful husband,
Steve,
who is *my* significant other.

Acknowledgments

I would like to thank all of my mother's lovely friends for sharing their stories of love and second chances. Thanks also to Jana Feldman Kreisberg, who shared her wonderful stories of the fabulous mother-daughter realtor team (Jana and her mother, Natalie Feldman). And to Claudia Phelps for filling me in on the life of a realtor.

And a special thank you to my wonderful and versatile editor, Nan Swanson, with The Wild Rose Press, Inc., who can edit in any genre and has worked with me on a variety of novels—from historical and romantic thriller to romantic suspense with paranormal elements, and now Women's Fiction.

Chapter One: The Jesus Tree

One Week Before Christmas
Atlanta, Georgia

When my brother Donny called to tell me our mother had seen the image of Jesus in a live oak tree on the golf course behind her retirement condo in Boca Raton, I knew I had to make a pilgrimage to Millennium Gardens to answer her cry for help.

It's not that I'm particularly religious, but there were two major problems with this sighting. One, my mother is Jewish, so she had no business seeing Jesus in a live oak tree or any other place. Two, it was the first anniversary of my father's death and she probably wasn't thinking straight.

For the past year, my mother had managed to avoid making some important decisions about the disposition of Palladino Properties, our family's residential real estate firm in Atlanta. In her grief, Dee Dee Palladino, the other half of our award-winning mother-daughter real estate team, had all but deserted me.

Dad's death not only left a hollow place in my heart, it left a gap in the business that was threatening to become a sinkhole. And my mother's extended absence was aggravating the situation. I'd done my best since the funeral to keep an eye on her. But with my busy schedule, and the fact that I worked and lived in Atlanta and she had taken up residence in Florida, my best didn't even come close to being good enough.

My brother was not doing much better. Donny, who used to play baseball for the Miami Kingfishers, bought the condo at Millennium Gardens in Boca for Mom after Dad died so she could be near her sister, our Aunt Helene, who also lived in The Gardens. He used it as a home away from home when he was in Miami making fan appearances and fulfilling his endorsement obligations.

The trouble was, my mother liked being near Aunt Helene so much that she'd stayed on for the past year, leaving Donny and me to run Palladino Properties alone. And my brother, who had agreed to help me out after Dad died, was not pulling his weight. All the time he spent with my mother was time away from the business, which had put an even greater strain on me and my marriage.

Mom still hadn't come to grips with my father's death. Otherwise she wouldn't have chosen to stay in a two-bedroom condo in Boca when she had a spacious home in Atlanta, one she hadn't stepped foot in since my Dad passed away. I knew she couldn't face that empty house alone. So I'd given her a deadline. I was determined to bring her home by Christmas. I needed her to come back to work at Palladino Properties, and she needed work to take her mind off my father.

But she hardly needed an artificial deadline when a real one was looming. The generous offer she'd received from billionaire investor Hammond Reddekker to acquire the family business was set to expire on Christmas Day.

Suddenly, she'd come to the conclusion—the

wrong conclusion—that she had to sell the business to Hammond Reddekker. Mr. Big-Deal Hammond Reddekker wanted to change the name of my father's company, which meant Palladino Properties would disappear forever. I was determined to make sure my mother walked away from that deal, to preserve my father's name and legacy and guarantee that Donny and I and my daughter, Hannah, who would hopefully join Palladino Properties when she graduated college, would always have a place in the family business.

No one, not even one of the richest men in the country, was going to swallow up my father's company.

If I didn't change my mother's mind, my father's entire life's work would vanish. And for what? A few dollars? Well, actually more than a few *million* dollars, but that would leave nothing tangible behind. Except me. And Hannah. So it was up to me to stop the sale and bring my mother back home to Atlanta, where she belonged.

After making my airline reservation to Ft. Lauderdale, I called my brother to let him know what time my flight would arrive the next day.

My mother wasn't the only one who'd been acting strange lately. My brother had been borderline secretive in the past few months...ever since my father died, really. Stanley Palladino wasn't Donny's biological father, but they had been as close as any father and son could be. Donny was definitely hiding something. Probably something he wasn't telling me about our mother.

"Have you seen the tree?" I asked, biting my bottom lip as I haphazardly stuffed my carry-on bag with some lightweight clothes. It seemed somehow incongruous to watch the gathering winter clouds outside my window when my bedroom was scattered with bathing suits and outfits suitable for the stifling heat of Boca. Who had time for swimming anyway, when there was work to be done?

"Of course I've seen it, Honey," he answered.

"And could you see Him? Jesus, I mean?" I made a final walk-through of my walk-in closet, snagging my favorite silver sandals off the shelf.

"Touchdown Jesus," Donny replied.

"Touchdown Jesus?"

"His hands are in the air in a victory sign."

"You see sports in everything," I said. "It's almost Christmas. We need to have Mom packed and out of Millennium Gardens by then, in time to make the Reynolds closing. Otherwise we'll be celebrating the holidays down in Boca." What was the difference, really? Christmas would be like any other day, even though it *was* my birthday. I had nothing to celebrate this year and neither did my mother. This year didn't even feel like Christmas.

Of course, Christmas in Boca Raton, Florida, was hardly traditional. It never snowed in Boca. There were no ice storms like we had in Atlanta. The only signs that Christmas was in the air were the non-denominational holiday light displays hanging from the lamp posts that lined Boca's wide boulevards. And the reindeer, gaily wrapped gifts, starfish and jellyfish, sand dollars, shells, and stylized stars they depicted couldn't be claimed by any religion.

"When Barbara looked at the tree from a different angle, she thought it looked like Abraham Lincoln," my brother continued.

"Oh," I said, bewildered, not knowing what to make of this troubling new development. Donny's wife Barbara was a high-powered divorce attorney, known and feared in legal circles (and in our family circle) as "Barbara the Barracuda." These were intelligent, practical people, not normally given to flights of fancy.

"Jackson thinks it looks like a rabbit, and the twins see Mr. Potato Head. But it's a definite face."

Eight-year-old Jackson, Donny and Barbara's midlife surprise, and his teenage twin sisters—Hayden and Taylor—were just kids, so who could blame them for imagining they saw Mr. Potato Head or wanting to pull a rabbit out of a hat.

The conversation stalled.

"Donny, what aren't you telling me? Is something wrong with Mom?"

"It depends on what you mean by wrong. She's—"

"She's what?"

"She's getting Bat Mitzvahed."

"Bat Mitzvahed?" I knew I wasn't hearing Donny correctly.

"She's, um, become more religious since Dad died, and, well, she's decided to have a Bat Mitzvah."

"Bat Mitzvahs are for thirteen-year-olds. Hannah had a Bat Mitzvah. Hayden and Taylor had Bat Mitzvahs. Donny, that's crazy. Women in their seventies don't have Bat Mitzvahs."

"Well, she's never had one before, so—"

"Most women her age get facelifts. My mother is getting Bat Mitzvahed?"

"I don't think it's crazy at all," Donny said. "I think it's nice. It's giving her something to do. And she's not the oldest one in her class. There are two men in their eighties and one woman who's 94. But don't tell her I told you. It's supposed to be a surprise."

"I'm surprised, all right. Do I have to buy a Bat Mitzvah dress?"

"If you want, I guess. Barbara's getting a new dress."

I smacked my wrist against my forehead. "It's a good thing I'm coming into town."

A low, vibrating sound rumbled under the bras still stacked on my bed.

"Hey, my BlackBerry® is buzzing. I've got to go. I'm expecting some news on the Lake Lanier listing."

"You're still using a BlackBerry? When are you going to upgrade to an iPhone?"

"No time," I stated.

After we said our goodbyes and I checked my message, I called my mother and broached the subject of the tree, NOT the Bat Mitzvah.

"So, Mom," I began casually, wondering how I would approach her, before I gave up the pretense of delicacy and succumbed to my habit of hurtling right to the point. "Donny says you saw Jesus in a live oak tree on the golf course at Millennium Gardens."

"That's right," she answered, as if seeing Jesus was a normal, everyday occurrence. "I called Mrs. Kane from 401—she's Catholic—and she came down to see it. She couldn't actually see Jesus, but she said it reminded her of the time she saw the Shroud of Turin. Then she turned to me, crossed herself, and whispered, 'Oh, Dee Dee, this is very important. You're blessed.'

"Mrs. Kane thinks I should take a picture and sell it on eBay, like that woman who saw an image of The Virgin Mary on a potato chip, but I want to keep it quiet," my mother whispered into the telephone.

"Well, then maybe you shouldn't have told the town crier," I couldn't help pointing out.

"She promised not to tell anyone."

"Let's hope she doesn't. You shouldn't be spreading this around." *Until you've had a thorough psychiatric workup.*

"Mrs. Rubin in 415 thinks the face in the tree looks more like a bearded rabbi carrying a Torah."

Oh, so it was a non-denominational holy tree.

"Honey, did I mention that two of the tree branches overlap in the shape of a cross?"

"No, I don't think so," I said evenly. The situation was even worse than I thought. My mother was either going to have to convert or be institutionalized.

"If people find out, they're going to be flocking here, especially at Christmastime," my mother added. "I don't want to start a riot or turn Millennium Gardens into a circus."

Too late, Mom, it already is a circus. In case you didn't know, Millennium Gardens got its name from the approximate age of its 15,000 residents. Gardens was really a misnomer. Other than some broad-based palms scattered around the complex like an afterthought, the sparse pink hibiscus bushes and some less spectacular landscaping, the complex seemed more guard-like than garden-like.

Practically every city in South Florida had its own version of Millennium Gardens. When my mother first saw the condo, she referred to the complex as "the barracks" because of its "Early American Army" architecture and the cookie-cutter four-story tan stucco and concrete block structures that stretched into infinity. Since then, she and "the barracks" had come to terms with one another. But it was still a love-hate relationship.

Millennium Gardens was a city within a city. I had to admit it contained just about everything a senior could want, including a medical center, roving ambulances, fire rescue vehicles, and an on-premises pharmacy, which also sold milk and deli sandwiches. It even had places of worship for every flavor of Judaism—Orthodox, Conservative, and Reform.

The entire complex was surrounded by barbed-wire fencing to keep the rest of the world out, with the help of some jovial, uniformed Rastafarians who monitored the gates and patrolled the grounds.

But occasionally some lost souls managed to slip out or, as my mother says, "had to be hauled away." Just yesterday she told me about an elderly couple in a condo at the end of her hall, found curled up in each other's arms in bed. Theirs had been a sweet and peaceful death. They weren't exactly a "couple" in the traditional sense, because they weren't married to each other. But they had made the decision to leave this earth together. Certainly theirs could be considered a "till death do us part" kind of commitment. And speaking of "till death do us part..."

"Mom, do you know what tomorrow is?" I asked tentatively.

"I don't need you to remind me," my mother bristled. "I don't need a calendar. I live with your father's death every day of my life. Of course I know what tomorrow is."

"I just don't want you to be alone," I said.

My mother responded with a wild, shrill laugh.

"Alone? Honey, I *am* alone. I've been alone for 364 days."

"Well, I wanted to be there for you tomorrow, so I'm coming down."

"So come. It's a free country."

"Mom," I pleaded, massaging the spot on my scalp like I do when I'm getting a headache. "I miss him too."

"I know," she answered faintly.

I held the phone tightly while she cried into the mouthpiece and I tried my best not to. The sound of my mother's tears unnerved me.

The BlackBerry was buzzing again. I looked at the message. I needed to call this client back as soon as possible. But my mother might be delusional or, at the very least, confused. I seriously doubt she really saw Jesus in that tree, though she firmly believed she did. I'm convinced Mom just needed something to hang on to. I think the fragility of life was partially responsible for her anxiety and for what she saw—or thought she saw—in that tree on the golf course.

"Fran from down the hall was rushed to the hospital a few days ago. She never came home. It was complications from pneumonia. She had a do-not-resuscitate order."

"Mom, I'm sorry. I know you and Fran were good friends."

"The funeral is tomorrow morning."

"Do you have a ride?"

"Yes."

People were dying all around my mother. Her complex was like a warehouse for the dead. I had to get her out of there.

My mother was obviously trying to tie up loose ends. She was divesting. According to my mother, by the time she entered assisted living, she'd be down to a shoebox, into which would fit all of her possessions. Then another resident would steal the shoebox and she'd have nothing left.

Recently, some of my Mom's friends had traveled that route, that downward path from independent living to assisted living to a nursing home, and from there to hospice and after that, who knew?

She didn't think I knew what she was doing, but even I could see she was planning for the end. She'd passed on her recipes for chicken soup and matzo balls and her challah-egg soufflé to me, and her recipe for potato latkes and split pea soup, which I had dutifully passed on to Hannah.

"Look, Mom, I've got to return a call, but I'll see you tomorrow morning, okay?" I said, my voice faltering.

"Are you flying all the way down here to check up on me, Honey?"

"Not to check up," I assured, sighing. My client was going to have to wait. My mother wasn't finished talking.

"I want to see you, and I'm going to help you pack and move you back to Atlanta," I said. *Where you belong.*

Every time I brought up the subject, she was ready with a handy excuse. "Aunt Helene and I have tickets to the Miami opera." "We want to catch that new gallery opening in South Beach." "There's a great show coming to the clubhouse." "We're going to hear a Japanese choir that sings in Hebrew." "Aunt Helene is still getting over Harold's death. She needs me."

But I knew the truth. My mother needed Aunt Helene more.

"Donny is going to pick me up from the airport," I said. *And yes, I wanted to see this big-deal tree for myself and try to make some sense of a situation that made no sense at all.*

"Have you told anyone else about this—apparition?" I ventured.

"Just Max," she replied. "Max says someone is trying to send me a message."

"Max?" I choked. My father hadn't even been in the ground for a year and she was already quoting another man to me? I stomped down my indignation and managed to sound calm.

"Max who?"

Someone else was beeping in, trying to reach me. I checked the number. It was my assistant, probably with some emergency only I could solve. But my mother was still talking.

"Max Fisher, the widower who lives down the hall in 411," my mother explained. "I told you about him. He was with his significant other, Jean, for six years. But she developed Alzheimer's. He's already booked a seniors' Christmas cruise to the Caribbean, but Jean's in a nursing home now, so she can't go. He was so upset when I talked to him on the phone. He's already paid for the cruise and he's thinking of canceling. I told him not to be so hasty. He won't go alone, and it would be a shame to waste the tickets. He asked me to go with him, and I'm considering it."

My mother paused for emphasis, and then started stuffing words into the gaping silence.

"And why not?" she challenged. "Do you think nobody but your father could be interested in me? You think I haven't had admirers before? Remember my old choir director?"

"Arnold Macovsky? The one with the six kids?" *The one who was too busy making babies with his wife to have time to even look at another woman? That Arnold Macovsky?*

"Exactly. You'll like Max. I want you to meet him."

Wonderful. I can kill two birds with one stone—see Jesus and meet Max.

The BlackBerry was still buzzing, so I knew it had to be important. The office would just have to wait. My mother was still too fragile to be rudely interrupted. *Slow down, Honey Palladino, this is your mother on the phone.*

Taking a deep breath, I tried to focus on the conversation at hand and began the role-reversing task of grilling my mother.

"How well do you know this Max person? Are you two dating?"

"Of course I'm not dating, not this soon after your father," she said defensively. "We've been out to dinner a few times. Sometimes we spend the evening sitting and watching TV. He keeps me company so I don't have to think about your father. When I slip and call him Stanley, he doesn't seem to mind too much. I don't think he hears very well."

"Are you crazy? You can't go on a cruise with another man. I know you aren't going to share a room."

"Private balcony staterooms are very expensive," my mother answered, "especially at Christmas. And the ship is going to some wonderful places—Barbados, St. Lucia, St. Johns, Antigua, St. Maarten and St. Thomas."

"That sounds like a lovely itinerary," I said, stalling for time, drumming my fingers on the end table. "But if you want to go on a cruise, I can take you."

My mother laughed.

"What's so funny?"

"You never have time," she insisted. "A relaxing cruise is just what I need. I can picture myself in perfect peace on my private balcony overlooking the ocean. You can lose yourself in an ocean."

"Private balcony staterooms are one thing," I countered. "But what about privacy?"

"I can always dress in the bathroom. It will be fine."

"But are you going to m-make out with M-Max?" I stammered.

"Make out?"

"Are you going to have sex?" I clarified. *Is that plain enough for you, Mom?*

"Honey, how can you talk to your mother like that?"

"Because I'm concerned about you."

"I'll let you know when I get back."

"Mom, don't you think you're too—I mean, is this appropriate behavior?"

"For a woman my age, you mean?" she shot back. Now I'd insulted her.

"I didn't say that. It's just that I don't know anything about this Max person. For instance, where did you meet him?"

"At my bereavement group."

"Your bereavement group?" I echoed, feeling faint.

I dropped a pair of flip-flops into my suitcase and slumped onto the bed.

"Yes, Aunt Helene told me about it. It's really sort of a social group. That's where everyone at Millennium Gardens meets their significant others."

Significant others? I wondered if I had time to catch an earlier flight. I knew I was being childish, but my father was the only significant other I wanted in my mother's life, even though he was no longer capable of being a significant other, except in the spiritual sense.

But I was hardly qualified to give my mother relationship advice when my own marriage was unraveling. I'd just found out that *my* significant other was cheating on me with a woman who was young enough to be his daughter.

My husband Marc doesn't think I know he's sleeping with his twenty-seven-year-old temp, Trisha. But he isn't exactly subtle. Maybe I am on the wrong side of forty, but I still can't believe he's betraying me. Still, how can I ignore the proof right here in my purse? Pictures don't lie. Husbands do.

When I arrived at the drugstore to pick up photos from our family Thanksgiving dinner, I was blindsided when, along with snaps of the turkey, I found pictures of Trisha that bordered on the pornographic. The only difference between Trisha and the bird was the turkey was dressed and Trisha wasn't.

And that wasn't his only betrayal. I had a feeling he was behind the deal to sell Palladino Properties. As a mergers-and-acquisitions attorney, he was in business to make acquisitions, and somehow he had influenced my mother and was working behind my back to sell our family business. I just didn't know why. So I'll admit I didn't want my mother to give up Palladino Properties, because, right now, the job was all I had. Well, I have Hannah, and my husband Marc, but I don't have him for much longer.

I considered myself a fairly rational person. But right now what I needed (besides a divorce attorney and a stiff drink) was a priest to help me unravel the mystery of what my mother saw or didn't see in the Jesus tree, and why. Where am I going to get one of those? I could call my rabbi, but she was going through her own divorce. My mother went to high school with a priest in Pittsburgh. *Before* he became a priest. And they were still in touch. Maybe I should call Father Dominick DeFazio.

"You think I'm crazy, don't you?" my mother asked quietly.

"I'm reserving judgment," I muttered, silently ticking off the dozens of tasks that had to be accomplished before my flight—the closings in progress, walkthroughs, appointments with inspectors, and a meeting with my assistant to make sure he monitored my listings, which currently ranged from a $260,000 condo in Decatur to a $3 million mansion on Tuxedo Road. Just an average day on the roller coaster that had become my life since my dad died and my mom dropped out of the picture.

Time was running out for my mother in Boca. Time was also running out for my marriage. I hadn't had the opportunity to confront Marc about his lies because I didn't have the time, but I was determined to have a showdown. I'd even marked it on my calendar. Christmas Day. There are no closings on Christmas Day. That was going to be our D-Day. "D" as in divorce.

I was planning to talk to Donny's wife about it at dinner tomorrow night. Marc was a lawyer, so he thought he had the advantage, but he hadn't counted on my secret weapon—Barbara the Barracuda, and right now a barracuda was exactly what I needed.

Or maybe what I really needed was a vision of my own, a vision of hope, of a new beginning, rather than the bleak prospect of an unhappy ending. Maybe my mother wasn't so crazy after all. I wondered what I'd see when I finally came face-to-face with the Jesus tree.

Chapter Two: The Shrine

Boca Raton, Florida

Leaving the Ft. Lauderdale airport, Donny drove me to his condo and used his key to unlock the front door. He moved my luggage into the guest room.

"I set up the scanner in your bedroom so it wouldn't disturb Mom," Donny said. "She, um, sleeps a lot." He looked deflated.

"Thanks, Donny," I replied.

"Honey? I thought I heard voices. I'm so glad you're here." Dee Dee smiled as she came out of her bedroom to greet us.

I folded the Bat Mitzvah Mom into my arms. Had she shrunk since the last time I'd seen her? Were those new lines under her eyes? Age spots on her hands that hadn't been there before?

Getting old bites, as Hannah liked to say. I never seriously thought it would happen to me. But it was happening, and without my permission. Even my hands with their ropy veins were beginning to resemble my mother's. My best friend Vicky and I had already found a few age spots of our own. We called them our Chef's Special Brown Spots, like the signature Chef's Special Brown Sauce they served in our favorite Chinese restaurant. Maybe Marc was trying to hang on to his youth by hanging on to his youthful temp. That actually made sense in a bizarre kind of way. I just wished he'd realize I'm not thrilled about growing old, either, and maybe we could help each other negotiate the minefield of aging.

I should never have let my mother out of my sight. The memory of her swaying over my father's grave still haunts me. If Donny hadn't caught her, I think she would have fallen—no, she was definitely about to jump—into the hole of freshly turned dirt to join her husband.

I took her small, shapely hands into mine and rubbed my fingers against her wedding ring. She still wasn't ready to let my dad go, to break the bond between them. Even though it breaks my heart, I had to admit it made me feel secure that she hadn't forgotten my father. It was also another reminder that my mother had a better relationship with her dear departed husband than I did with my live, lying one, and that her marriage—even beyond the grave—was in better shape than mine.

My mother had been heavily involved in the negotiations with Hammond Reddekker, but lately her focus hadn't been on business and her heart hadn't been in the acquisition talks. Her recent pronouncement that she was going to pull out of the company completely was not entirely unexpected. The final decision was hers, but right now Palladino Properties was my life and I didn't know what I'd do without it. Maybe that was selfish, but that was how I felt.

While my mother walked into the kitchen to fix us lunch, Donny approached me about the buyout.

"Not now," I cautioned. "We just got here. We can talk about that later."

Donny grumbled.

As I surveyed the living room in disbelief, he announced proudly, “So, sis, how do you like the changes I’ve made to the place?”

“You’ve redecorated,” I noted, rubbing my fingers against my jaw and across my mouth, trying not to register my shock. “It’s very...retro,” I said charitably.

Taking my remark as a compliment, Donny smiled one of those big goofy smiles that lit up his green eyes and his entire face, while I continued to look around the darkness in confusion.

Walking into the living room of my mother’s condo was like walking back in time. The blinds were closed and the lights were dimmed, except for strategically placed spotlights designed to enhance the vintage photos on the wall. It was obvious my mother didn’t really “live” here. She just existed. The atmosphere was as sterile as a museum. I wondered if I needed a ticket for admission.

“Is this supposed to be some kind of a shrine?” I asked in the hushed tones that the room demanded, thinking that maybe it was something like the Elvis shrine Mrs. Shelby down the hall had in her spare bedroom. “Did you do all this for *your* dad?”

Okay, now it was official. Both my mother and my brother were skating on the edge of sanity. And it was my job to pull them back from the brink. Work was the perfect prescription. It was the only way to help them get over the pain of losing a husband and a father. It was the way I planned to cope with a marriage that had turned to mush. If I could convince my mother *not* to sign my father’s company away.

“Yeah, and I already know what you’re going to

say," Donny blustered. "*Stanley Palladino* was my dad."

"I wasn't going to say that." I frowned; however, I *was* thinking it. It was still spooky how well my brother could read me.

Donny had obviously set the place up as a memorial to honor his *real* father, a World War II flyer who was shot down in a bombing mission over Europe. Donny never knew his real dad. The only remnant of him was an out-of-focus and now faded picture—the only picture Mom had of him. Donny had set it up on the sideboard on a lace runner, in a place of honor, next to his team picture of the Kingfishers, his wedding picture, a photo of Barbara and the children, and a high school graduation shot of Hannah that Marc had taken. That was the only trace of my husband in this condo. Which was appropriate, because I was trying to erase all traces of him from my life. But I'd been in love with my husband for twenty years, so it was hard to break the habit, even for a serious indiscretion.

I circled the room. It was a throwback to the '40s. Donny was obsessed with World War II, and it showed in the way the place was decorated.

"Is this what you've been doing down here the last few months?" I asked in disbelief, thinking of all the time he had wasted.

"These are great books, huh?" Donny said, hefting a particularly bulky volume from the coffee table and placing it gingerly into my hands. He indicated several other books with World War II themes displayed around the room, as well as a wealth of wartime memorabilia hanging on the walls.

"Look here," he said eagerly, picking up each book

in turn. "*The World at War 1939-45; Bombers: the Aircrew Experience;* and *Bomber Missions: Aviation Art of World War II.* You wouldn't believe what I had to go through to get these. Go ahead, don't be afraid to handle them."

Flipping through some of the pages of the book in my hand, in an effort to humor my brother, I glanced at color photos of Superfortresses, pin-ups painted on the planes, and personalized jacket art worn by fearless young men dressed in leather flying jackets with fur collars to ward off the cold in the cockpit. My eyes skimmed the words—"dangerous missions," "strategic targets," "intrepid bomber pilots." I tried to muster up some excitement because these books meant something to my brother, but they were echoes of a past I wasn't part of and couldn't relate to.

I returned the book to Donny, who pressed the button on a wall panel that sent soft background music from the 1940s spilling into the living room.

"I've piped the music into every room in the house," Donny announced proudly. Apparently you couldn't even go to the bathroom unaccompanied by the big band sound.

My mother and Donny's father met at a USO dance at a women's club in Pittsburgh during the war, and Donny was obviously trying to recreate those happy memories.

"Your father was very handsome in his uniform," my mother used to say, when Donny asked about his dad, which was often. "He was an exceptional dancer. He had the most gorgeous green eyes. You have his eyes." But Mom didn't have much else to tell about their compatibility off the dance floor. They danced to all the greats—Glenn Miller, Artie Shaw, Tommy Dorsey. The romance lasted for several months. They fell hopelessly in love. He went off to war and got himself killed. End of story.

When Donny asked to see their love letters, so he'd have a tangible record of his parents' history and get a better mental picture of his father, she told him they must have gotten lost after all those years.

Looking around the condo gave me the creeps, because I didn't think now was the time for my mother to be dwelling on painful memories of her first dead love while she was still recovering from her grief over her second one.

But how could I be critical when I had a lifetime of memories with my dad, and Donny didn't even have one real memory to cling to. So he'd created his own memories in a cramped condo in Millennium Gardens.

"Stanley Palladino was a good dad," I said, feeling the need to defend my father, especially now that he was gone. Why hadn't he been enough for my brother?

"You don't have to tell me," Donny said, "but he wasn't my *real* dad." Donny lowered his voice so our mother wouldn't overhear. He had heard the story; we both had, more times than we can count.

My dad adopted Donny and gave him his name when he married my mother. She and her baby boy were making a new life for themselves when they moved from Pittsburgh with my grandmother and Mom's younger sister—my Aunt Helene—to Atlanta, where she took a job as a typist at my dad's real estate agency. She worked herself up to agent, and after a couple of years of courting, she agreed to marry him. The rest, as my dad used to say, was history. My birth was part of their history.

"Your mother was the most beautiful woman I'd ever seen," Stanley Palladino was fond of saying when he told the story of their romance. "She was prettier than any model on the pages of a fashion magazine. She refused to marry me so many times I stopped counting, but I never stopped asking. Then one day when I arrived at her apartment for dinner, little Donny greeted me at the door and said his first words, 'Da Da.' Your mother burst into tears. I'll never forget that night. I caught her at her weakest point and closed the sale," Stanley grinned. "She finally said yes. Of course, I'd been carrying the ring around in my pocket for more than a year. Let that be a lesson to you, Honey," he used to say, tapping a long finger to my nose. "Persistence pays."

Speaking of my nose, sometimes I think Donny is lucky. Maybe it would have been nice to have been adopted. It would be handy to have a non-existent parent where I could lay the blame for my physical flaws. This nose? It must have come from my *real* father. Stanley Palladino's nose looked just fine on Stanley Palladino, but on me, it was a different story. And there was absolutely no way to get past my fat ass, literally or figuratively. That big butt? Right again. My *real* mother.

Actually, I got my tendency for substantial hips from Grandma Lewis, my mother's mother. Probably as a result of the eight years she lived with us and admonished Donny, Helene, and me to "eat everything on your plate because the children in Europe are starving." Grandma Lewis must have been the founding member of the clean plate club. I'd spent most of my adult life fighting the Lewis genes so I could fit into my own jeans. Thank God for Talbots® Woman. Other than Mom, I didn't really know where Donny's genes originated. But Donny was pretty much perfect in my eyes and owed no apologies to anyone. Everyone adored Donny, and I got to bask in the glow of that adoration, so I couldn't complain. Even though it was obvious everyone preferred Donny.

I picked up a picture of Donny and my dad that sat on the pass-through between the kitchen and the living room. Donny was probably eight years old when that picture was taken, dressed in a dirty Little League uniform, with smudges all over his face. It was taken right after his team had won the championship game and my dad was beaming into the camera, bursting with fatherly pride.

Stanley Palladino was thrilled to have a son. He took Donny to Little League, taught him how to throw a ball, went to all his high school baseball games, and was as proud as any father when Donny, the hottest prospect in the country, was recruited by the coach of one of the top SEC East teams and later as a pitcher for his first major league team. But as much as Donny loved Stanley Palladino, I knew that my brother still secretly longed for his own father, even after all these years. Donny was a grown man, but he couldn't stop searching for clues and connections, no matter how tenuous, to a man he never knew.

Stanley Palladino's death forced him to lose a father all over again. After mourning my father, he turned to his past with a vengeance and became obsessed with finding out all he could about his real father. Did I think it strange that my brother redecorated his condo to recapture memories of his father after all these years? Yes. Might I have gone to the same lengths to preserve my heritage if our situations had been reversed? Quite possibly.

"You still miss him a lot, don't you?" Donny asked. "So do I." The sadness was still fresh for both of us, even a year later, I thought, as I wiped the tears from my face, blurring the moisture I saw sparkling in Donny's eyes. I guess my mother wasn't the only one affected by the anniversary of my father's death. Stanley Palladino had not been a big man in stature, but his presence in our world had loomed larger than life.

Donny took the picture from my hand and placed the silver filigreed frame back on the granite countertop.

"Hey, we'd better not let Mom see us like this," Donny whispered. "I don't want her falling apart again."

Donny was a strapper, probably the biggest baseball player in history; so big, in fact, he could have played defensive football. He reminded me of a big stuffed bear I once saw at the Museum of Natural History in Miami. But Donny was not all brawn. He was also sensitive and very smart. Not many people knew that about my brother. Donny didn't just slide through college on a baseball scholarship. He majored in botany, and his favorite pastime was puttering in his garden in Atlanta and ensuring that Jackson and his girls drank in everything he could teach them about tending indigenous plants.

No one would have guessed that "The Slugger" grew tomatoes, green peppers, and cantaloupe in a compost heap behind his backyard. And no one would have suspected that beneath that bulk beat a soft, sensitive, and generous heart. I wished I could patch that gaping hole left by the loss of his real father, but I couldn't. No one could.

Donny walked over to the couch and began turning the pages of another one of the World War II picture books.

"My dad was a hero," Donny stated, "like the guys in this book. Do you think he would have been proud of me? I hope I've made him proud. I'm the only thing left of him in this world, except my kids."

"Oh, Donny," I sighed, facing him. "How could you not? You're the best person I know. Whoever had a hand in making you must have been pretty great. He certainly did something right."

"Then why did he have to die?" Donny bit his lip, and I could tell he was close to tears again. He tried to blink them away. At that moment, he looked as young and vulnerable as that eight-year-old in the photograph.

"I wish I could answer that."

"And how come Mom never wants to talk about him?"

"I guess it's too painful to love someone and lose them like that," I answered quietly.

"I always thought that if I asked her it would seem disrespectful to Stan—to our dad—I mean. Now that he's been gone for a year, I have some questions."

"I'm not sure now's the right time," I cautioned, indicating with a slight turn of my head that my mother was within earshot—right in the next room.

"Questions only Mom can answer," Donny persisted. "I wish I could have known him. I wish he could have known my children. Do you think they—the ones who've passed on—can see what's going on down here?" And now I knew he was talking about both dads.

That question was easier to answer. I talked to my dad, my dead dad, all the time, in my mind. His presence was tangible. I felt him looking down on me, watching out for me, watching over me, from wherever he was. I guessed Heaven. Heaven would be lucky to get a good man like Stanley Palladino. I didn't think that made me crazy. It would have made me crazy if I couldn't have reached out to him. I still asked his advice, and I thought I heard him answer.

"I believe that," I assured my brother. Inevitably, my thoughts drifted back to what my father would have wanted me to do about the sale of Palladino Properties. It was hardly the right time, but someone had to confront the elephant in the room. It was a topic I knew was on both of our minds.

"Do you think Mom is really going to sell the company?" I asked, motioning for Donny to follow me into the guest bedroom, out of hearing range.

"She has her mind made up. It's really too good an offer to pass up, don't you think?" Donny reasoned, walking behind me and closing the bedroom door.

"But is it what Dad would have wanted?" I asked.

"Probably not. But Mom's plan was for them to sell the company so she and Dad could retire, travel, take time to live life. She didn't expect him to die. But Mom thinks that's still what Dad would have wanted. It's not what we want, but we have to respect her wishes. It's her decision."

"Dad would have wanted her to move on with her life, to find happiness again, but she's not ready. And I don't think she's ready to make any decisions about the business, either," I insisted.

"I think she'll come around, once we get her back to Atlanta," Donny said. "Look, I'm heading back to the hotel to see Barbara and the kids. I'll say goodbye to Mom and apologize because I can't stay for lunch. I promised I'd take the kids swimming. Let Mom know we're taking her out to dinner at her favorite place. I made reservations at The Addison for seven o'clock tonight. Meanwhile, you talk to her about the possibility of a merger. She listens to you."

After Donny left, I walked into the living room and found my mother sitting in the dark on a yellow chintz couch.

"Hey, Mom, let's let some light into this place," I suggested gently, walking toward the sliding glass doors and pulling up the honeycomb shades.

"The light hurts my eyes," Dee Dee said, holding up her hands in front of her face. Seeing my vital, vibrant mother like this was so unbearable, I thought I was going to cry, and I couldn't cry in front of my mother. I was supposed to be supporting her. I'd left her alone way too long. She needed me and I needed her. But I wasn't about to dump my marital problems on my mother when she didn't even have a husband anymore.

I turned around.

"Honey, don't step on the fringe," she warned as I approached the Oriental carpet. "I just combed it."

"You comb the fringe on the Oriental carpet? Since when?"

"It gives me something to do."

The situation with my mother was much worse than I'd ever imagined.

The wall phone in the kitchen rang. I walked over

to answer it.

"Yes, this is the Palladino residence. Who's calling? She did? Well, thank you so much for letting us know. Just leave it at the Service Desk, and we'll be by later this afternoon to pick it up. I appreciate it."

"Who was that?" Dee Dee asked from the club chair.

"A woman calling from Sam's Club. Apparently you left your wallet at the register yesterday, and she turned it in to the manager."

"Oh," said my mother, her face twisting in an embarrassed frown. "I was shopping for your visit, and I had to get out my ID at the checkout, and, well, I—"

"Don't worry. We'll go over and pick it up after lunch," I said smoothly, adding, "Does this happen a lot?"

"It's happened before. I...sometimes forget things."

"We all do," I said, not wanting to sound critical.

"You won't mention this to Donny, will you? He hovers enough already. I don't want him to think..."

"It will just be between us," I assured her.

"I wish you had brought Hannah." Dee Dee sighed.

"Hannah has finals," I said. "Then she's going to Aruba with her friend's family for Christmas break." *The only way I'd get Hannah here would be to tell her that Grandma Dee Dee had seen Channing Tatum's face on that live oak tree.*

I could really use my daughter's support now, and I'd really love to see her, but I'm not ready to tell her what is happening between her father and me.

"I know you're anxious to see the tree," my mother said.

"If you want to show it to me, after lunch," I

answered evenly, like I wasn't chomping at the bit to get down to the golf course. But I needed to stop eating so much or those Lewis hips would come roaring back.

"Actually, you can see it from here," Dee Dee said, "if you stand out on the screened-in patio."

I followed my mother out to the tiled patio and opened the sliders that overlooked the golf course, offering a scenic view of the lake. The birds were chattering madly and they seemed to be mocking me. Even the birds were louder in Boca. Apparently it was mating season all year round here. There was a foursome playing under the window and golf carts traversed the green in the distance. I guess these people are retired and don't have to—or don't want to—work anymore. I squeezed around the glass coffee table and the padded lounge chair to get a better view.

"Most of the trees were uprooted in the last hurricane," my mother explained, straightening the cushions on the chair, her hands fluttering nervously across the leaves of one of the potted plants. "I can't even remember the name of the storm. We were at the end of the Greek letters, I think. Half of those trees were damaged by lightning. I remember the night the lightning hit this particular tree. There was a big flash, and the boom shook the whole building. It sounded like the earth was coming to an end. It nearly scared me to death. And when I looked outside, I saw smoke and the tree was on fire. The rain finally put it out, but the lightning bolt had stripped the bark completely off the tree. The trees that weren't hit by lightning lost a lot of foliage. My Jesus tree was one of the only ones left standing. It's almost completely denuded. The leaves are beginning to grow back, and I'm afraid they will hide His face."

From this vantage point I could see uprooted trees scattered around the golf course. No one had come to collect them after the storm. There was a lone, leafless live oak tree directly in the path of my mother's line of sight. The bottom of the tree was charred. The top branch was thick and pure chalk-white. But I couldn't really see much from where I was standing.

"You can see it better if we go downstairs," my mother suggested.

So we took the elevator four stories down and walked behind her building onto the golf course.

"Watch out for these dead branches," I cautioned, taking hold of my mother's hand to help her negotiate around the uprooted trees. "I don't want you to fall." When older people fell, it was the beginning of the end. Their brittle bones never healed. Then they had to be put into a home. And before you knew it, they were gone.

I'd already lost my father. I couldn't stand the thought of losing my mother, too. She wasn't just my parent. She was more of a friend. Working together builds that kind of closeness. At least it used to. Some phone calls between us were strictly mother-daughter. Some were business-related. Some calls were more informational. Some were, "Why didn't you call me?" She was a wonderful mentor and a great role model. I imitated everything she did. How many people got to spend working daylight hours with their mothers? It was pretty special. I hoped to repeat that experience with my own daughter, when Hannah came to work at Palladino Properties after she graduated. If there still was a Palladino Properties.

I had so much to pass on to Hannah, lessons that Dad and Mother taught me. Lessons about honesty and integrity and ensuring that our clients come first. My mother treated every client like she was *their* mother, and she took care of them like she'd always taken care of me. Now it was my turn to take care of her.

When I moved closer to the live oak, the sunlight filtered through the tree to warm my face, and I was surprised to find a figure etched into the bark.

"It looks like John F. Kennedy," I said in awe, squinting as I looked up.

"No, it's definitely Jesus," my mother stated, pointing. "It's there as plain as day. Can't you see those two branches forming his outstretched arms? I know it's strange for a Jewish woman to see Jesus on a tree, but I know what I see."

I took a deep breath and tilted my head this way and that, circling the tree, approaching it from various angles.

"I don't see it," I apologized. "I mean I see a face, but..."

"Then maybe you weren't meant to see it," my mother snapped abruptly as she turned and stomped back to the condo.

Chapter Three: Swimming with the Sharks, or, Who's Stirring the Pasta?

"I'm starving," I announced to Donny and Barbara.

"Well, tonight is your night," Donny said.

"Every night is my night," I interrupted with a smirk.

"Where do you want to eat? There's a nice Cuban restaurant we just discovered, but it's pretty far away. Or there's a closer place with authentic Italian cuisine. The chef is from Naples."

"I'm in the mood for Italian."

"You're always in the mood for Italian." Donny laughed. "I don't know why I even suggest other options."

"It's too bad your mother couldn't make it," Barbara said. "She claims she was too tired."

"She's always too tired," Donny complained. "We'll take her to The Addison tomorrow night. And anyway, I think we need this time to talk alone."

"I agree."

The hostess at Café di Napoli made the appropriate, expected fuss over The Slugger. Her eyes never left Donny's as she nearly tripped over herself leading us to our table. Of course Donny took the time to autograph a menu with a special message to her son. I wondered whether the woman's son would ever see Donny's signature. Or if she even had a son.

The hostess was reacting the same way all women reacted around my brother—either they were tongue-tied or their tongues were hanging out, panting. I am used to women giggling, gawking and gaping at, even groping, my brother in public. Whenever I take Donny on an appointment with a client, the wife inevitably spends more time leering at Donny than looking at the house and the husband is so star-struck talking sports with The Slugger that they literally trip over each other to sign the contract.

Apparently the chef's head had been stuck in the manicotti for the past thirty years, because he had no idea who Donny Palladino was. Nevertheless, he was properly solicitous.

"We have a lovely simmered octopus," announced Chef Ricardo, after Donny, Barbara, and I were comfortably seated at a cozy table. "It looks scary, but it's really wonderful. And you should try the lasagna, just like my mama makes it in Napoli." He gestured with his hands, smacking his lips lightly with an air kiss.

I took my food seriously, so it was a little disconcerting to see the chef out here talking to us when he should be back in the kitchen stirring the pasta. It reminded me of the pilot who walked the aisles making small talk with the passengers when he should be flying the plane.

In the middle of the chef's presentation, Donny's cell phone rang incessantly and my BlackBerry didn't stop burping. My daughter Hannah called the sound "making raspberries." Marc called my BlackBerry by the more popular term, a CrackBerry, because he thought I was addicted to it. Maybe he was right. But the BlackBerry was my lifeline. Like Donny, he also urged me to get one of the new iPhones, but I wouldn't give up my BlackBerry.

"What wine do you suggest?" I asked Ricardo. "Or maybe I won't have wine tonight."

"A woman without wine is like a flower without water," Ricardo gushed.

Jeesh! What a flatterer. But he *was* really cute. I wondered what he thought of my trim new butt. I was starting to notice other men now. I had to, in my current situation. I had to start putting myself out there.

"Let's try an appetizer," I suggested. "How about fried calamari?"

"We don't deep fry anything here," Ricardo admonished, as he reviewed the list of antipasti. "Our *Frittura di Calamari* is flour-dusted, only lightly fried, and served with marinara."

"That sounds great," Donny said. "We'll start with that."

"We have two entrée specials tonight," the chef continued. "Our *Prosciutto e Mozzarella* with imported buffalo mozzarella and *Parma Prosciutto*. It's in the shape of the Leaning Tower of Pisa. Or our *Pasta Tri Coloré*—homemade ravioli covered with tomato sauce, pesto sauce, and a seafood sauce, in red, green and white, arranged on the plate like the Italian flag."

I rolled my eyes and ordered the *Linguine Al Frutti di Mare*—a mix of seasonal shellfish, sautéed with extra virgin olive oil, garlic, white wine, and cherry tomatoes, served on a bed of linguine. Donny and Barbara both ordered the *Brodetto Di Pesce* with shrimp, scallops, calamari, clams, and mussels, poached in their own broth, with a touch of marinara served on the pasta of the day—Ricardo's favorite. They always ordered the same thing because they were so in sync.

Even before the meal arrived, I was seriously studying the dessert menu. Since I discovered that my husband prefers women with big asses, I'd decided to quit this ridiculous diet I'd been on. I lost a ton of weight so he'd like me more, and now he thought I was too bony.

The slimming-down process didn't happen overnight, either. For weeks I carved time out of my hectic schedule to go to the gym, and forced my best friend Vicky to sweat along with me. I even cut down on potatoes and their evil spawn, potato chips. The trouble with diets was you had to exercise restraint, and I hated to exercise. In the end, the result of my dedication and deprivation was a trim new butt. But by then my butt was no longer of interest to my husband.

Since I no longer had to worry about what Marc thought of my butt, I considered the Tiramisu for dessert. Or maybe something else from the *Dolce* menu—*Torta Caprese, Crème Caramella, Panna Cotta, Cannoli,* or maybe a sampling of all five of them.

If Mom decided to sell the agency, I wouldn't even be able to snag a job as one of those double-wide Wal-Mart greeters, not without the Lewis hips.

But hey, if men liked younger women, I should be able to do pretty well at Millennium Gardens—a classy, forty-something chick like me with a trim new butt. And, I could drive at night. Apparently, that was a big commodity around there.

The trouble was, I didn't want another man.

After the chef retired to the kitchen, where he

belonged, Donny and I returned some calls.

"We got the listing on the Neel Reid house on West Paces Ferry, and that great country French estate home in Roswell," I reported. "Oh, and there's finally some interest in the high-rise condominium in Midtown. And bad news, one of our clients has found some termite damage in the garage. I need to call someone to have it checked out."

"Well, on the bright side, we finally closed on that European traditional in Buckhead," Donny said. "But the two closings on our Country Club of the South listings had to be postponed because of the weather. Supposedly Atlanta is expecting a major ice storm. I rescheduled the closings for after New Year's."

"My personal assistant says the Hightowers are still wavering on that English Tudor in Ansley Park," I added.

"They're the kind who like to kick the tires," Donny observed. "After all, the house was built in the early 1900s. I think they're waiting for one of us to come back to Atlanta. The property is pretty pricey. They need some hand-holding."

"I think Mrs. Hightower wants to do more than just hold your hand," I suggested. "You know, if this sale doesn't go through and we get Reddekker and Mom to agree to a merger, I want us to expand into the Northwest Florida and South Florida markets, pick up some properties on the Gulf and the Atlantic."

"All those plans go out the window if Mom sells," Donny pointed out.

"The desirable waterfront properties in Florida will complement our portfolio on the Georgia Coast. Atlanta has the Chattahoochee River and Lake Lanier, but we're too landlocked. Hey, while we're here, why don't we scout out some of these oceanfront properties, maybe snag some new listings? We're letting our Florida licenses go to waste."

"Great idea," Donny agreed, "but we *are* on vacation."

"You know there is no such word in our business, Donny. I can't remember the last time I had a real vacation. Let me just make this one call to Mrs. Martin." I dialed the number, but she wasn't home, so I left a message.

"Grace. It's Honey Palladino. Just wanted to let you know that we had two showings on your house yesterday, but two of the buyers decided they wanted to live in Dunwoody. Third time's the charm apparently. We've got a loan approval letter on the third prospect. They're good buyers, so start packing and stop worrying."

"Our condo at Atlantic Station is attracting a lot of interest," Donny noted, dipping a piece of crusty bread into the plate of olive oil the server had just put on the table, after which she accidentally/on purpose pressed his hand. I guess she's also a Donny Palladino fan. Barbara glared. I started work on my second piece of bread.

The server brought out the calamari, and I picked out all the crispy, squiggly pieces and put them on my plate.

"Glad to see you eating again, sis," Donny observed.

"Glad to be eating again. This is my coming-out party. Now what were you saying about Atlantic Station?"

"That's a hot area, but condos have been overbuilt in Atlanta," Donny explained, with a nod to Barbara. "But the inventory levels are dropping. The biggest problem we have is the traffic. The city has no natural boundaries. If people are willing to drive and commute an hour to get to a new house in the suburbs, they're going to do it. But some people are so sick of the commute, they're moving back in to the city even for an older house, even though they have to downsize."

"There's certainly more optimism out there in the housing market," I echoed. "With interest rates about to rise, people want to lock in lower rates. The economy is beginning to recover and housing is rebounding strongly."

"Which is why Reddekker wants to acquire us," Donny pointed out.

"Okay, you two, that's enough," Barbara interrupted, delivering a verbal hand-slapping. "Why don't you put away your toys?" My sister-in-law didn't like being left out, and she hadn't been able to get two words in edgewise since we sat down at the table. Maybe she was mad that I stuck her with the round, rubbery pieces of squid.

"That's enough about Palladino Properties," Barbara scolded. "When you're with family, you should be fully engaged." Donny shot his wife an apologetic look, flashing his irresistible smile and crinkling his killer green eyes.

"Oh, talk about family, that reminds me, sis, I forgot to tell you what my Little Slugger did the other day," Donny said.

"What?" I asked, smiling, eager to hear about the latest antics of my beloved nephew, who was a major trickster.

"He went on a field trip with his class to the Georgia Aquarium, and you know how they don't allow backpacks for security reasons? Well, Jackson started pitching a fit when they tried to take his backpack away."

"Jackson has separation issues," Barbara interjected.

"So they made an exception," Donny continued. "That night when Barbara checked to see how he was doing on his bath, she heard him talking to someone and she found a baby penguin splashing around in the tub with Jackson."

"Seriously?" I asked.

"He had hidden the little fellow in his backpack when no one was looking," Donny said.

"What did you do?" I asked, wide-eyed.

"Well, I called the Georgia Aquarium," Barbara said. "What else could I do? I told Jackson that the baby penguin missed his mother and all his friends, and then I bought a family pass to the Georgia Aquarium so we could go back and visit as often as he wants."

"Isn't that the cutest thing?" Donny said, smiling. "That's my boy."

With Palladino Properties business and Jackson's penguin-napping episode behind us, I cleared my throat and tried to work up the nerve to talk about more personal matters.

"Barbara, Donny, actually there's something I've got to tell you."

Donny looked concerned. Barbara looked like she would explode if she heard any more talk about Palladino Properties.

"I want to divorce Marc," I announced abruptly.

Donny didn't look surprised. Barbara perked up. Now I had Madame Divorce Attorney's undivided attention.

"What did that bastard do to you?" Donny growled. Donny had a quick temper that blew itself out as rapidly as it came on, like a fast-moving hurricane. He must have inherited that temperament from his real dad, because our mom never even raised her voice to us and *my* dad, Stanley Palladino, was as gentle as a St. Bernard. Donny's inclination was to throw a punch first and ask questions later, especially when defending his family and friends. And he didn't consider my husband one of his friends.

I laughed, gratified that my brother was leaping to my defense and taking my side before he even heard the story.

"It's not what he did to me," I pointed out. "It's what he's doing with his temp, Trisha."

"I knew it," my brother fumed. "I never liked your husband. He thinks he's better than the rest of us. Can't ever be one of the guys. What happened to his regular secretary?"

"She's out on maternity leave."

"Wait a minute. I think I saw this chick Trisha in Marc's office the other day when I dropped by and asked him to deliver a contract to you. What does he see in her? She ought to wear a sign on her butt that says Wide Load Coming Through."

"Apparently Marc has developed a taste for big butts," I said.

"Nothing wrong with your butt," Donny observed.

"Thank you," I said as we high-fived each other

like boisterous children. Barbara rolled her eyes.

"How long has he been cheating on you?" she asked sympathetically, patting my hand and affecting her most concerned attorney-client demeanor.

I shrugged. "Who knows? But it galls me every time I have to go through that smug little twit to speak to my own husband at work."

"You know Trisha probably deserves half the blame," Barbara said. "You have no idea how many women are after my husband. And they're not even subtle about it. That's why I have to travel with him. Every woman who approaches Donny is on the prowl. I have my hands full peeling women off him."

"Barbara, you know that's not true," Donny objected innocently.

I had to laugh because it *was* true. The same thing happened to me whenever Donny and I went anywhere together. While Donny is not exactly handsome in the classic sense, his particular combination of rugged features exudes sex appeal and seems to be irresistible to most women. There hasn't been a package like Donny's since the days of Joe Namath. Or Russell Crowe. I could go on.

"But I know your brother would never cheat on me, because I'd cut him off at the knees," Barbara smiled sweetly as she sliced her sharp knife cleanly through the fresh bread the server had just brought to the table.

Barbara was tiny but fierce, and everyone in the family, including me, was a little afraid of her. Actually, Barbara reminded me less of a barracuda than of a type of fish I'd recently seen at the Georgia Aquarium, called the Rosy Wrasse. Apparently, wrasses all begin life as females, but dominant females eventually change sex and become male. Barbara Palladino was a dominant female, but Donny was devoted to her. And she adored him. I knew the real reason she traveled with my brother was because she wanted to keep her family close and she couldn't stand being away from him. I could have learned a lesson from Barbara. She was as busy as I was yet somehow she managed to create a stable marriage and a happy home, a home her husband was anxious to return to. Beneath all that brashness, maybe the barracuda was really just a guppy.

"How did you find out?" the Barracuda/Rosy Wrasse/Guppy asked quietly.

I proceeded to tell them about the Thanksgiving pictures.

"I also know of at least one overnight trip they took together," I noted.

"Good." Barbara nodded.

"Barb, how can you say that?" Donny protested

"It means he's sloppy. Most men are so arrogant they never think they'll get caught, so they make stupid mistakes. Women, on the other hand, wives and mothers, will do anything in their power to believe their husbands have not been unfaithful. Do you have any proof besides the photos?"

"Well, a few weeks ago he told me he was going to a firm retreat in New York. When I mentioned it to Vicky, whose husband is a partner at Marc's law firm, she told me the firm retreat was in California. So I know he was lying. I called the office and Trisha wasn't there either."

Do you have any other evidence?"

"Evidence?"

"Yes, you need to go through his credit card receipts, look through his pockets, his wallet, his desk, even his dirty laundry, to learn all you can about his dirty dealings. Find any suspicious-looking bills for extravagant dinners, out-of-the-way hotels, personal gifts, things like that."

"I think I should move out of the house," I said. "I can't stand the thought of being around him, knowing he's cheating with another woman. And now Hannah isn't coming home for Christmas break. She's going with her friend's parents to their time-share in Aruba. I know it's because she senses the tension between us."

"Moving out would be a mistake," Barbara advised. "Georgia is an equitable distribution state, which means that all marital property acquired during the marriage is subject to division. You own half that house and you need to stand your ground, no matter how uncomfortable things become. You have to act like nothing's happened, so he doesn't become suspicious. If he tries to sweet talk you into bed, make excuses; you have a headache, it's your time of the month. Lock the bedroom door if you have to."

"Barbara, my time of the month has pretty much come and gone, and the point is he's not interested in sleeping with me anymore. If I wanted him to sleep with me, I'd have to lock him *in* the bedroom." I wiped the tears away from my face with the back of my hand. I hated being weak, but it hurt every time I thought about Trisha and Marc, Trisha under Marc, Trisha on top of Marc, or any combination thereof.

As if he could read my mind, and we were so close that most times he could, Donny shifted uncomfortably in his seat and offered me his napkin.

"It's okay to cry, sis," Donny said.

Barbara was unperturbed and she smelled blood. Maybe she was more shark than barracuda. Same distinction.

"Hannah's almost twenty-one, isn't she, so there won't be a custody issue. We'll make sure he continues to pay for her education, any major expenses, her wedding, things like that."

"Her wedding?" I asked blankly. My daughter was not even close to getting married, and the thought of Hannah walking down the aisle without Marc being part of the festivities made me sick. Or maybe it was the calamari churning around in my stomach.

"I want custody of the Gold Wing," I said, lifting my chin, trying not to break out into tears again.

"Isn't that some kind of motorcycle?" Barbara asked.

"Yes. He went out and bought the biggest, baddest, blackest bagger money can buy—the 2013 Honda Gold Wing F6B Deluxe. It's a sleek, powerful, luxury touring motorcycle with all the goods and plenty of room for Trisha's fat ass. He bought it when he turned fifty a month ago."

"That Wing is an old guys' bike," said Donny. "Marc can deny it all he wants, but he's going through a classic midlife crisis. He's never even driven a motorcycle."

I glared at my brother. "You knew about it?"

"Guys talk."

I sneered. "Old guys talk. I've been doing research on this bike. It's supposed to feature a lighter, leaner package."

"I've seen Trisha. There's nothing light or lean about her, unless you count her brain." Donny snorted.

"Do you know that monster cost more than twenty thousand dollars?" I added. "Complete with all the creature comforts like a passenger backrest and heated grips." *Though I don't know why Marc needs creature comforts now that he has Trisha.*

"I think he loves that bike even more than he loves Trisha. So I want to take it away from him." I wasn't usually this vindictive and vengeful, but in this case it felt really good. Maybe I needed to sunbathe at one of the Millennium Gardens pools and bake out all the bitchiness.

"That can be arranged," Barbara said. "That's a boatload of money. Did he tell you he was going to buy it?"

"Of course not. He just came home with it one day. He won't let me near his most precious possession."

"While we're on the subject of possessions, I want you to make a list of all your possessions, your personal possessions, his, and the things you own jointly," Barbara instructs. "And I'll need copies of your most recent tax returns. Also any financial information you can get your hands on, bank and money market account numbers and his pension plan information, IRAs, things like that. He may be hiding money from you, but I've got a good accountant. If Marc's hiding anything, we'll find it. My guy is like a bloodhound when it comes to the money trail."

Okay. A barracuda and a bloodhound. A divorcee's dream team.

"So you'll handle my divorce?" I asked. I hoped so, because I can't exactly call 1-800-DIVORCE. Marc and I were pretty well known in the community, and it would be a high profile case, especially with Barbara handling it.

"Of course. We'll be back in Atlanta as soon as we get your mother packed up. Just call my office and make an appointment at your convenience. I can't wait to sink my teeth into that horny bastard. And to think I actually liked him. He's a top-notch attorney, too. Oh, well, I guess I'm not such a good judge of character. Meanwhile, I'm going to get a private detective on Marc and Trisha right away. Especially now that you're out of town, their guard will be down. He'll check Marc's cell phone records, tap into his computer at home and at the office, see what sites he likes to visit."

"Sites?" I asked, confused.

"You know, porn sites."

"Marc would never do that," I argued.

"Did you ever think he would cheat on you?" Barbara reasoned. "How well do you really know your husband, Honey?"

I thought I knew everything about Marc. But I couldn't explain the Thanksgiving pictures of naked Trisha.

"We've been married for more than twenty years," was all I could manage.

"Still, I'll bet he has a private e-mail account. My guess is he's made his personal travel arrangements over the Internet. Maybe he even has a little love nest tucked away somewhere."

I didn't even want to think about that. "It sounds complicated," I lamented.

"Divorce takes time," Barbara pointed out. "It's more than just an irritation or a bump in the road. You have to be committed to this process, Honey. But you're ahead of the game. You don't use his name professionally, so you won't have to change it back."

"What did you ever see in him anyway?" Donny asked, before he excused himself and jumped up to pull out Barbara's chair so she could go to the ladies' room to freshen up and call the kids.

"Be right back, sis," Donny said. "I want to talk to the kids before the sitter puts them to sleep."

I took a sip of my wine. Looking back, I tried to remember what it was I ever saw in Marc Bronstein and realized that I first noticed him because of something he saw in me.

My identity had always been tied up with being Donny Palladino's little sister. Few people looked at me in my own right. To most people I was an afterthought. Donny more than tolerated me tagging along with his friends like I was one of the boys. But if I developed a crush on one of the guys on his team, he'd always deliver a stern lecture to the object of my affection and quash any chance of a blossoming romance. I'd nursed some serious crushes over the years, but no one was "good enough for me," according to Donny, and no one wanted to antagonize Donny Palladino. I always thought Donny was just being overprotective. But maybe I simply wasn't worth the effort.

When I first met Marc Bronstein at a college fraternity party, he'd never even heard of Donny Palladino and he didn't know the difference between a batting average and a blitz, a sacrifice and a sack, a squeeze play and a sweep. And that was fine with me.

Usually the first thing people noticed about me was my nose and, as my Grandmother Lewis used to say, that I was "big-boned." My father said my nose gave my face character. Marc also thought that my nose was cute and my butt was perfect.

I'd spent most of my life around hunky baseball players whose only goal was to make it to the major leagues. An education was just a necessary stop on the route. Marc was sexy, smart and ambitious. He had goals. He was already in law school. And after we met, I developed a goal of my own. To make Marc Bronstein fall in love with me.

Marc's definition of getting to first and second had nothing to do with baseball. And I was determined not to let him strike out. When I finally got my diamond, it had nothing to do with the infield. Of course my brother thought I was making the biggest mistake of my life.

My brother thought he was an expert on marriage even though he got married very late in the game. Women were literally falling at his feet, proposing marriage and making other less traditional propositions, so he'd never felt the need to get tied down.

But when Donny accompanied a teammate who needed moral support to an attorney's office while he was being sued for divorce, he sat in on a property settlement session and saw Barbara in action. He described his future wife as a lioness, a fiery avenging angel, protecting a woman's rights. When she spoke, with such conviction, he imagined her astride a stallion, wielding her sword, dispensing justice in defense of her client. Unfortunately, thanks to Barbara, his friend's wife took him for everything he had. That meeting signaled the end of his friend's marriage but the beginning of a new life for Donny. The moment he laid eyes on Barbara, something just clicked. He fell right then and there, and after that he never looked at another woman the same way again.

I'd never seen anything like it. Donny and Barbara were the proverbial odd couple. He was a hulking, handsome hunk. And she was this diminutive but ferocious lady lawyer, all business. Attractive, yes, but nothing like the brainless, busty, clingy model-types Donny had gone for in the past. They had a happy marriage and three beautiful children, so now he was eager to offer advice. And his advice had always been that Marc Bronstein was the wrong man for me. Turned out big brother was right after all.

I always thought I'd marry a baseball player or an athlete, and that was the image, the standard I'd carried around in my head since I first dreamed of love as a teenager. But when I looked at Marc Bronstein, I saw something different. He wasn't big and brawny but compact and confident and solid in his own way. He looked good on paper. He had all the right credentials. He was everything I *never* wanted in a guy but at the end of the day he made me laugh, like my father, and I liked that about him.

Most important, he was in love with me. I was so sure of that then. Where did that love go wrong? When did we drift so far apart that he felt the need to find satisfaction with another woman? I guess the joke was on me.

Maybe that was because, with me, everything was a joke. But I wasn't laughing now. Stanley Palladino could find the humor in any situation. In addition to my nose, I got my sense of humor from my father. Sometimes that was a blessing. But it could also be a curse. Grandma Lewis had a Yiddish expression for people like me. "*Lacha la veinalach.*" Roughly translated, it means "Don't get too happy, because soon you'll be crying."

Grandma Lewis didn't know a thing about laughter. I don't think she ever laughed a day in her life. No wonder my mother fell in love with my father. Growing up in a joyless house with Grandma Lewis, it must have been refreshing to come home to Stanley Palladino. Our lives were so empty without his laughter. In fact, the silence was practically deafening.

My husband is cheating on me, Daddy. I'll bet you never would have believed that could happen. I can't find the humor in that, and I doubt you could have either.

Betrayal hurts. And because of Marc's betrayal, our marriage was irretrievably broken, irreparably damaged. Take your pick. I had nothing more to say to Marc. I recalled the last honest conversation we had.

"Do I have to buy a damn house to get your attention?" Marc accused.

I guess I *had* been working hard since my dad's death. I didn't have a choice. The truth was Marc and I had been working hard since he signed on as a summer associate with his law firm and I was starting out in the real estate field. Looking back to all those years ago, I realized we hardly had time to conceive Hannah. I was on call 24/7, catering to the whims of buyers. Apparently I wasn't catering enough to my husband's whims, so he found somebody who would. Trisha, whatever her qualifications, was certainly available and willing. And, she was right under his nose. An irresistible combination.

Is that where I went wrong? I thought we had a

solid marriage. Did I take Marc for granted? Maybe we didn't spend enough time together.

All I knew was I couldn't stay in a marriage where I wasn't wanted, wouldn't stay in a house with a man who preferred another woman. Not a minute longer than necessary. I had to get out of there fast.

I drained my glass. The curtains in the restaurant fluttered from the movement of the whirring fan. The steady motion of the blades seemed to be whispering, "Slow down, Honey."

"Daddy, is that you?" I whispered.

I put the wine glass on the table as Donny and Barbara returned to the table. Her smudged lipstick gave them away. The lovebirds were at it again. Donny helped his wife into her seat and turned his attention to me.

"I guess we should talk about the offer from Hammond Reddekker," I began. "Marc is against a merger. He thinks Mom should just sell Palladino Properties outright and get out of the business altogether, which leaves us out in the cold."

"Marc has no business sticking his nose into it," Donny answered. "He's not a member of this family anymore."

"Well, technically he still is," I pointed out.

"Not for long," Donny barked. "After Barbara gets through with him, he won't have a dime, and then just see how fast Miss Trisha melts into the woodwork."

I was furious at Marc, true, but the thought of him alone in the world and penniless didn't make me feel any better. I didn't want that for him. I was still pretty numb and trying not to feel anything, but I had to admit I still had feelings for my husband. Damn him.

To get my mind off my crumbling marriage, I told Donny about Max's cruise proposal.

"Are you serious? She met this guy at a bereavement group?"

"Yes, apparently a lot of people at Millennium Gardens hook up that way."

"I don't want my mother *hooking up* with anyone." Donny frowned. "And how come I didn't know about this?"

"I think it was a last-minute thing. Max's significant other has Alzheimer's, so he had an extra ticket. Mom thought it would be a shame to let it go to waste. I hope she knows what she's doing."

"She just lost her husband. It's too soon for her to be dating."

"It's been a whole year. Maybe she's ready to move on."

"I'd better not catch that Max guy sniffing around her," Donny blustered.

"He'll be doing more than sniffing if she goes on that cruise with him. The plan is they're going to share a cabin."

"That's why we're going to get her out of Boca as soon as possible, *before* the departure date. There's no way I'm letting my mother go on a cruise with that operator."

"Have you met Max?" I asked.

"No, and I don't want to. My mother is still in mourning. The last thing she needs is a man. And neither do you."

Chapter Four: A Chicken in Every Freezer

While Donny thought that a man was the last thing my mother needed, a man was exactly what Aunt Helene had in mind for her older sister. A feeling of intense relief washed over me when Aunt Helene showed up at the condo just as my mother and I got back from our trip to Sam's Club to retrieve her wallet. I was anxious to ask my aunt more about Mom's forgetfulness, to find out if it was a pattern, but I could hardly do that right in front of her. And besides, I had promised my mother I wouldn't mention it to anyone.

"Honey, you look great," Aunt Helene said, hugging me tight.

"For a premenopausal woman?" I quipped.

"For any woman."

We looked at my mother and exchanged worried glances.

"Why don't I leave the room so the two of you can talk about me behind my back," my mother offered, pretending to be offended.

"We weren't going to talk about you," I denied, looking at my aunt for confirmation, "Were we?"

"Of course not," Aunt Helene said. "What *should* we talk about?"

"How about Max, for starters?" I suggested as we sat on the living room couch.

Aunt Helene laughed. "She must have told you

about the cruise. It's sponsored by the Millennium Gardens Social Club. A lot of the residents are going. There's going to be a lot of hanky panky going on aboard that ship when people aren't standing in the buffet line. It's a hot ticket."

"Yes," I said, "she told me about the cruise, but not about the hanky panky."

"*She* is right here in the room with you," my mother cautioned. "So stop talking around me."

"Sorry," Aunt Helene apologized perfunctorily, without pausing for a breath. "But even if you are in the same room you wouldn't be able to hear us. Honey, did you know that your mother has a severe high-frequency sensorineural hearing loss?"

"Is that serious?" I asked, stricken. Apparently there was a lot I didn't know about my mother. She seemed to be deteriorating right before my eyes. Aunt Helene was an expert on the subject of hearing loss. She had been a speech/language pathologist before she retired.

"I've been testing her for the past fifteen years. Your mother can't hear high decibels. For instance 'cheese' is a high-frequency sound. Dee Dee, turn around."

"Helene, I don't want to do this in front of my daughter."

"Just turn around," Aunt Helene said impatiently.

My mother obliged reluctantly.

"Cheese," said Aunt Helene. "Now what did I say?"

"Tube," my mother answered.

I was horrified.

"It's okay, Honey. She's compensated, especially if

you look her in the eyes, use expressive facial movements and speak clearly. She can hear the low frequency sounds, like ‘boat’ or ‘bone’ or ‘go’ or ‘sane.’ Let’s try another one. Tick,” my aunt said purposefully.

“Tock,” my mother answered.

I laughed. Okay, this was all a joke. There was nothing wrong with my mother.

“You think this is funny?” Aunt Helene asked.

“No, but I want you to stop torturing my mother,” I insisted, turning her around and kissing her on the forehead.

“I didn’t mean to upset you. I just thought you should know.”

“Has she seen a doctor?”

“Yes, and he agrees with my diagnosis.”

Okay, my mother combed carpet fringe, my brother was stuck in the 1940s, and my aunt was practicing medicine without a license. I had my work cut out for me.

“Did you know she’s also seen a doctor for cataracts?”

“No,” I said, alarmed. “She never said a word.”

“If you have something to say, please say it to my face,” Dee Dee said to her sister.

“I told her not to see Dr. Frank,” Aunt Helene said, ignoring her. “He’s not very friendly.”

“I don’t need a friend,” my mother countered. “I need an ophthalmologist.”

“All I know is that after my cataract surgery, when I went in for a recheck, Dr. Frank looked into my left eye and said everything was fine, and I said, ‘You did the surgery on my right eye.’ They’re operating a laser mill down there."

I took my mother's hand.

"It's okay, Honey," my mother assured me. "I'm not falling apart."

"Exactly," Aunt Helene said. "Your mother is still an attractive woman, which is one of the reasons I came over here. There's a big dance at the club tonight, and I've been trying to talk her into going. She refuses." Aunt Helene folded her arms and looked directly at my mother.

"I'm tired, and Honey just got here," my mother protested. "Besides, Donny and Honey are taking me out to dinner at The Addison."

"But, Mom, a dance sounds lovely," I said. "It's just what you need. I think you should go. I'm sure Donny and Barbara will understand. We can save The Addison for another night."

"They're going to have big band music," my aunt added. "I know you like that. Didn't you used to dance to all the big bands when we were girls?"

My mother sighed and got a wistful look in her eyes. "That was a long time ago, Helene. I've forgotten how to do those dances."

"You're not getting out of this. There's a man in my building—a very handsome man—who also lost his wife recently. He shouldn't be alone right now. I convinced him to go to the dance and told him I was bringing my very lovely, recently widowed sister. He's from up north too. But he's worked most of his life in South Florida, and he and his wife moved to Boca to be closer to their son and his family."

"I don't care where he's from, or why he's here. I told you I'm not interested in dances or dating," Dee

Dee snapped, jumping up from the couch. "Just because he lost his wife and I lost my husband doesn't automatically mean we were meant to be. If he's that handsome, I'm surprised the vultures around here haven't gotten to him yet."

"You mean the brisket brigade? Well, actually, Mrs. Goldman in the next building thawed out a chicken she had in the freezer. And Mrs. Klein down the hall already has a Mojo chicken from Publix ready to go, in her refrigerator. Mrs. Kennedy is roasting one as we speak, so it will be nice and fresh. He's had roast chicken three times already this week. I think he's ready for a taste of something new."

"Roast chicken?" I asked, not understanding.

"Every widow in the complex keeps a roast chicken or a casserole in her freezer to bring over when one of the men here loses his wife or significant other," Aunt Helene explained. "Either that or they leave a trail of brisket gravy dripping down the hallway so they can find their way back in the middle of the night. Millennium Gardens is a regular Peyton Place. If a woman is interested in getting a man, all she has to do is defrost a chicken and go out and grab him. They're all just lonely, ready for action, and ripe for the picking."

"What about Max?" I wondered.

"Well, he's lonely too. He's missing his significant other, Jean."

"Significant other?" I prompted, anxious to know more.

"Significant others are very common down here," Aunt Helene answered. Apparently the phenomenon was as pervasive as Early Bird Specials. Aunt Helene knew what she was talking about. Her significant other—Harold Cohen—passed away two months ago.

"It's a different culture in this complex," she continued. "Many of the couples who live here are well off, but no one wants to mix up their finances, or get less Social Security by remarrying. And they don't want flak from their children, who are worried about losing their inheritances. So instead of getting married, they become significant others. But it's not a legal arrangement, so it raises a lot of other issues."

"Speaking of chickens in the freezer, I forgot I have to put away the groceries," Dee Dee said. "We picked up some things from Sam's Club while we were out."

"I thought you just went to Sam's Club yesterday," Aunt Helene said, her eyes narrowing.

"So I went back. Is that against the law?"

My aunt rolled her eyes and threw up her hands.

I gave my aunt a look that said, "I'll explain later." My mother turned to me and said, "Sit and talk to your aunt and I'll be right back. But don't talk about me."

"Mom, let me help you with those groceries," I offered, getting up.

"Sit, sweetheart," she said, pressing me back down on the couch. "You're probably still tired from your flight yesterday. Your aunt never gets a chance to spend time with you. She misses you." I watched my mother walk into the kitchen. Was she moving more slowly than I remembered?

"You came to take her home, didn't you?" accused Aunt Helene.

"Yes," I replied honestly. "I think it's time. We need her at the office. She can't stay here forever."

"Did you ever ask her if she wanted to come back, to the business, I mean?"

"I've been asking her every week since she got here."

"And she's been stalling, am I right?"

I nodded in agreement.

"There's a reason she's procrastinating," my aunt said. "Has she told you she's made a decision about selling the company?"

"Yes, and that's one of the reasons I'm here. To talk her out of it."

"She's made up her mind," my aunt protested. "It's a great deal of money."

"She can still get the money. But instead of selling outright, Palladino Properties could become an affiliate of one of Hammond Reddekker's holding companies. We'd become part of one of the premier real estate providers in the country."

"I know that was the deal your mother initiated, but she told me she doesn't want to go through with that."

"Do you know how great this acquisition would be for Palladino Properties? The potential for growth? The resources we could offer our clients? Hammond Reddekker could infuse a lot of capital into our business, enough resources for us to upgrade our entire operation, improve our Web site, and compete with the national firms. And I came up with a campaign that would highlight Donny in a series of television ads that could put Palladino Properties on the national map. 'Palladino Properties: Your Home Base.' It would feature footage of a young, powerful Donny Palladino hitting the ball out of the park, rounding the bases, and sliding in to home. Now women across the country will fall under Donny's spell all over again, but this time *off* the playing field."

"That sounds nice, but your mother is worried about taking on so much responsibility. Her goals have changed."

"When is the last time you talked to her about this?"

"Right before you came. She's afraid to tell you how she feels. She doesn't want to disappoint you. She wants to do what's right for you and your brother and your father's memory, but that's not what's right for her at this stage in her life."

I sighed. "Then I need to talk to her again."

"What you need to do is *listen*, Honey, to what she's trying to tell you. Her heart isn't in it anymore. This was your father's dream, not hers."

"Well what does she intend to do with the rest of her life? Wait for the end in Millennium Gardens?"

"Is that what you think we're doing here? Waiting to die? We're living very fulfilling lives. Every Friday night they play Cuban music at the clubhouse and they teach salsa dancing and Zumba."

"I didn't mean anything by that," I apologized to my aunt, who looked like she was on the verge of walking out. "But my mother had a very active life in Atlanta. She still has a lot to give. Donny and I need her to come back."

"Whose needs are you looking out for? Hers or yours?"

"She needs to face what's happened," I argued, "and look at life from a realistic perspective."

"That's easy for you to say, Honey. You haven't lost your husband."

My aunt's words stung, but she didn't know that was exactly what was about to happen to me.

And I knew Aunt Helene was not just talking about my mother's loss.

"So how are you doing, really?" I wanted to know, taking her hand.

"I'm fine," she answered, patting my hand and placing it back on my lap.

Aunt Helene never struck me as the type to shack up—or, as Hannah would say, hook up—with someone. My aunt had always been very conventional. But apparently things were different here at Millennium Gardens. She had essentially been shacking up with her significant other before he died.

"Aunt Helene. Why didn't you and Mr. Cohen ever get married?"

"I loved having him around," she confided. "We had a very pleasant relationship and we got closer and closer, but I didn't want the responsibility or commitment of being married."

"Why not?"

"He had his own apartment. I had mine. We were on separate tracks but managed to meet in the middle ground. I like my privacy, doing my thing at my time. Harold was the same way. He preferred watching football games and the fights and being quiet. I went to bed at 11:00; he went to bed at 2:00. I liked to watch nature shows and he was interested in the stock market. Why does it do this and that? Why is it up one day and down the next day? He liked to wear his hair long. I like a man with a hair cut. If we had a disagreement, we repaired it and kept going." She sighed. "But I like my home. I like thinking of your uncle. After so many years being involved with one man, I didn't want to have to adjust to another man as a husband."

I was thinking about my own marriage and the adjustments I'd soon have to make, and then we got to talking about love the second time around.

"It's not exactly the same," explained Aunt Helene. "Being older, you look at things a little differently, and it could be exciting, but in a very different way. There's another dimension to it. When you're young, your hormones take over more so than logic."

What about sex? I wanted to ask, but didn't have the nerve. Aunt Helene, however, seemed to anticipate the question.

"Sex is up to the individual, and what their needs are. Not only up to the individual, but it has to do with who can perform sex. There are some who think about sex an awful lot but that's about all they can do. Unfortunately, Harold and I were in that category."

What category did I fall into? My husband was certainly "performing sex," but not with me. In fact, I couldn't remember the last time we had "performed sex."

I was fascinated with the subject of significant others. After all, my mother seemed about to get involved with one—Max—a man I had yet to meet.

"Do any of the significant others end up getting married?" I asked.

"I've had friends who did get married," Aunt Helene answered. "From the outside it looks great. I don't know what goes on behind closed doors. Some significant others maintain their apartments. A lot of women who have gotten remarried gave up their apartments and were very sorry because the relationship didn't work out and they got divorced within a few months. Then there's the problem of who gets the apartment—who leaves and who stays. Harold and I were content the way it was. I didn't need marriage. I keep very busy with my girlfriends. But I also like the idea of having a date all the time, and I liked the affection. When Harold and I cruised together, we shared a room. It never bothered me. Of course he was eighty-seven years old. When we cuddled, that was terrific. The cuddling, the head on each other's shoulders, was sufficient. I didn't want to go any deeper. There comes a time in your life when sex is not the most important thing. Does that shock you, Honey?"

"No," I said, grinning. In light of what was happening in my own marriage, concepts about sex and acceptable behavior were already beginning to shift.

"When you get to be as old as I am, nothing shocks you anymore," Aunt Helene laughed.

"You're not old. You're younger than my mother."

"Age has a way of creeping up on you when you least expect it. Your mind is as active as always, and you want to go all the time. But I have arthritis. My hip hurts a little bit. Oh, well, you just go on, try to exercise, eat well, keep your weight down, and the rest is in God's hands. Women may not think anything about living with a man or having sex with a man, if the man can, that is. But it's not the safest thing. There are men here with AIDS."

"Are you serious?" I asked, my mouth opening in surprise.

"Yes. It's a low percentage, but men go out of the Gardens looking for women. Just the other day there were people here from the health department giving an educational lecture, and they were distributing condoms in different colors—blue and pink ones—in the clubhouse. They were warning women, 'You don't know who this man has slept with before. You meet a gentleman for the first time, he takes you out to dinner, and he expects to be paid for dinner. He'll say, 'Let's go to my house and have sex.' Harold wasn't like that. I wasn't in love with Harold like I was with your uncle," Aunt Helene admitted, "but being with him still gave me a good feeling."

"Do you think you'll ever find someone else?" I asked. "Stop me if I'm being too nosy."

"No, it's okay. I don't think I want a long-term relationship anymore," Aunt Helene answered, throwing back her head and laughing. "Even the term long-term is relative around here. I have fond memories of both my men. But I'm getting on in years, and I like the idea of total independence. I don't want to be the kind of woman who goes out looking for a man, like some of the women here. If a man asked me to go to dinner or a movie, and I think he has a brain in his head, I would go. I do believe in destiny, finding your soul mate or perfect match. If it's going to happen it's going to happen. I guess you're never too old for love or sex."

I blushed.

"You know there's no shame in a woman going out with a man, going to his house, living with him. In a community like this, surrounded with older residents, it's accepted behavior. Well, not by everyone. There's this group, Seniors Against Sin, that's distributing these awful red flyers all around the complex. It's disturbing.

I haven't gotten any. I guess because I'm not currently in a relationship. But some of my friends have been singled out. Everyone here knows everyone else's business. It's putting us all on edge."

"Have you called the police?" I asked, wondering if I should be worried.

"No. I mean, they'd just ignore us and think we're a bunch of crazy old fools. After all, they're just flyers. It's not like anyone is holding a gun to our heads. We've told the Homeowner's Association about it."

My mother came out of the kitchen carrying a tray. "Here, I cut up some nice apples, and I've got some cheese and crackers. Eat. What did I miss?"

"We were just talking about those Seniors Against Sin flyers."

"Oh, yes. I got one of those taped to my door."

"Probably because you're seeing Max."

"I'm not *seeing* Max," my mother protested. "He's just a friend."

"And I was telling Honey about the concept of significant others," Aunt Helene said.

"You mean like Birdie Rosen and Ben?" my mother asked.

"A perfect example," she replied. "Just last week Birdie Rosen's significant other, Ben, went into the hospital for open heart surgery and he never came out. When they were together, he treated her like a queen. When he went shopping for groceries, he'd buy one for him and one for her because he knew she was on a moderate income. He was not a rich man, but he was comfortable. He even paid whenever they went on dates or trips. They were going to take that Christmas cruise with their friends Max and Jean. The one Max has invited your mother to take with him. But after Ben died, where did that leave Birdie? Ben's children were very appreciative of the fact that she had taken such good care of their father for all those years, but Birdie was still an outsider and they weren't willing to share a penny of their inheritance with her. Since Ben never made specific provisions for Birdie in his will, she was left high and dry."

"That's sad," I said.

"But around here, those are the realities of life," Aunt Helene said.

"At least Birdie and Ben found a little bit of happiness in their final years, which is why I'm encouraging your mother to go to this dance. I don't think I've seen her smile since your father died."

"Exactly," Mom said. "I'm in my final years, so what do I have to smile about?"

I knew what my mother meant, but I didn't want to share my aging anxieties with her. She didn't need the extra aggravation.

"Mother, that's morbid and in *your* case, premature," I argued. "You're still young. And you're beautiful. Why don't you go to the dance? You can stay for a little while, and if you feel uncomfortable, Aunt Helene will take you home."

My mother hesitated.

"Okay, I'll go with you. I even brought a dress for just such an occasion."

"But I have nothing to wear," Dee Dee said, "except black."

"Oh, well, now you sound like Cinderella," I teased. "I think we need a shopping trip. Aunt Helene and I will be your fairy godmothers and find you something special to wear to the ball. And it's turning cold in Atlanta. I'd like to buy you a holiday sweater. Nothing practical or classic. Something trendy and fun. We can make an afternoon of it—go to the salon, the works. You could use a nice haircut. Maybe I'll even let Rumpelstiltskin mangle my hair."

Aunt Helene's hairdresser—I call him Rumpelstiltskin—has a heavy hand on the heat and his endless blow-drying has a tendency to turn my golden hair into straw. Some people go to their hairdressers for a haircut and blow-dry. Everyone went to Rumplestiltskin for his advice. The best place to go for window treatments, where to buy tile, who could build a cedar closet, the best painter, the best restaurant, the best hotel to stay on vacation—and the best gossip.

Aunt Helene lifted a few strands of hair from my head. "He can get rid of this gray, too."

"I don't have any gray hairs," I objected. "They're Arctic Blond. But I'm due for a cut. I'm always too busy to go to the salon in Atlanta. So, Mom, what do you say?"

"I say I need more than a new hairstyle and a dress. What I need is a facelift. All of my friends are getting facelifts."

"Well, aren't you lucky you don't need one," I replied, licking the hot tears from my mouth. Losing confidence was a sure sign that my mother was growing old. A facelift was the last thing she needed. Touching up my mother's face would be like marring the Mona Lisa. Only my mother never smiled anymore. Maybe because she had no more secrets.

Chapter Five: The Silent Bullfrog

"Mom, I think we have to talk about this merger," I said after Aunt Helene went home.

"You mean the sale," she answered stubbornly.

"Well, that's what we have to talk about," I replied.

"Why don't we go out to the pool, relax a little bit before our hair appointments," my mother suggested. "We can talk there. Did you bring a bathing suit?"

"Yes," I acknowledged, thinking, Who has time to swim? I was going to be gone the entire afternoon, between shopping and the salon. But this day was about my mother. "I'll go change."

After a restless night in a strange bed, listening to '40s music in the background, I woke up disoriented, with big band sounds pounding in my head. No wonder my mother was on the verge of insanity. Marc was not the only one going through a midlife crisis. But Marc didn't have to deal with an internal furnace that woke him up several times a night, never able to get comfortable enough to fall back to sleep. And Marc's bedclothes weren't drenched in sweat. But since I was a woman, I guessed my midlife crisis didn't count, because I didn't go acting out all my fantasies for the whole world to see.

I had been too tired to unpack last night, but now I started hanging my clothes in the closet. My hand paused on the frothy lime green cocktail concoction that had originally belonged to Vicky. I planned to wear it when we took my mother to The Addison. The one Marc called my “mildew” dress. Vicky had purchased it for a Holy Land Foundation Dinner at her church, but when she put it on the evening of the event, she decided it was too risqué even for her, and especially for the bishops and monsignors. But I didn’t have Vicky’s cleavage problem. When I’d tried to return it, Vicky refused to take it back.

This dress should be worn to shake things up, I thought. Marc doesn’t like me in flashy colors. But after what he did to me, I shouldn’t have to answer to him anymore. And I wasn’t going to see Marc on this trip anyway.

I squeezed into a leopard-print, figure-hugging bathing suit. Not that anyone here would be alert enough to notice my figure, but it never hurts to look your best. I put on a long black eyelet cover-up, grabbed my wide-brimmed hat, sunglasses, and a file folder, and pulled my cell phone and BlackBerry from my purse.

When I returned to the living room, my mother was staring at my manila folder.

“You’re not going to bring work out to the pool are you?”

“Well a few Faxes came in that need my attention. I have some phone calls to return, and I brought the thumbnails that the agency did on the TV campaign I want to show you.”

“Honey, why can’t we just be a mother and daughter going out to the pool for a relaxing swim? Does it always have to be business between us?”

“We’re going out there precisely to talk about the

business. You have a deadline coming up in a few days. I want to make sure you've considered all the consequences of an outright sale."

"I've already been over this with Marc, and he says that is what's best for—"

"Marc doesn't speak for me," I said abruptly. "He has nothing to do with this."

"He's been helping me structure the deal," my mother said.

"I don't want him involved in my business," I said.

"Honey, maybe there's something else we need to talk about. Is there something going on between you and Marc that I don't know about?"

"No, there isn't," I denied hotly. "Okay, I'll leave all this stuff here, except the notes on the ad campaign. I think you'll want to see those. Let's go."

We walked out the door and took the elevator to the pool in front of her building.

It was unusually warm for December, and we pulled together two matching lounge chairs. It had been too long since I'd really relaxed. I stretched and settled myself in a position to soak up the sun.

"This is nice, isn't it, Honey?" Dee Dee smiled. It was worth taking a break from work just to see my mother smile.

"Yes," I sighed, surprised to feel the stress and strain slowly drain out of my body. I must have dozed off, and before I did I vaguely noted my mother covering me with her towel and slipping my hat lower down on my face.

After the sun worked its magic, my inner lounge lizard decided to take a dip in the heated pool and swim a few laps. As I was about to climb up the ladder, I noticed a frog splashing about frantically in the pool. Frogs are quick to jump into a pool, but then they can't get themselves out, and eventually they succumb to the chlorinated water before they even know they are in trouble. I guess it's something like a lobster being slowly boiled in water that starts out cool. So I set out to rescue him. I chased him around the pool a few times. Naturally he was scared. I imagined I could hear his little frog heart beating out of cadence. Winded, I finally caught him in my cupped hands and placed him carefully on the decking.

He wasn't a cute little green creature at all, but a big bullfrog with a yellowish-green back and brown markings. And he was staring up at me, impudently.

"Go on, hop away, now," I urged, motioning him along.

I tapped him lightly with my forefinger, but he refused to move. Maybe he was waterlogged or stunned. He tilted his head and skewered me with his bulging black frog eyes.

"Okay, what do you want from me? A kiss? Maybe you're so grateful I saved your life that you want to grant me three wishes?" If I did get three wishes, I knew what they'd be. That my father would come back to us. That my mother wouldn't sell the company. That Marc would still love me.

There was no answer from the frog.

"What?" I challenged.

I climbed out of the pool and stood next to him, dripping water on the decking and onto the silent frog. He hopped back a step. I nudged him gently with my toe, and finally he turned and hopped away slowly, like he was out for his morning constitutional, without a care in the world.

I laughed. When I returned to my lounge chair, I toweled myself off.

"That was fun," I admitted. It had been years since I felt so relaxed. I had a lot of work to do, but for the life of me I couldn't remember what it was.

"Okay, Honey, you wanted to talk about Mr. Reddekker's offer?"

"Mom, do you know how lucky you are that Hammond Reddekker, probably one of the richest, most successful men in this country, singled our company out? What a tribute this is to you and Daddy and what you built together."

"With a lot of help from you and your brother," Dee Dee acknowledged.

"Daddy had such big plans, and I have plans of my own. Imagine what Palladino Properties could become with Mr. Reddekker's financial backing and connections," I stated. "It would put us right on the national map."

"I'm exactly where I want to be on the national map," Dee Dee protested.

"What, here in Millennium Gardens?"

"What's wrong with Millennium Gardens?"

"Well, for one thing, if you stay here, your brain will atrophy."

"You're wrong about that," Dee Dee disagreed. "Do you think all we talk about are bowel movements and early-bird specials? You can't imagine all the activities they have here for us. I've made a lot of friends. My sister is here."

"And your children and grandchildren are not," I argued.

"That's the only drawback. Donny visits a lot"—I guess she didn't have to say, "And you don't"—"and I'll be making frequent trips back to Atlanta."

"Mom, I told you about the national TV spots I planned for Donny. Here, I have some sketches for you to look at."

Dee Dee examined the contents of the folder and handed it back to me.

"It's brilliant, really, Honey, but all this is not for me. I've had my time. I'm in a different place now. The future is for you and Donny."

"But Mom, that's exactly my point. If you sell, there is no future for Donny and me, or for Hannah. I think she wants to come to work for Palladino Properties after she graduates."

"You can still work in the real estate field. Mr. Reddekker is offering me a small fortune. You and Donny will be getting part of that."

"Mom, I know you're not making this decision based on the money. Daddy left you well provided for. But do you think he would have wanted you to give away his company?"

"I'm not *giving* it away," Dee Dee argued. "I think I'm making a smart business decision."

My mother looked over at me and sighed. "You're mad at me, aren't you. That's really what this is all about. That's why you took time out of your busy schedule to come all the way down here."

"I'm not mad," I denied quickly, but the minute the words tumbled out of my mouth I realized they weren't true. I was furious with my mother.

"I never thought you would do this to Daddy or to us," I said, lifting my chin.

"I'm disappointed in you, Honey," my mother said. "Don't you think I know how much that company meant to your father? And I know how much it means to you. But I don't have the capability to run the business on a national scale. I think the best way is to sell outright. Your husband agrees."

I definitely didn't want to hear about my husband right now, and how he was plotting with my mother behind my back to take away the one thing that meant the most to me.

Things went from bad to worse after that, when my loofah fell apart in the shower. I mean, what did that say about my ability to hold it all together? I pouted as the sponge unraveled into two long yellow mesh strands and sagged onto the white tile floor.

After I stepped out and toweled, I dried my hair and decided I was calm enough to call Marc at his office in the middle of the day. I was obviously failing in my mission to change my mother's mind. Now it was time to enlist my soon-to-be-ex-husband's help in changing my mother's mind about the buyout. He owed me that. But time was one thing I did not have enough of.

Trisha did not answer. The receptionist said Marc was at lunch. I looked at my watch. It was 3 o'clock in the afternoon. That was some long lunch. Then I called Marc's cell phone and got him on the fifth ring. He sounded sleepy and satisfied. I swear I could hear the sound of Trisha's laughter in the background. I wondered if they were in our bedroom. My first reaction was, God, I hope the sheets are clean and the bed is made and that Trisha doesn't look in my messy closet or dresser drawers. I didn't want that home wrecker to find out what a horrible homemaker I was. How pitiful is that?

Barbara had said I couldn't act like I knew about their affair, not yet. So I had to pretend everything was okay. But my blood was boiling. And my suspicions were confirmed. I was so mad I couldn't even remember what I wanted to say, so I hung up the phone.

About an hour later, my cell phone rang and I answered it. It was Hannah, and she was hysterical.

"Hold on. Calm down, honey. Where are you calling from? Aruba? What's wrong? I can't hear you if you don't stop crying. Where are the Winslows?"

"M-Mommy. I c-came home to s-surprise you," she sobbed.

"Oh, honey, that's wonderful. I'm down visiting Grandma for a few days, but I'll be home soon."

"Don't come home," she said frantically.

"Hannah, you're not making any sense. Have you called your father? He'll come home early from work. As a matter of fact—"

I could hear Marc's raised voice in the background. "Hannah, give me the phone. Let me talk to your mother."

"Oh, your dad came home to see you. That's wonderful." How convenient that Marc was already home.

"No," she screamed. "I'm going to tell her."

"I said give me the phone," Marc ordered in a voice I had rarely heard him use in our entire married life.

"Hannah?" I asked nervously. "Is everything all right?"

"No," Hannah sniffled. "I came home to try to find

you, and all I found was Dad in his bathrobe. He wasn't alone."

Oh, God in heaven! Marc, you bastard. I'm going to strangle you. How could you?

"He's here with this woman, and she's barely dressed."

The images of Trisha in the photographs would never leave my head, and it was a hundred times worse because now my daughter would be seeing them live and in person for the rest of her life, too.

"Honey," Marc had the phone now. "I can explain."

"Marc," I said evenly. "I want you to get rid of that trash and put my daughter on the next plane to Ft. Lauderdale. *Now*."

"Honey, baby, I'm sorry. I'm so sorry. I didn't mean for this to happen."

"I don't care what you meant to happen. And you should be apologizing to our daughter. I want to see my little girl now, you miserable bastard. What have you done to us?"

I couldn't catch my breath. I was hyperventilating.

"For God's sake, put some clothes on," I heard him shout at Trisha. "Get in the bathroom."

"I'll bring her down to Florida," Marc said to me.

"I hate you, I hate you," I could hear Hannah screaming in the background. "I hate both of you."

At this point I didn't know if she meant she hated me or Trisha. This was beyond horrible.

"Put Hannah back on the phone," I demanded. He did.

"I'm not going anywhere with *him*," Hannah cried. *Him* being the interloper, the stranger, the liar, the cheat, not the father who had loved and treasured her all his life.

"Sweetheart, I'm so sorry you had to see that. I wish I could be there for you right now. I don't want you to fly alone in your state of mind. So if your father wants to bring you down, it's okay."

"Are you guys going to get a divorce?" She hiccupped.

"We don't need to talk about that now. I just want to see you. So hurry down here, okay?"

"I love you, Mommy," she whispered, still choking on her tears.

"I love you too, baby. I'll see you soon." At least Marc had the decency not to get back on the phone. *Divorce is too good for the cheating scum. I am going to bypass the divorce phase and go straight to the lingering and painful death phase and maim the miserable creep as soon as he steps foot in this condo.*

How could I explain this to Hannah? And would I have enough time before they got here to plan Marc's demise and give him what he deserved? I needed to call in the reinforcements. I needed my best friend Vicky.

Chapter Six: The Boss from Hell

"Vicky? Did I get you at a bad time?" I whispered into the BlackBerry when I was back in the guest room.

"No, I'm on my way in to work."

"It's almost the end of the afternoon!"

"Hello. Don't you listen to the news? We're in the middle of a major ice storm here, and I should be home snuggling with my honey in my warm bed. But of course Grant went into the office. It's unnatural for me to get to work before ten anyway. Yesterday I got in at nine and my boss was shocked. I told her not to expect me to sustain that level of punctuality. It's already turning out to be a really bad day."

"What's wrong?"

"Well, the boss from hell is out of town, and I forgot to call ahead to the hotel and find out the thread count of the sheets. Now she's on a major rampage. She claims she couldn't sleep. Like the princess and the pea."

"What?"

"She refuses to stay at a hotel if the bed sheets don't have a thread count of at least 300. She prefers 100 percent Egyptian cotton or pure silk."

"Are you serious?"

"Totally. I think she's convinced she's a member of the aristocracy or the royal family."

"And she's the CEO of one of the largest

corporations in the country?" *Note to self. Now I know what I'm going to buy my best friend for Christmas. A set of Frette deluxe bed sheets.*

"Hard to believe, isn't it? And she makes me buy this special liquid hand wash—Molton Brown—that they use at Buckingham Palace, for her executive washroom. It costs more than $25 a bottle, and she insists I get it at Neiman Marcus. And you know how her Royal Pain in the "HighnAss" expects me to take the seeds out of her grapes? Well, yesterday she caught me with a grape in my mouth, trying to spit out the seed."

"What did she say? *We* are not amused, as in the royal 'We'?"

"No. She yelled and screamed and lectured me on the value of being sanitary. I think she was just outraged because our stock is tanking, but I was hoping she'd fire me."

"And?"

"No such luck. She told me I'd better not put that grape in the good crystal bowl."

"Can't you just buy her seedless grapes?"

"She prefers the taste of the big red seeded ones, so I'm the unfortunate one stuck with pitting them. She can't fire me because no one else will do what I do. It's humiliating. I don't know why I put up with her."

"Because she pays really well? And she can't run the company without you? I thought you said it would be a cold day in Hell before you worked for Annabelle Crawford again."

"It's pretty damn cold out here right now," Vicky answered. "And working for her is like childbirth. You forget how much it hurts the first time and then you find yourself pregnant again. There's that—and the ironclad employee agreement I signed."

"It's always something," I said. "No job is worth that aggravation."

"I know. But being assistant to the CEO is my dream job. Other than wanting to be CEO myself someday. And I'm the best Assistant To in this city."

"Okay, who am I to stand in the way of Annabelle Crawford's high thread count? But I know you didn't get your MBA to spit seeds out of your boss's grapes."

"Actually I'm getting plenty of opportunities to practice the skills I learned in business school—accounting and marketing. Accounting for my whereabouts every single minute of every day and doing Annabelle's marketing at the grocery store, not to mention picking up and delivering her dry cleaning. Keeping track of that woman is like herding cats."

"You know you can always come to work for Palladino Properties," I offered. "We could really use you right now. If this merger goes through, you'd make a great CEO. Mom, Donny, and I can sell houses, but managing a business, that was Dad's forte. We don't have the time or the expertise."

"Are you kidding? I'd kill for the opportunity to be CEO of a Hammond Reddekker company."

"Let me talk to Mom and Donny. Maybe you coming to work for us would make a difference to my mother. She says she's made up her mind about selling, but I think there's still a chance she may agree to a merger. She's not in a very good place now. But I need your help on a personal level. Can you drive and talk at the same time?"

"Of course I can. I'm a woman; I can multitask.

What can I do for you?"

"Well, first I want to check on Winnie the Pooh."

"You mean Winnie the Poop?" Vicky asked dryly. "When I undertook this assignment of dog sitting, I didn't realize she would be doing her business all over my house, including on my formerly priceless Oriental rugs."

"Sorry. You knew she's not potty trained."

"That's an understatement."

"She's too old to leave in the kennel. She's losing control of her bladder."

"Aren't we all? Hey, Honey, you know, I don't mind dog sitting, but why didn't you leave her with Marc?"

"Because I don't trust him," I answered. "He has loose morals and he's a bad influence on my dog."

"You want to explain that?"

"Not really," I said, changing the subject.

I still hadn't told Marc about the last time I picked Winnie the Pooh up at the animal hospital where we boarded her and that after I settled my bill the doctor's daughter, who was the office manager, had motioned me into one of the empty rooms.

"We've noticed that Winnie is deteriorating since the last time he was here," she began.

"*She*. Winnie the Pooh is a *she*. And that's because she hates the kennel. And I've kept her here too long."

"No, we noticed it the first day you brought him in," the doctor's daughter explained calmly. "He paces and circles and falls down on his hind legs. He's blind and he can't hear, and I just wanted to let you know it might be time to think about—"

She left the thought out there hanging like

somebody's dirty laundry.

"No," I said vehemently, before I broke down in tears and realized, and then voiced, "I'm not ready."

She handed me a tissue. Marc should have been there. *Why isn't he here to help me handle this emergency? Oh yes, he's too busy making it with Trisha.*

"Do you want me to call the doctor in?"

"No," I replied. "Is she sick?"

"No," she answered.

"Is she in pain?"

"No."

"Well, then, why do you want to kill her? Just because she's old?"

She sighed. "That's not how we refer to it. It's just that we know it's best for *you* to keep Winnie alive but is it best for *him*?"

"Winnie is a girl!" I shouted. "How many times do I have to tell you? Winnie the Pooh is a girl!" I'd been boarding her there for seventeen years and they couldn't even get that right.

"I need more time," I said, grabbing Winnie the Pooh and rushing out of there, vowing never to return. Which is why I'd designated Vicky to watch my dog.

"By the way, how is Winnie the Pooh getting along with Rex?"

"He's been sniffing her butt."

"She's an old lady, at least in doggie years."

"Rex doesn't care. He wants to hump her. He's a male dog."

"Sounds more like a horn dog."

"And now that your dog is peeing all over my house, Rex wants to mark his territory. He's all worked up and he's frightening Kayla."

"Kayla?"

"Our new guinea pig. Grant brought her home yesterday."

"Whatever for?"

"Now that he's seen Rex with Winnie he's worried that Rex is lonely. So what's up?"

Where should I start?

"Well, my mother saw Jesus in a tree on the golf course and Marc is screwing Trisha, his temp, and Hannah walked in on them in our house today—"

"Stop, wait, halt, this is too much even for me to process on Georgia 400 in the middle of an ice storm. Luckily, I'm the only driver stupid enough to be out on the road. But my boss needs me to Fax her a report I wrote before she goes into her 4:30 meeting and—forget about me, let's start with Marc screwing his temp. Are you sure about that?"

"I have pictures," I said, "Barbara calls it evidence."

"Your sister-in-law Barbara? Barbara the Barracuda?"

"Yes, she's my divorce lawyer."

"You're divorcing Marc?"

"What else can I do? Hannah is a mess. No child should have to go through that. No wife should have to."

"When did Hannah see them? I thought she was in Aruba with Ellie's family."

"Well, yes, she was supposed to be, but apparently the Winslows are getting divorced, and I guess Hannah feels if she wants to experience marital enmity, she doesn't have to fly all the way to Aruba when she can get plenty of it right in her own home."

"Oh," Vicky said. "And that made you feel like dirt."

"Exactly."

"Vicky, I don't have time for this. Isn't there some place I can just fly to and get a quickie divorce?"

"You don't have time for your own divorce?"

"No, there's too much going on, what with the merger or buyout or whatever it turns out to be. And now this Max person wants to take my mother on a cruise, and—"

"Hold up. Who's Max?"

"He's some totally nice old man whose significant other was just hospitalized with Alzheimer's and he has this extra ticket for a seniors Christmas cruise, if he survives that long, and my mother thought that—"

"Do I need to come down there?"

"No, I'm okay."

"Actually, it sounds like your mother has it all together," Vicky said. "On the other hand, there's *my* mother. She went to get her botox shot yesterday and she told the doctor she didn't want to look like a guppy. And the doctor said, 'You don't want to look like Angelina Jolie?'"

"So your mother is doing okay?"

"You know she's been dating this Senator and she's been spending most of her time at his farm in Virginia," Vicky continued. "Last week they were in town and she insisted he buy her a nice piece of jewelry from Tiffany's. Well, he told her there's not going to be any jewelry buying on this trip, because Holland, that's his name, has his heart set on a new manure spreader. She argued that she'd like him to buy her an emerald to go with her eyes, and he said, 'Not unless it comes in John Deere green.' It's all about priorities, Honey. I say if your mother wants to go on a cruise and find a little well-deserved happiness with an old geezer, let her. She's been through a lot, losing your father. Now let's get back to Marc."

"Hannah and Marc will be flying in tomorrow, and I've got to get my mother packed up and moved back to Atlanta. That deal has a deadline, and we can't keep a man like Hammond Reddekker waiting. And we have a closing the day after Christmas."

"The only things that are going to be closing around here are the roads. And I'm not sure Marc and Hannah can even get out of Hartsfield tomorrow. Everything is socked in."

"Well, maybe they'll drive. They said they'd be here tomorrow, and I need a game plan. That's the real reason I called you, to get your opinion about how I can ambush Marc the minute he walks in the door."

"What did you have in mind?"

"Well, I thought about hitting him over the head with a frying pan. My mother has this nice, heavy cast-iron skillet."

"That has possibilities," Vicky said. "What else?"

"I could have Donny tackle him. Then I could tie him up and let Donny read *Bomber Missions* to him, with piped-in music from the 1940s in the background."

"That sounds kind of kinky. Not to mention cruel and unusual. Not even Marc deserves to be tortured like that."

"I've had to listen to it."

"I'm sure it wasn't torture to you. You love your brother. And your brother can barely tolerate Marc."

"He just doesn't trust anyone who isn't passionate about baseball. My next option is to enlarge the picture of Naked Trisha and hand it to him in a frame with a note saying that I've e-mailed a copy to all his partners at the firm. But it would need to be bigger than an 8x10 because Trisha's ass is sticking straight up and it practically takes up the whole image."

"Don't do that," Vicky said quickly.

"Why not?"

"Um, well, you have to consider the Raunch Factor and the fact that his partners would probably get off on that. You know she used to be a stripper in Café Exotica, that place on Cheshire Bridge by the Expressway, right?"

"No, I didn't. That makes me feel so much better."

"And she's also a life coach and an exotic photographer."

"Exactly what does a life coach do?" I asked.

"Whatever it takes," Vicky answered. "And besides, the firm only pays its temps the going rate—the lowest salary you can pay before they get going. So Trisha probably figures Marc owes her."

"Well, what evil, twisted, vengeful plans can you suggest?" I asked eagerly.

"How about forgiving him?" Vicky said quietly.

"That's not the right answer. Is that the best you can come up with?"

"Look, you've seen Trisha," Vicky said. "Her butt is as big as those whale sharks we saw at the Georgia Aquarium. Marc is obviously trying to send you a message. He's only interested in one thing—well, two things, three if you count her butt, maybe four if you count her butt twice. You don't think he's really serious about her, do you?"

"That's not the point," I reasoned. "I think too much of myself to tolerate that kind of behavior."

"Did you ever think he might be going through a phase or something?" Vicky asked cautiously.

"Like a midlife crisis? That's not an excuse to act out. I don't have time for his games. I need to get back to work as soon as possible."

"Well I can tell you absolutely nothing is happening in Atlanta. The city is shut down. No cars on the road, except mine, plenty of abandoned cars strewn all over the highway, though. Oh wait, there's another one. I'm almost at the office and some idiot guy is waiting at the red light. Apparently he doesn't realize it's legal to make a right on red. Now it's green and he still won't go. The jerk. What is his problem?"

"Maybe he's waiting for another color," I said.

"Funny. Well, I guess I'm not going anywhere. And neither is anybody else. Nobody's looking at any houses. Grant and I had a tango lesson scheduled for tonight, and I was supposed to take Rex to his doggy agility class, but those have both been canceled."

"Talk about canceled. I'm sorry, but Marc and I will have to cancel our New Year's plans. I don't think we'll even be spending New Year's together."

"What are you planning to do?"

"Probably a load of laundry."

"Don't you know it's bad luck to do laundry on New Year's?"

"What?"

"Yeah, if you do, you'll wash away the ones you love."

"Well Marc's already taken care of that." I sighed.

"You two need to work this out ASAP. Isn't saving your marriage more important than doing a load of laundry?"

"I don't know if there's a marriage left to save."

"You two have been married for more than twenty years. That's got to be worth something."

"That's 140 years in dog years," I replied.

"How come I'm just finding out about this?"

"I was too embarrassed to tell you. You're always talking about how great Marc is, how great it was that we found each other. How lucky I am."

"Well, I might have exaggerated a little," Vicky admitted. "Marc hasn't completely evolved. But you're my best friend, so naturally I'm going to say that."

"You didn't know about this, did you?" I asked suspiciously. Marc and Grant worked at the same firm, and they were best friends. Grant was a criminal attorney. Most of his clients were hip-hop artists, and they got into a lot of trouble. Grant was probably used to this kind of bad-boy behavior. "Has Grant said anything to you?"

When I didn't get a response I blew out a breath.

"Honey, you know I can't talk about what goes on at the firm. Grant would kill me."

"I'm hanging up now," I said, "on my lying former best friend."

"I only lied to protect you."

"You could have given me some warning."

"What did you want me to say, that your husband is sneaking off with his fat-ass temp every day at lunch?"

"Every day?"

I massaged my forehead. I could feel a whale of a

headache coming on. *In my next life I want to come back as one of those spotted whale sharks at the Georgia Aquarium. The whale shark is the biggest shark and the biggest fish. Nobody messes with a whale shark. Whale sharks are not aggressive, and they eat enormous amounts of squid. I am not aggressive, at least not in relationships, and I like squid, but only if it's fried. I can picture myself gliding mindlessly through the placid waters of the Georgia Aquarium, sucking up sustenance like a giant Hoover.*

"I've got to go," I said, contemplating my new, unencumbered life as a whale shark, swimming in my giant tank without a care in the world except where my next meal of fried squid was coming from. And I didn't want to cry in front of my best friend.

"Honey!" Vicky pleaded.

"I'm not mad, just tired," I said, resigned. "I'll call you later." I hung up the phone.

Was I the only one on the planet who didn't know my husband was cheating on me? *I guess the wife is always the last to know.*

Everything used to be easier with my best friend. Well maybe easier for me, sometimes not for her. When we were fifteen, I went out and bought a package of Miss Clairol hair color because Vicky, whose hair was red, decided she wanted to live her life as a blonde. I succeeded in turning my best friend into an Easter chicken. After rinsing her out, I wondered out loud, "Does she or doesn't she...cluck?" I thought it was funny. Vicky wouldn't stop crying for days. But we got past that. I hoped we could get past this.

But right now, besides my mother, the only other woman I was concerned about was Hannah. And I couldn't wait until my daughter got there. Meanwhile, first things first. I'd go to this dance tonight with my mother. And hope there was something around the corner for her. Maybe for both of us.

Chapter Seven: Swing Dancers

This was the last thing I needed. Who was I kidding? I wasn't ready for this. It was a year ago that Stanley was taken from me. A whole year had passed and I could remember the pain as if it were yesterday. I still wore my wedding ring like a talisman. Helene gently suggested I take it off for the dance, but I refused. It was still too much a part of me.

The room was crowded and the walls were closing in. I was suffocating. I looked across the dance floor, trying to focus on the horizon and stop the world from spinning.

The decorations committee had outdone themselves turning the clubhouse into a World War II-era canteen. The mood was kind of romantic. It was very realistic—too realistic, in fact.

Honey was very popular. She hadn't sat out one dance. She looked so beautiful. What a shame Marc couldn't be here to see her in her stylish green dress.

Looked like it was mostly women dancing with women. There weren't many available men at Millennium Gardens. Oh, there was a married man asking one of the girls who didn't have a husband to dance. Everybody got a little chance. That was nice.

And this was my big chance, according to my daughter and my sister. I was sure this man Helene wanted me to meet would be all wrong for me. The thought of another man was too much. I didn't want another man. I wanted Stanley back here with me.

"This was a m-mistake," I whispered, terrified, literally swaying, but not to the music. I reached out my arm to get my sister's attention and found myself clinging to her shoulder to keep upright. "It's too soon. I want to go home." *Stanley, why did you have to go and die on me and leave me alone? You promised you'd spend the rest of your life making me happy. Well, you lied. You're gone and I'm miserable. I miss you so much.*

I knew I wasn't being entirely fair. Stan had taken wonderful care of me for a lifetime. If he could have stayed here on this earth a minute longer, I know he would have. That's just the kind of man he was. But his big heart had simply given out. He fought leaving me, every step of the way. First the operation, then the pacemaker, then, suddenly—and I wasn't prepared for it; I guess no one ever is—he was gone.

I was feeling exactly the same way I did at Stan's funeral. I could still see all those well-meaning people lining the gravesite with their pitying looks. It was unseasonably warm for December, and I'd been standing outside for so long my legs could hardly support me. I was feeling faint and had trouble catching my breath. I shudder to think what would have happened if Donny hadn't caught me. I might have fallen into the open grave.

He was gone, and I knew that by myself I was way out of my element with this business deal. I wasn't prepared to operate Palladino Properties on the scale this merger would entail. Not without Stan. That's why I made the decision to sell. Honey and Donny would just have to understand.

And that's why the cruise with Max sounded so inviting. Maybe I could get off on one of the more remote islands and never get back on the ship. People would think I'd gone overboard and then I'd be free to live my life the way I wanted to. They already thought I'd gone over the edge, and maybe that was where I should go, over the edge of the world, where no one could find me.

I realized I needed help. But whenever I approached Honey about asking Marc to review the contract, her reaction was so vehement that I dropped the subject. So I'd had to go behind her back. Marc believed that selling the company was the right thing to do. And I trusted his judgment. Something was obviously going on between the two of them, but it wasn't my place to interfere in my daughter's marriage, so I stopped asking. My mother interfered a lifetime ago, and it cost me everything.

Stan would know just what to do if he were here. I could sell houses, but Stan always took care of the big picture. In fact, Stan always used to tell people, "Can my wife sell houses? Yes, indeedy." That's when he started calling me Dee Dee. And the nickname stuck.

"Don't you like the way it rolls off your tongue?" I remembered Stan asking. "Dee Dee Palladino."

I missed Stan's cornball sense of humor and the way he drew a crowd, like a circus barker. I missed a lot about Stan. But here I was alone at a dance. My daughter and my sister were right here with me, but they may as well have been a thousand miles away.

And a dance was the last place on earth I wanted to be. Why had I come? I was all dressed up and looking desperate. Feeling desperate. I spent all afternoon getting my hair done and buying a new outfit. Stan used to think I looked good in anything. In fact, he was always telling me, "Dee Dee, you would look good in a burlap sack." But these people, who could know? They were sweet, but really, when it came right down to it, they were all just strangers.

"We just got here," Helene soothed, sensing my discomfort. "I understand that you're nervous. The first time out in a social situation without Stan. Just stick with Honey and me. You look beautiful in that dress. It's your color. And doesn't Honey look fabulous in her green dress? Apparently she's not at a loss for company. I guarantee, Dee Dee, you're the most beautiful woman in this room, by far. Oh, here comes the man I wanted you to meet."

I looked up at the giant of a man ambling awkwardly toward us. He was as nervous as I was. There was something about him. Something familiar, something tugging at the back of my mind. As he got closer, I resisted the impulse to run. Too late. He was already here.

"Dee Dee, I'd like you to meet Daniel Moore," Helene said, as she introduced us.

Daniel Moore. It couldn't be. How many years had it been since we had last seen each other? His hair had gone gray, his face was fuller, but he was still as big as a bear. Not stooped over like most of the men here. But tall and imposing. And still as handsome as ever. It *was* the same Daniel. *My* Daniel.

There was no mistake. I couldn't even move, but he reached out and took my trembling hands into his. Hands I thought I'd never feel again. Warmth I hadn't known since Stan died, and before, since the day Daniel had left me to go overseas.

He flashed that dazzling smile I remembered but, my God, he didn't even recognize me. How could he not know me? But he knew me as Dorothy Lewis, and he'd been told my name was Dee Dee Palladino, of course. When he last saw me I had long ash-blond hair like Honey's. The blond was faded now and I was wearing it short. *Have I changed that much? I guess I'm an old lady now.* But he still looked the same to me.

He really filled out that tux. Big and broad-shouldered, he towered over every man in the room, and he still had the ability to focus those green eyes like a laser, like I was the only woman in the room. His eyes were still bright. *Why does he look so familiar? Of course. He looks just like—like Donny.* I had to get out of there.

"It's very nice to meet you," Daniel said, tugging my hands almost imperceptibly, sensing my inclination to bolt. He seemed genuinely interested. "Would you like to dance?"

I pulled my hands away and widened the distance between us.

"I-I don't think so," I said, starting to turn away. Part of me was afraid he'd remember. The other part was afraid he wouldn't.

"Come on, I promise I won't step on your toes. I was considered quite a good jitterbugger in my day." The best, I thought.

When I didn't object again, he pulled me onto the dance floor and we came together like we'd been dancing this way forever. We picked up the old familiar rhythm right away and didn't miss a beat. First we danced to a jitterbug medley, then to Patty Andrews singing, "I Can Dream, Can't I." Those songs were followed by some GI Jive, an Ellington medley, a Goodman instrumental jitterbug, a tribute to Harry James. The words to the songs brought back all the old familiar places. "I'll Be Seeing You." "I'll Never Smile Again." "You Made Me Love You." "They Say That Falling in Love is Wonderful." "Apple Blossom Time." It was so easy to go back to the moment when Daniel and I had first danced together.

If we continued to dance so smoothly and comfortably he would surely recognize me. We had spent months in each other's arms on the dance floor, dancing to some of these same songs. I faked some missteps and apologized, mumbling something about my feet bothering me, but then I couldn't help getting into the spirit of the music. I had come here determined NOT to have a good time. I was fighting it, but—

"Don't worry," he assured. "I'm a strong leader."

I tripped again, but after another misstep or two I let myself be carried away. We went into a couple of routines. It was like riding a bicycle. It all came flooding back.

"You've been holding out on me. You're good."

"Rusty, I'm afraid," I smiled shyly. "Stan, my husband, wasn't much of a dancer."

"Neither was my Natalie," he said.

The pressure of his hand around my waist and at my shoulder made me blush. It was good to feel a man's arms around me again. My response to him hadn't changed. Suddenly I was nineteen and in love again. How could he not sense who I was? After everything we had meant to each other. I had changed on the outside, but inside I was still that same naïve girl who had fallen desperately in love with a man who went off to Europe and never wrote. Not even one letter.

It wasn't hard to remember the last time I'd seen him. We'd been slow dancing to "I Don't Want to Set the World on Fire." How did the rest of the song go? Something about starting a flame in our hearts… And suddenly we were on fire and needed to get closer. It had been building for months. The time spent in his arms, the stolen kisses, the caresses, both of us wanting, needing, longing for more. So he had danced me out to my car.

It was just beginning to rain. The windows were fogged up, so we switched on the radio, climbed into the back seat, alone in our own little world, and I saw only him. Knowing it would be our last night together for years, maybe, we could hardly keep our hands off each other. It was the first time for both of us. Each time he touched me in places we'd never touched before, he sent out sparks. Together we had exploded like fireworks on the Fourth of July.

"I'm leaving in the morning," he said, as if that wasn't the only thing in the world I could think about.

"I know."

"I don't want to leave you," he whispered.

"I don't want you to leave."

"I want us to get married as soon as I get back," he said, as we stared into the dark window and relaxed in each other's arms. "Would you like that?"

"Oh, Daniel, yes, I'd love to marry you."

I still remembered his expression, like he couldn't believe I'd said yes. Even in the darkness I could see he was beaming.

"I can't afford—I don't have a ring to give you right now."

"That doesn't matter," I said. "The only thing that matters is that you love me."

"You know I love you. I've never said that to anyone before. Do you love me?"

"Yes. More than anything."

"I think I fell in love with you the moment we danced our first dance."

"I knew you were the one as soon as I saw you in your uniform."

"Everyone in the room was in uniform," Daniel laughed.

"You were different," I'd said. "When I looked into your eyes, the others fell away."

"All I could see was you," he echoed.

Afterward, I drove him to my house, fixed my lipstick, straightened my dress and made myself look presentable, eager to share our good news with my mother. But nothing could have prepared me for her reaction. When we opened the door, my mother was already standing there with her arms folded.

"Where have you been?" she accused. "It's after midnight."

"It's all my fault, Mrs. Lewis," Daniel said. "I'm shipping out tomorrow. We had a lot to talk about. I asked Dorothy to marry me tonight and she said yes. I know I'm the luckiest man alive, and we wanted you to be the first to know."

My mother stood there as large as a barn, as stern and stubborn as a billy goat, and as immovable as a troll.

"I can see that you've been doing more than *talking*," she said, dripping with sarcasm. "You want to marry my daughter? I don't care much for you. From what I've seen, you have nothing to offer her. My daughter could do a lot better. I came to this country as an immigrant, with nothing. I want better for my daughter."

"Mother," I pleaded. "That's rude."

"We love each other, Mrs. Lewis," said Daniel, refusing to take offense. "I have some money saved and I intend to send Dorothy all my pay. And when I get back..."

"When you get back, if you get back, she won't be here."

"How can you talk to him like that?" I screamed.

"Go upstairs, young lady."

"No, I won't. He's leaving tomorrow. It's raining outside. I'm going to drive him home." And I could tell my mother was thinking, "You see, he doesn't even have a car." I didn't care. I was determined to spend every last moment I could with him.

"As long as you're living under my roof, you'll follow my orders."

"No, Mother," I said recklessly and pulled Daniel back onto the front steps. I knew I would suffer for the insubordination later. But I didn't care. The rain was pelting us as we raced to my car. I looked back. My mother's face was bloated in the front porch light and her fists were raised in indignation.

"Daniel," I said, launching myself into his arms and kissing him when we made it safely to the car. "What are we going to do?"

"Sweetheart, I'm sorry your mother feels the way

she does, but I don't intend to let that stop us. She may be stubborn, but I'm twice as stubborn. I'll write to you every day and think of you every minute, and when I get back we *will* be together." He had sounded so confident, so sure.

I drove to his house, tears streaming from my eyes. Fog was enveloping the city. I pulled the car up in front of his driveway. It wasn't a house, really, just a space above a radiator shop. But I didn't care where he lived or how he lived or what he had or didn't have.

"Daniel, don't leave me. Please, not yet." I couldn't bear to let him go. He held me tight in his strong arms and kissed me. I remember being almost numb from the cold and the rain, or maybe it was because I knew in a short time I would be utterly alone.

"Hush, sweetheart. I won't leave you. We can stay here all night. Until morning, if you'd like."

We came together again, desperately, and finally when the light broke he pried me gently from his arms.

"Always remember how much I love you. Please wait for me."

I never saw him again, until tonight. A few months later, when I showed signs of being pregnant, my mother was furious and full of I-told-you-so's. She sold our house and moved my younger sister Helene and me to Atlanta, where she had relatives. She left no forwarding address.

She passed me off as a young war widow, and to this day I'd never had the courage to tell Donny the truth about his father. I didn't have the nerve to tell him there was no marriage and there were no love letters. That his father had gone off to war and forgotten all about me. That I was just another girl sweet-talked into "bed" by a smooth-talking soldier creating a false sense of urgency with the story that he might never come home again. It was the oldest line in the book, and I had fallen for it. What a fool. I'd thought Daniel was different.

But the revised scenario I'd created in my head wasn't exactly correct. Daniel had been the hesitant one when it came to making love.

"I don't think we should take any chances, since I'm leaving tomorrow," he had said, gathering me into his arms. "We'll have plenty of time to be together like this when I get back. Don't think I don't want to, baby, but..."

"No, Daniel, no. I don't want to wait."

"Once I—once we—then you're mine *forever*," he spoke softly, his green eyes fixed on mine, shining like a cat's in the dark.

"I'm already yours," I whispered, loving the romantic sentiment and the riskiness of it all.

In the end, our emotions and our desperate need for each other had overwhelmed us and we'd lost control and all sense of propriety. But I had instigated our spiral toward disaster.

When the disc jockey in the Millennium Gardens clubhouse began to play "In the Mood," the tempo changed and I was jerked out of the past.

The dance after that was a slow one, and Daniel must have missed his wife or the touch of a woman, because he was holding me close, and not casually close.

"Let's take a break and rest for a while," I suggested, breathless, purposely separating myself from the warmth of his embrace. "I want you to meet my daughter, Honey, but she's been out on the dance floor all evening."

We walked out onto the balcony overlooking the clubhouse lobby, but we could still hear the strains of music in the background. I looked down. There was Max, all dressed up in his tuxedo and fast asleep on the couch in an upright position. He'd gone to all this effort and then been too tired to make it upstairs to the dance. I'd promised him a dance, too. Poor, sweet, vulnerable Max. There were other people asleep on the chairs, people who weren't dressed for the dance.

Many of the seniors hung out at the clubhouse all day so they didn't have to run their air conditioning. And some of them even bathed every day at the clubhouse so their own showers wouldn't mildew and they wouldn't waste water.

"My sister said you just lost your wife," I began, looking up at Daniel.

"Yes, I miss her very much. She told me about your husband. I'm sorry. I haven't held a woman in my arms for a long time. I hope I haven't overstepped."

"No," I said. With that permission, he took my hand and gazed into my eyes. And, okay, I couldn't look away from those beautiful green eyes or that handsome face any more than I could all those years ago. His hands rubbed against my wedding ring and he gave me a questioning look.

"I-I'm not ready t-to…" I stuttered defensively.

"I understand," he said, gently pressing my ring finger against the palm of my hand and holding my hand tightly in his.

"I just took mine off tonight, as a matter of fact," Daniel admitted sheepishly.

We talked for more than an hour, danced some more, and as close as he held me, he never suspected a thing about our past. But I could still feel the pull between us, the same magic, as if it were yesterday.

"Can I walk you home?" he offered. "It's a nice night. The moon is full. Corny, I know, but..."

It was exactly the right thing to say. I was used to corny. But I wasn't prepared to be alone with him. It felt good. Too good. It felt right, but...

"Well, my sister and my daughter..."

"I'm not going to kidnap you. I'm sure they'll understand. Here comes Helene now."

"I'll see that she gets home," Daniel promised Helene as she walked up.

"But you haven't even met Honey," I protested.

"If she's as good-looking as her mother, I can't wait to make her acquaintance. But as you said, she hasn't been off the dance floor all evening. So I'll probably never get the opportunity to meet her here. We'll have plenty of time for that later."

His words hinted of the future. The future he'd once promised, that had never come to pass.

Helene smiled knowingly, her eyes twinkling.

We walked home, hand in hand. He bumped up against me "accidentally" and I didn't move away. It was a cool night, and Daniel wrapped his jacket around my shoulders.

When we got to my door, I hesitated.

"Aren't you going to invite me in?" he asked.

I twisted my hands in front of me, and he stilled them with his own.

"Okay, I guess it would be all right," I said, unlocking the door. Someone had taped another red flyer to my door. Another one of those irritating Seniors Against Sin notices warning me to "Stop Sinning Now." I crushed it and threw it in the trash can.

"What is that?" Daniel asked.

"Oh, nothing," I said, shrugging. "Just some junk mail. Why don't I fix us some coffee," I suggested, anxious to have something to occupy my hands. What I really wanted to do was touch his face and assure myself that I was not imagining him. That this was not a dream.

"Coffee sounds great. I'd like that."

Things were beginning to heat up, and not just the coffee. Something was beginning to percolate in the pit of my stomach.

Chapter Eight: *Déjà vu*

Looking around the dark room, I experienced a feeling of déjà vu. It sure took me back. Someone in this house was obsessed with World War II. A serious collector. I picked up one of the books on the coffee table. *The Mighty Men of the 381st: Heroes All*. I had some of these same books at home.

Then I looked at the picture on the sideboard. It was pretty fuzzy, but it could have been a picture of me. Any one of us, I guess. Back then, all soldiers looked alike—young, innocent, and blindly patriotic. The man in the picture wore a busted-up hat like officers wore back then, and wings. I remembered taking the cardboard out of my own hat and mashing it down, trying to impress the girls. One girl in particular. But I hadn't been an officer, then. And I'd lost my wings when I washed out of flying school.

Next to the soldier's picture I saw a boy, a boy who looked a lot like my own son. The low light must be playing tricks on me.

At that moment, Dee Dee came out of the kitchen carrying a tray and I couldn't see anything else but her. God, she was a beautiful woman. She was breathtaking, the kind of woman who defied time and age. What was it about her? She looked and felt oddly familiar, like someone I could come home to. I had felt that way holding her on the dance floor. When she was in my arms, it was as if we were transported back in time. She looked a lot like the girl I used to love. It must have been the music and the mood, and probably a lot of me wanting her to look like the girl I remembered. The lights playing tricks again.

"Dee Dee?" I asked. I liked saying her name. "Is that your husband?" I pointed to the picture on the sideboard.

"M-my first husband," she stammered, flustered, accidentally knocking the picture face down onto the lace runner. "He was killed in a bombing mission during World War II."

"Was he a pilot?" I asked, and she looked at me blankly. *Bad memories?*

"No, not a pilot, but he was part of the flight crew."

"Maybe I knew him. I flew Diamond Ls, B-17s, with the 381st Bomber Group."

"I'-I'm sure you didn't know him."

"Maybe not. I was an engineer with the 533rd Bomb Squadron, Eighth Air Force. Was your husband based in the European Theatre?"

"Yes, but I—well, I didn't know much about what he did, and then he—I mean the Army Air Corps notified me that he had died. And so I don't think you knew him. It was a big war."

"In the simplest terms, yes." I laughed. "It certainly was that. You interested in World War II?"

"Not me. My son. He never knew his father, so—"

"This is your son?"

"Yes. My son Donny."

"He looks just like his father." Dee Dee jumped.

"I don't make you nervous, do I? It's just that he looks so familiar."

She exhaled deeply and turned pale.

"M-my son used to play baseball for the Miami Kingfishers."

"Wait a minute. Palladino. Not Donny Palladino? The Slugger? He's your son?"

She nodded. "You've heard of him?"

"Sure, who hasn't? My son grew up on my stories about the war. He's sick of hearing me talk about it. But if your son is interested, I still have my bomber jacket, with the hash marks on the sleeve, the stripes, battle stars, ribbons, some air medals, a Distinguished Flying Cross. It's pretty well preserved. He might want to see it. I'd love to show him. It's still in my closet."

Dee Dee blanched.

"Did I say something wrong? Are you okay?"

"I'm fine," Dee Dee answered, but I could see that she wasn't. I waited until she had regained some color in her cheeks.

"Well, the offer stands. And if you wanted to—"

"See your etchings?" Dee Dee smiled, recovering.

"Well, there now," I said, raising my hand to caress the curve of her cheek. "You're even more beautiful when you smile. I've been waiting to see your smile all night. It was worth the wait, by the way."

Dee Dee pulled away nervously.

"Coffee's almost ready, I think."

"Tell me about your family," she asked. It was obvious she was eager to change the subject.

"Well, there's only my son. You're not going to believe this, but he's a professional football player. You may have heard of him. Barry Moore. What are the odds? That our sons are about the same age and both played professional sports. I wonder if they know each other."

Dee Dee's eyes narrowed.

"You know, I played a little ball myself, not professionally, but I always thought I had a talent," I continued. "I grew up in a tough area. When I first moved to my neighborhood, you had to run the gauntlet. They'd line up about ten kids, and the youngest one was maybe five or six and the oldest maybe eighteen or twenty-one, and you had to fight the whole bunch. So I went up to the top and put up a pretty good fight, and after that I was accepted.

"I learned how to take a knife away from somebody. How to throw somebody down. Generally how to defend myself. In those early years I was a good athlete. I played basketball for a church team because the church was warm and they gave us hot chocolate to drink. And then we'd play some softball. You'd bring a sandwich and stay all day because there was no place else to go. By the way, I had a wonderful time tonight. I don't want to leave."

****

I was feeling trapped. I was still thinking about Daniel's son, which was too weird to contemplate. Somewhere out there Donny had a half-brother. A half-brother he would probably love to know. Donny was obsessed with family. And when Daniel made the offer to show my son his uniform, I thought I wasn't going to be able to hold it together. Donny would love someone to talk about the war with, especially his own father. And I had cheated him out of that.

"The coffee's getting cold," I said. We sat together on the couch and he poured. Cozy. Uncomfortably cozy.

Then he asked me to dance. He got a kick out of the piped-in music. The fates were conspiring against me.

"Where or When" was playing, and we both experienced the strong sensation that this wasn't the first time we'd been together. Daniel mouthed the words along with the music and stared into my eyes.

I looked up at him and whispered the lyrics back to him. He was frowning, and seemed to be straining to remember something important. When he couldn't, he mouthed the rest of the lyrics, about having loved before. The music was building to a crescendo that mirrored our emotions.

"Is this music piped into the bedroom?" he asked softly, gently rubbing my back, making me go weak with those clever hands and hypnotizing me with those fathomless green eyes.

I nodded. I was shaking, and so was he. We both knew what was about to happen. What I knew had already happened so many years ago.

He danced me into the bedroom expertly and took my face into his hands. Then he kissed me. And I definitely remembered this kiss, this marvelous sensation. I remembered everything, the way he had touched me, the way his skin had felt under my hands. His heat. Even his smell. It was all coming back, and one thing led to another. Whether it was the music or the man or the moment, when his warm lips touched mine, I surrendered. It was more than a woman missing her husband and a man missing his wife. It was our special moment. What we shared was magical. I never felt this way when I made love with Stan. Never, not once.

I'd fought getting close to Stan for a long time, still tied to my memories of Daniel. When Stan finally wore me down with his unique brand of persistence, he was hard to resist. You can resist for only so long a person who loves you as much as Stan loved me and loved my child. But the first time Stan touched me I nearly jumped out of my skin. He was a gentle and ardent lover, but sex with Stan was just pleasurable, not passionate. It was familiar, but there were no fireworks. I did love him, and he was a wonderful husband and father. But I was always in control of my emotions with Stan.

It was this man I was missing and this man I felt like I was coming home to. It surprised me that I would ever feel this way again. I could almost feel the moment when the iceberg blocking my heart melted. I could hear the crack as it broke away, and I welcomed what followed with relief.

When Daniel and I fell into bed it was like we had tumbled back in time. Only for a moment did I hesitate.

And then there was nothing standing in our way.

After we made love, I blushed and turned away as we listened to "I'll Be Seeing You." I sat up in bed suddenly and pulled the sheets around me.

"Don't be embarrassed," he said. "It was wonderful. You were wonderful. And so familiar. I'm the one who has to worry about embarrassment. At my age, sometimes it's hit or miss, I'm afraid." Daniel smiled sheepishly and offered his familiar lopsided, boyish grin as he held me in his arms.

"I think this time you hit the bull's-eye." I laughed. "You know, this is probably foolish. I'm an old woman."

"Well, if you're an old woman, then I'm an old man. Are you calling me an old man?"

"No." I laughed. It felt so good to laugh again.

"I haven't felt this way since..."

"Before your wife died?" I guessed.

"Before I met my wife," he answered honestly. "You know, I almost didn't go to that dance. Your sister practically had to drag me into the clubhouse."

"I didn't want to go either," I admitted.

"What if I hadn't gone? What if I hadn't met you? In one evening, you've given me back something I thought I'd lost. I think it's obvious that I'd like to see you again."

"I'm going back to Atlanta with my daughter in the next few days. I've been avoiding going home, but it's way past time. I have to get on with my life."

"I think there's something good happening between us. But we need more time to see where it's going. Will you give us that time?"

I shrugged. I wasn't making any promises. But I knew the answer to his question. There was no future for us. I was going home. But something was holding me back from saying the words.

"If you leave, I'll be on the next plane," he insisted, sensing my hesitation. "I won't let you get away from me. I let that happen once before. Is there anyone I have to go around to get to you? I don't mind obstacles."

Some obstacles can't be overcome. I began to cry, and he folded me into his arms.

"Sssh, tell me what's wrong," he said softly.

"I have a lot of decisions to make," I explained. I began counting the fingers on my right hand, saying one thing, but thinking another.

"First, I just told my son and daughter that I'm selling our family business. A man named Hammond Reddekker is offering me so much money I would be foolish to turn it down. But I can't guarantee that he will find a place for my children." *Donny still idolizes his "dead" father. My son is entitled to know that his real father is still alive, and that he has a stepbrother. But if I tell my son his father is not dead, that he's right here in Millennium Gardens, he will hate me forever for lying to him all these years. Donny would have his father back, but I'd risk losing my son.*

"Or I can turn down the offer and we can continue to run the business, independently." *This man has a right to know he has another son. But if I tell him who I am, he'll surely hate me for being dishonest.*

"But if I go through with the deal, the merger, I ensure my husband's legacy to his children. My granddaughter Hannah has already expressed an interest in joining the business when she graduates from college." *I could build a life with this man, whatever life I have left. I loved him once. I think I may still love him.*

But you never wrote, I thought. If you had written, contacted me, given me reason to hope and wait, things might have been so different for us. If I'd had the courage to fight my mother. But back then, my mother controlled my life. And I had a new life growing inside of me. The baby had to come first. I was completely on my own, with no other means of support. I needed my family, especially in those days when people weren't so forgiving about unwed mothers.

Which road should I choose?

"Tell me about the war," I said, eager to know

what had happened to Daniel during those lost years since we had last seen each other.

"Well, the short version is, I enlisted on March 18, 1941. I was a top-turret gunner on a B-17 crew. We flew thirty combat missions. I was discharged on September 25, 1945, with a 52-20. The Army gives you $52 dollars a week for 20 weeks. I could either have looked for a job or taken advantage of the GI Bill of Rights. I never did get to college. I blew my opportunities because I was obsessed with looking for someone, a girl I used to know. Never found her, but in a roundabout way I found a career and a wife."

"What do you mean?" I asked evenly, hoping my voice didn't betray my feelings. *You looked for me?*

"Well, I got pretty good at digging out information, so I became a private investigator, then a cop, and then chief of detectives. I'm retired from the Palm Beach County Sheriff's Office. Forced retirement, actually. I wasn't ready to leave, but they have age limits. Always dreamed of going solo, opening up my own detective agency, maybe right here in Millennium Gardens. These people could use my help. I know I could do some important work here. But dreams have a way of going by the wayside. At least my dreams. And after Natalie died, well, I just didn't have the heart to start over."

"Do you ever think about that girl?" I ventured, my hand and my heart trembling to finally be able to talk about our past. To actually have him back beside me. Real. Not in my imagination or my dreams.

"All the time. She was pretty special. You remind me a lot of her, actually. I wrote her almost every day. But my letters were returned, unopened. I sent her money, but she didn't want my money or me. And she never wrote to me. I figure she found somebody else. Somebody better."

Letters?

"Her mother didn't think much of me. I thought she might have sent back the letters without showing them to her daughter, but I was on the other side of the world. There was nothing I could do until I got home. When I finally did, years later, I tried frantically to find her, but she had disappeared without a trace. If her friends knew anything, they weren't talking."

Could it be? Could my mother have done such a horrible thing? Knowing I was pregnant with Daniel's child? Knowing how much I loved and missed him, how I pined for him, and how much Donny needed his father? No wonder she pushed me to marry Stan. To my mother, Stan represented safety, security, status. There was no question he would be a good provider for her daughter and grandson and, indirectly, for her. And Stan didn't disappoint. He provided for all of us. There was nothing he wouldn't do for us or give to us.

"Did you love her?" I couldn't resist asking.

"More than I loved my own life. God, yes, I loved her. I was an emotional wreck the whole time I was over in Europe. I'd begun to think her mother was right. That I wasn't good enough. That she had moved on. And then when I imagined her with another man, well, that was another kind of hell. There were times when I actually didn't want to come back, if you know what I mean. Not if there was nothing left for me to come home to. It would have been so easy, you know. I thought about it, too, but I couldn't risk anyone else's life. We, the guys, were a team."

"Do you still have the letters?" I asked, twisting my hands around the sheets.

"Yeah, sure, I saved them. I never showed them to my wife. But I couldn't destroy them. That would be like letting her go, and this way a part of her stayed with me. But I had to get back to a normal type of life."

"When did you meet your wife?"

"I found her when I was looking for my sweetheart. I went down to City Hall to check the records, forwarding addresses. Natalie was the office clerk, and she did her best to help me with the search. But one day, after almost a year of trying and following dead ends, she put her hand on mine and said, 'I think it's time to give up. You're never going to find her.' Her hand was warm and gentle, and she was there and my sweetheart was gone, and one thing led to another. She got pregnant and I married her. It was the right thing to do. It was too late for regrets and longing for what could never be."

I sighed deeply and thought back to the night before my wedding to Stan. The night when I found out Daniel was still alive. My best friend from Pittsburgh had flown down for the wedding and she was helping me pack for my honeymoon. I hadn't heard a word about Daniel since he'd left, and when I asked my friend if she had, she hesitated.

"Well, your mother said that I wasn't—"

"I want to know what you know," I demanded, interrupting her. "Is he—d-dead?" I held my breath. I was prepared for the worst, but I had to know either way.

"No," my friend said.

I could still remember the relief I'd felt. I had been

certain he was dead. Otherwise, he never would have abandoned me and our son.

"He did come to see me, asking about you," she said. "And there was a girl with him. She was draped across his chest, all clingy, like, you know, there was already something between them. At least she wanted me to think so. And your mother had made me promise not to tell you if he should come around. She said that it was the best thing for you. That Daniel had ruined your life. And so when he did show up, I told him I didn't know where you were. I'm sorry. Your mother can be pretty forceful. And then he and the girl were obviously—"

I broke down. That was the first I knew for sure Daniel survived the war. I experienced a range of emotions in the space of an instant. *Daniel's alive. Thank you, God, for bringing him home safely. Even if it's to another woman's arms.* I was so happy, grateful. I had thought maybe if I flew back to Pittsburgh, if I could just reach him on the phone, tell him where I was, he'd come after me.

But I was on the verge of getting married, and then there was the matter of that girl with Daniel. And our baby. What would Daniel think about being saddled with a baby? He'd made all sorts of promises, the kind new lovers make. We both had. But none of those promises had been kept, because the war had turned the world upside down. And I needed a father for my son. Stan had been there when I needed him. He was wonderful with Donny. Donny had really taken to him. Daniel was obviously ready to move on. So I cried myself to sleep and woke up the next morning, bleary-eyed but resigned to marrying Stan and going on with my life. I walked down that aisle with a smile and never told Stanley. I'd made a commitment to him, and I was determined to stick by it.

It wasn't an unhappy life. Stan couldn't have been more adoring. Of course I loved him. I discovered just how much after he was gone. His death devastated me. But something had always been missing in our relationship. Some spark of me that I'd hidden deep inside in a place I'd never let Stan enter.

"Did you love your wife?" I asked Daniel.

"I grew to love her. She was a wonderful person. It was a different kind of love. She loved enough for both of us, you know. I think we can only feel one great love in our lives. And Dorothy was mine."

"Dorothy," I said, holding my breath. "Was that her name?"

"She was a beautiful girl. And she had the biggest blue eyes, eyes that were a lot like yours, eyes you could get lost in, and the biggest heart."

I was going to cry. I had to get Daniel out of here before he saw my tears.

"My daughter will be coming home soon, so you'd better go," I choked.

Just then I heard the key in the lock and we rushed to get dressed, like a couple of guilty teenagers about to get caught in the act.

****

"Mom?" I called out, walking into the living room and dropping my purse on the coffee table. "Are you home? Aunt Helene just dropped me off."

"Uh, yes, Honey, I'll be right out." I heard a lot of commotion behind the door, giggling, strange noises, and a deep, unfamiliar voice.

My mother was coming out of the bedroom with a man, a rather remarkably handsome giant of a man. He was built like the Incredible Hulk. He looked familiar, but I knew I'd never seen him before. *Hold on here, the bedroom?* My hand flew to my heart.

"I was, uh, just showing, I mean…" My mother sputtered, looking from the Incredible Hulk back to me.

"This must be Max," I said, trying to regain my composure. Well, I guess they couldn't wait until the cruise.

"Max?" the man asked, puzzled. "Is that my competition?"

"No." Mom laughed. "Max is just a man in my building, a friend I met in my bereavement group."

"Oh, yeah, your sister tried to get me to go to one of those bereavement meetings, but I prefer to suffer in silence. Hi," said the man, coming toward me. My mother was obviously too flustered to make the introductions, so he stepped up to the plate. Cocking his head, he flashed me a look of recognition, and then he said, "I'm Daniel Moore. You must be Dee Dee's daughter. It's a pleasure to finally meet you in person. Your mother was trying to introduce us at the dance earlier this evening, but you were a popular partner. We kept missing each other."

I would definitely have remembered meeting you.

"You must be the one Aunt Helene was talking about," I said.

"Right, that's me, the widower, otherwise known as the eligible bachelor. You look just like your mother, by the way, except for your nose," Daniel pointed out.

"I got my dad's nose," I stated.

"I didn't mean anything by it." Daniel laughed,

tapping his finger lightly to the tip of my nose, like my dad used to do. "It's a beautiful nose."

Okay, this man has potential, even if he's not Max and my mother has become a loose woman.

"I've spent my whole life trying to live down this nose," I said, crinkling it.

"Don't," he said, squeezing it affectionately.

"Mr. Moore." I nodded to him. *You two are so busted.* All the telltale signs were there. Her smell was all over him. My mother's lipstick was smeared. He'd lost the bowtie to his tux, and I was ready to bet if I were to go into the bedroom I'd find it tangled up in the sheets. My mother had taken a man to bed. How did I feel about that? How did I feel that another man had taken my father's place so soon? A little wobbly. But Mom looked so happy, like a young girl again. Her face was flushed with that well-loved look. A look Daniel Moore obviously put there. *Well, okay, Honey Palladino, you're just being a prude. This man has put a smile back on your mother's face. So stop being so unreasonable and selfish and, okay, a little envious.*

"Look, I'd better be going," Daniel said awkwardly, putting a possessive hand on my mother's shoulder.

Oh, yes, I noticed the way he was touching her.

"I'm going to play golf with my son tomorrow," he said, looking at his watch. "Actually it's already tomorrow, and then I'm on the hook for dinner, but I'd like to see you the following morning, for breakfast, if you're free. Although I don't know how I can wait that long."

"No, I don't think..." Dee Dee objected.

"I make a mean omelet." Daniel laughed. "Hey,

I'm offering to cook for you. It doesn't get much better than that."

I looked at my mother. She hadn't looked this happy since, well she'd *never* looked this happy that I could recall.

"Go ahead, Mom," I said. And her face lit up because I had given my permission for the breakfast, and maybe for the rest of it.

"Well, okay," she agreed.

"I'll be by to pick you up at nine," Daniel promised, and he was acting as giddy as a schoolboy with his first crush. He looked like he wanted to kiss my mother but thought better of it because I was in the room. And she looked like she wanted him to. Instead, he touched her hand and gazed at her with those gorgeous green eyes. Oh, he was a hunk all right. The Incredible Hunk.

"Until tomorrow, then," he said wistfully to my mother. She nodded. She was walking on air.

"Honey, you're invited to come if you'd like," Daniel offered, rather halfheartedly, I thought.

Oh, yeah, the last thing these two needed was a middle-aged chaperone. A third wheel. Then again, maybe that was exactly what they needed.

"Thanks, but I think I'm going to be packing," I replied.

Jeesh. My mother was dating. It was beyond weird.

"Honey, it was nice meeting you," Daniel said before he walked out the door.

"Mom, is this guy Jewish?" I asked, after I was sure he was gone.

She tilted her head and considered the question. "You know something? I don't even know." My mother laughed at the absurdity of the question that a Jewish mother would typically ask her daughter. "Your father wasn't Jewish. And at my age, what difference could it possibly make?"

"Well, then, I hope you didn't tell him about your Jesus tree. I don't want him to think you're crazy, at least not until the second date."

My mother laughed again. She'd laughed more in the last few minutes than I'd seen her laugh in the past year.

"Actually, we never got around to talking about that."

"Probably would have been inappropriate under the circumstances," I said, gesturing to her bedroom. "You two obviously had other things on the brain. I wasn't wild about the idea of Max, but I have a nice feeling about this guy, Mom. I like him. He seems familiar somehow. He's substantial. He could be a linebacker. He's in pretty good shape for an old guy. And those eyes, wow!"

My mother blushed.

"Meeting him tonight is a sign," Dee Dee said wistfully, looking like she had a secret she wasn't prepared to share.

"A sign?" I asked, confused. Was she talking about her tree again? What should it matter if she saw Jesus in a tree if it could bring her some comfort? Make her feel less alone in the world.

Chapter Nine: The Q-Tip Brigade

One by one, my mother's friends were "dropping like flies." Her words, not mine. Mom's intimate group of girlfriends, "The Awesome Eight," had been decimated to "The Fabulous Four," much like the demise of the Big Eight accounting firms. Mom's friends used to run in a pack. They were as close as sardines. There was hardly room to maneuver between them. And I was a part of that. I thought my mother's friends would always be there, for her and for me. But sometimes, as Donny liked to say, life throws you a curve ball.

One of the last friends to go had been Maxine. We called Maxine the Black Widow because she'd already outlived two husbands and was afraid of marrying a third time. She'd been going with Harry, her significant other, for fifteen years. The way Maxine figured, she was keeping Harry alive by *not* marrying him.

I was sure Maxine, who had been in the synagogue choir with my mother, was now in heaven singing soprano with the angels.

"I wish I could have told her to give my love to your father," my mother had said last week, after we'd had a good cry over the phone when we learned about Maxine's death. We didn't even have the finality of a funeral. Maxine had requested that her ashes be scattered over the Pacific Ocean off Hawaii. Although I didn't think my mother could have survived another funeral.

With my father gone, all the husbands of the Fabulous Four were dead, and friendships had become even more important.

My aunt knew my mother was missing Maxine, so she invited some friends over to her place and arranged for us to drop by. Donny had left Jackson with us so he and his girls could finish their holiday shopping. Jackson was cute, but he was also boisterous—in my brother's words, "all boy"—and my mother and I had him by the hand so our little whirling dervish couldn't get into any serious trouble.

My aunt set out a platter of homemade chopped liver and crackers, a vegetable tray and dip, a fruit plate, some home-baked sweets, and diet sodas.

"I'm going to wreck this joint," Jackson said, pulling away from me.

"Oh, no, you're not," I countered, shaking my head. Jackson was big, as big as Donny had been when he was a boy, and honestly I thought he *could* wreck the place if given half a chance.

"Would you like something to eat?" I asked, trying to get my nephew's mind off thoughts of havoc and pandemonium.

"It's all rabbit food," Jackson frowned, eyeing the table suspiciously.

"No, it's just healthy food. But I do see a brownie over there. Why don't you go over and get one, but just one, or your mother will kill me."

I released Jackson's hand and he lumbered over to the table, under my watchful eye.

"Wait, let me take your backpack," I called, afraid

of what he might put into it.

Jackson turned at the table and greeted me with a full-face scowl.

"Okay," I said, backing off, remembering what my sister-in-law had said about Jackson's separation issues.

I turned my attention to my aunt.

"We've got a roomful of Q-Tips here," Aunt Helene confided to me.

"Q-Tips?" I wondered.

"Gray hairs," my aunt explained, as she took me by the hand to make the introductions. "And most of them are paired up."

My mother did not belong in this place, with these people. She was still young and beautiful.

"Honey, I'd like you to meet Carol and Hank," Aunt Helene said before I could get my mother out of there. "Honey is Dee Dee's daughter. And that adorable little boy over there"—Jackson smiled and shot us an angelic look—"is Dee Dee's grandson." Then she leaned over and whispered, "Carol and Hank are significant others." In her normal voice she continued, "Hank is the vice president of the Millennium Gardens Boca Raton Community Center."

"It's very nice to meet you," I said, offering my hand.

"Carol and Hank just returned from a romantic trip on the French Riviera," Aunt Helene remarked.

"It's a convenient arrangement, going together on our vacations," said Hank. "We've each got a ready-made roommate for double occupancy reservations."

"It's been so great since we found each other," Carol admitted. "Isn't he the handsomest man in sight? And add to the bargain, he drives at night."

"I think Carol's really good-looking," Hank echoed.

"I think he's blinded by my good cooking," answered Carol, "or maybe he's just blind."

"It's good to know, when we're dating, I don't have to worry...she's right there waiting," Hank said, taking hold of Carol's hand.

"We've got a great understanding; we're content without wedding banding," Carol quipped.

"I heard you two are going to take a trip out to Vegas soon," Aunt Helene said to Hank.

"Yes, we both like to gamble," Hank said.

Maybe I should take a gamble on life. Here I was with this cute couple, who weren't officially a couple, laughing, rhyming, bantering like seasoned vaudevillians with their routines, teasing and enjoying each other's company, and just being together and alive. It didn't matter that they were in their seventies or older. Watching Carol and Hank, I realized there is no limit on happiness or second chances. They were in the ecstatic throes of their new romance. It was selfish of me, I realized, but I was jealous of their obvious show of affection.

"Being alone was very lonely," observed Hank, "after I lost my dear one and only. Then I met this lovely charmer."

"And I met my knight in shining armor," Carol agreed.

"No disrespect was intended, when my new honey picked up where my dear wife ended," Hank explained.

"Now, we're significantly blended," Carol said.

I wanted to learn more about this significant-other business. Before I knew it I would be approaching the

Big 5-0. My empty, loveless life had turned out like Y2K—absolutely nothing was happening. Marc had Trisha. Who did I have? Where could I sign up for *my* significant other?

"So, Dee Dee, you and Daniel looked really good on the dance floor last night," Carol commented. "The whole condo is talking about it. We noticed he didn't get home till the wee hours of the morning."

My mother blushed.

"I thought you and Max were an item," she pressed.

"Max is just a friend," my mother explained.

"When am I going to meet this Max person?" I wondered.

"I've invited him to drop by," Aunt Helene said. "And Daniel, too."

"Helene, you didn't," my mother protested.

"It will do Mr. Big and Bulky Gorgeous Green Eyes good to know he's not the only man in the picture."

The doorbell rang as if on cue, and an elderly gentleman shuffled in behind my aunt. She spoke loudly into what was apparently his good ear before she introduced me to the infamous Max.

"So you're Dee Dee's daughter." Max smiled, extending his free hand and displaying some missing teeth. "What a beauty. It's easy to see where you get your good looks. You and your mother could be twins, except for your nose. It's so nice to meet the daughter of my lady."

"Your lady?" I said, flabbergasted, giving my mother a questioning look. My mother raised her shoulders, perplexed.

"She's the most appealing woman in my life," Max said proudly.

I couldn't believe this. I examined Max from the top of his frayed white hair and his hearing aid to his shiny oxfords and mismatched socks. With the Coke-bottle lenses Max was sporting, I was surprised he could even see me. Well, he certainly didn't have any problem spotting my nose. The Palladino nose had struck again.

There was no cause for concern about my mother sharing a stateroom with this man. As he leaned precariously on his cane, Max looked like he had one foot in the grave and no important equipment in working order. That was it. My mother felt sorry for him. She needed someone to take care of again. She was a born nurturer. At his stage in life, Max would be fast asleep as soon as his head hit the pillow. But he *was* kind of cute. I wondered if he had a son, a much younger son.

At this point, Jackson came up to me, his hands and face smudged with brownie goop, and announced, "I have to go to the bathroom."

I wondered how many brownies he had eaten. I walked him over to the guest bathroom, washed and dried his face and hands, and told him I'd be waiting right outside the door.

After a few minutes Jackson's voice boomed out of the bathroom, loud enough for everyone in the room to hear. "Aunt Honey, I can't poop."

"I know what you mean, kid," Max answered jovially.

Sighing, I said, "Okay, then we'll try again later."

I hoped Aunt Helene would stop talking long

enough to let Max sit down. He looked like he might not make it to the chair. My suspicions were confirmed when he told me he takes ninety-eight different medications a week. I guess that's the new pick-up line among septuagenarians and octogenarians.

"My wife was the first Jewish Rockette," Max announced proudly.

Jeesh.

"You weren't really planning to go on that cruise with him, were you?" I whispered to my mother when Aunt Helene settled Max into an easy chair on the other side of the room. And not a moment too soon. "He can barely walk. I don't think his heart could take that much excitement."

"Probably not," she admitted. "But Christmas is right around the corner. He'll be so disappointed if he can't use those tickets. He's such a nice man."

"I'm sure he is," I answered, "but still."

"He's just a companion, someone to go out with occasionally. I'm hoping some woman will come along between now and then and snatch him up," my mother said. "You know, defrost a chicken. What about Shirley Weinstock?"

"She's sort of seeing Paul Sellers," said Aunt Helene, coming in at the tail end of the conversation.

"I thought Paul was married," Dee Dee said.

"Well, he is," Aunt Helene admitted. "But he has Alzheimer's and sometimes he forgets he has a wife. When that happens, he comes into Shirley's bed and lies down next to her. I think she has her hands full."

"I guess we can always call Merle. She's dating someone, but she doesn't take him seriously. She thinks he's looking for a nurse with a purse."

When I looked puzzled, my aunt explained.

"It means he's looking for a woman who can take care of him and also support him financially. But Merle is just looking for excuses to move on to the next guy."

"Well, she doesn't sound nice enough for Max," Dee Dee pointed out.

"You're probably right," Aunt Helene agreed. "There's always Cher. Sonny and Cher have broken up again."

"Sonny and Cher?" I asked.

"Yes, Sam Wexler's nickname is Sonny, and he's been dating Charlotte Simms—we call her Cher—for years. But Cher dumped him. They had just returned from a cruise and she traded him in for a new model, complained he fell asleep at the Black Jack table. And that he spent too much time in Phoenix taking care of his sick daughter. He was gone for weeks at a time. She was very lonely. So she took up with some new guy. Left town with him for a while. That was before you got here, Dee Dee. But she kept her place at Millennium Gardens. Now she's back and determined to get together with Sonny again. But Sonny's moved on. He's with a new significant other—a woman named Rose Blanco. Cher is furious. There was quite a scene at the clubhouse last night after you and Daniel left the dance. It got pretty ugly. I thought she was going to pull Rose's hair out. Except that Rose doesn't have much hair left to pull.

"She and Sonny break up and make up on a regular basis," Aunt Helene continued. "But the word is that he's not giving in to her this time. So she's available now. And Max is on her radar screen. You should have seen her sniffing around him at the dance, after she woke him up. You'd better watch out."

"I don't have designs on Max," my mother said. "If she's free and he's free, then—"

Aunt Helene shook her head. "We call Cher 'Mattress Back.' She has a reputation of going from one man to another. She's like a doorknob—everybody's had their hands on her."

"I think Max deserves someone more loyal than Mattress Back," Dee Dee reconsidered.

"Unfortunately, Max is ripe for the picking. He's lonely and rich *and* he's got an unused cruise ticket. That's an appealing combination. There aren't many single men left around here. Uh-oh, here she comes now, dressed to kill. None of the other women will give her the time of day. She's such a vamp."

"Well, then why did you invite her?" I asked.

"I didn't. She heard I was having a get-together and she invited herself."

Mattress Back came on into the room and headed straight for my mother. Dressed in a tight V-necked red sweater and winter white slacks, she was pretty well preserved for a senior. Still rosy and plump in all the right places. A little too made up and trashy-looking for my taste. The blood red lipstick was a little over the top. And the high-heeled sandals were a bit much. Judging from the way she was put together and her provocative walk, her spindly heels click-clacking against the ceramic tiles, it was obvious she was trolling for fresh meat. And my mother was an obstacle she wanted to eliminate. She would have been funny if she weren't so pitiful. But at the same time, there was something decidedly sinister about that woman.

"You're Helene's sister Dee Dee, right?" Cher

grumbled, eyes flashing, mouth turned down in an unattractive frown. "Rumor has it you and Max are going on a Caribbean cruise."

"I haven't decided yet," my mother said, inching away from Cher. "He had an extra ticket, and I—"

"Well, don't count on going," Cher interrupted viciously. "Charlotte's back, and I don't think Maxie is going to have any time for you anymore."

My mother's mouth fell open, and Cher strutted off in Max's direction.

"She's all wrong for Max," my mother managed when she finally recovered. "She'll eat him alive."

"That's the plan," my aunt acknowledged. "Just look at her. She's moving in for the kill."

"We can't let her get her hands on Max," Dee Dee said, alarmed. "What about Birdie Rosen, the woman who just lost her significant other?"

"That's a great idea," Aunt Helene agreed. "Two lonely people. Temperamentally suited. I've invited her too. I'll see that they reconnect as soon as she gets here. I'll have to think up an excuse to get that bloodsucker away from Max. Don't you worry about it. You need to focus all your attention on Daniel when he arrives."

The doorbell rang and Daniel appeared in the doorway, big and burly, his bulk barely fitting into the door frame. He peeked into the room, zeroed in on my mother, and broke out in the biggest, sloppiest grin.

Charlotte's eyes bugged out when she saw Daniel, and she wiggled off of Max's lap and intercepted Daniel before he could get to my mother.

"Hey there, Green Eyes, I'm Charlotte. You must be new. I haven't seen you around here, and I would have noticed *you.*" She placed a plump hand on

Daniel's arm and began rubbing it. She arranged herself so that Daniel could get a good look at what she had to offer. Her gold bangle bracelets jangled and she jiggled. Then she started massaging his ring finger.

"No ring, I see," she said, batting her eyelashes like a woman half her age, sidling closer to him and grasping his arm in an octopus grip.

Daniel squirmed uncomfortably. "I moved here about eight months ago, and then I lost my wife soon after. I, uh, just took the ring off."

"Well, I'm sorry," Cher purred insincerely, winding her leg around Daniel's. "That's rough. I know you're lonely. Well, Charlotte will fix you right up. I know just the thing. I've got something nice to drink back at my place to get us in the mood, if you know what I mean." She licked her full, wet, red lips and smiled crookedly. "My place is just down the hall."

I wondered if prostitution was legal in Florida.

"I, uh, I'm here to see Dee Dee," answered Daniel, obviously flustered. He looked over at my mother uncomfortably.

Cher turned to Dee Dee and glared.

"Well, now, I'm not one to talk, but you know Dee Dee has a thing for Max over there. They're going on a Christmas cruise together. So you come on with Charlotte. Did anyone ever tell you you have strong arms? Such a big man. I'll bet you're just a little old teddy bear. Why don't we go to my place and find out how cuddly you are under all those muscles." Daniel stood stock still, looking shocked and absolutely terrified.

Aunt Helene chose that moment to come to his rescue.

"I think Daniel has a previous engagement with my sister," she said, grabbing Daniel by the elbow and wrestling him out of Charlotte's steely grip.

Charlotte hissed like a viper when her tasty morsel was taken away.

Jackson picked that moment to barrel though the bathroom door, almost knocking Mattress Back flat on her face. I leaned in and kept her from losing her balance.

Cher glared at Jackson.

"He's just a little boy. He didn't mean anything by it," I apologized.

Cher's eyes were still flashing, so I got Jackson out of her path as quickly as possible and headed in my mother's direction.

"Dee Dee," Daniel breathed in relief when he arrived at her side, placing a brief kiss on her lips. He turned to me. "Honey, it's nice to see you again. And who have we here?"

"I'm Jackson," my nephew said.

"That's my grandson," Dee Dee smiled. "Donny's son."

"Well, Jackson, it's a pleasure to meet you." Daniel shook Jackson's hand.

"What a fine-looking young man you are," Daniel added. "I'll bet you're going to follow in your father's footsteps."

Jackson beamed. "I'm going to be on the team someday."

"Okay, champ, I want to introduce you around," I said, taking Jackson's hand. "We'll be back."

"Sorry about that scene at the door," Daniel said. "I don't know what happened. And I'm sorry to be so late.

My son would have been disappointed if I'd canceled our dinner. Don't think I didn't want to, though."

"That would have been rude," Dee Dee said, blushing. "And don't apologize for that she-monster. I just had the *pleasure* of meeting her."

"Let's not talk about her," Daniel whispered. "I'm just lucky I got out of the doorway alive. She's about as subtle as a hooker. And I think she might be dangerous. All I could think about the whole day was you and when we could be together again. Can we get out of here? I want to be alone with you."

"Daniel, this is my sister's party. We're her guests. We can't leave now. We just got here."

Max looked like he was getting agitated in his chair in the corner. He was tapping his cane on the tile floor in an effort to get my mother's attention.

"Hey, that guy over there is giving me the evil eye," Daniel said.

"Oh, that's Max," my mother said.

"That shark at the door said you and Max were an item and that you were going on a cruise together."

"No. He has an extra ticket to the cruise. His significant other is too ill to go, and I think he just wants company, not me in particular. I think any warm body will do at this point."

"You're not going with him, are you?" Daniel challenged.

"I don't think so, but I want to make sure he has someone nice to take. It would be a shame to waste the ticket."

"Just so it's not you. I don't want your warm body next to anyone's but mine."

My mother blushed again and looked awkwardly at

me. I smiled and rolled my eyes. I couldn't believe what was coming out of this man's mouth.

Hank walked over to Daniel.

"Hank Adams," he said, introducing himself. "I'm the vice president of the Millennium Gardens Boca Raton Community Center. In charge of security. Helene tells me you used to be with the Palm Beach County Sheriff's Office."

Daniel extended his hand and flashed his badge. "That's right. I'm retired, but I like to keep my hand in."

"That's good to know. I might have a job for you, if you'll come by my office at the Community Center. I'm sure you've seen those Seniors Against Sin flyers around the complex."

"Yes, as a matter of fact, I've pulled a few from my own front door."

"We're trying to keep it sort of hush-hush. We don't need any outsiders knowing our business, so if you have some time, I could use your help. I'd like you to look into the mystery for us. Also, I'm going to be going on the Millennium Gardens Christmas Cruise, so I'd appreciate it if you would keep your eyes and ears open while I'm gone."

"I'd like that," Daniel said.

"Oh, and let me give you a little friendly advice. Keep away from Cher. That woman is poison. I'd stick with the beauty you've got right here."

My mother's face lit up at the compliment.

Daniel nodded in agreement. "I intend to. And thanks."

The doorbell rang and my aunt ushered Birdie Rosen into the room. Ignoring Charlotte, she pulled up a folding chair next to Max's seat and gestured for Birdie to make herself comfortable.

"Max," Aunt Helene said, smoothly. "You remember Birdie Rosen, don't you? I think you two have a lot in common."

"I was sorry to hear about Ben," Max said respectfully. "He was a good man."

"Yes, he was," she said and began to cry. "Oh, I promised I wouldn't do that."

"Don't apologize," he said, gallantly offering her a handkerchief from his coat pocket. He patted her shoulder while she dabbed her eyes.

"We were very close. We helped each other out. Remember when he had his hip operation and he stayed at my house for three weeks? And then he stayed with me for a month while he recovered from his knee operation. I took care of him quite well. And he was a good companion. He adored me. I can't say… It's hard for me to say I loved him like I loved my husband. I cared for him. Saying 'I love you' is extremely romantic, don't you think? At this stage in life, romance is not really the proper word, don't you agree? It's affection, consideration, deep friendship, and caring for each other. I felt a lot of goodness for him. I felt appreciated. He felt the same way. He was happy with me and I was content with him. So it worked fine. But now he's gone, and I'm afraid I'm not handling it very well at all. And we were all supposed to go on that cruise together. But now—"

"I understand," Max nodded.

"He was a very intelligent man," Birdie continued. "I like a man who's intelligent. We could have a conversation about the toaster and sit and talk for hours or feel comfortable just sitting and not talking."

I had a feeling this woman carried on conversations with a lot of inanimate objects.

"Exactly," Max concurred.

"I think of him a great deal," Birdie said. "I miss him terribly. Even when we didn't see each other, we phoned back and forth. But I'm doing all the talking. I was sorry to hear about Jean going into the home."

"Yes, she's a lovely woman," Max said, and his eyes welled up.

Birdie placed a sympathetic hand on Max's knee.

"Did you know that my wife was the first Jewish Rockette?" Max asked.

"Really?" Birdie said. "We're all alone in this world now, and that's a shame. But I have a nice chicken I could warm up and bring over to you. Maybe some matzo ball soup to go with it."

Max's eyes brightened. The deal was sealed.

"Did you know I take ninety-eight different medications a week?" he chirped.

Looking at Birdie and Max together, I knew he was going to be just fine. It was a match made in heaven. She couldn't stop talking and he could barely hear. Love at any age couldn't be sweeter. I wondered how long it would take for Max to withdraw his cruise invitation from my mother and extend it to his latest lovebird, Birdie Rosen.

Aunt Helene came up behind me and put her hands on my shoulders as we both glanced at my mother and Daniel.

"You know, my Harold was a handsome man, built solid, but not nearly as good-looking as Daniel."

We laughed. Heck, even I thought Daniel was

good-looking. Mom's new guy was in great shape for a senior citizen. He must have some great genes. He and my mother were huddled in a corner. They couldn't seem to get close enough. They were oblivious to everyone else in the room.

"Look at the two of them," Aunt Helene said wistfully. "They were made for each other."

"I lost my father not that long ago, so I can't come face-to-face with the fact that there's another man in her life so soon after," I confided. "It's a little difficult to adjust to. But I can't deny he makes her happy. And one thing I know with certainty—my dad loved my mother beyond anything, and he would have wanted her to be happy."

"The main thing is no one should be alone," Aunt Helene said, "whether you develop close relationships with other women and you get together and do things or find a significant other for male companionship. The Gardens is a wonderful place to live."

I was beginning to understand what my mother saw in the place. She had friends here, she was making a new life for herself, and, from the looks of it, she was beginning to fall in love.

"We're all in the same boat," Aunt Helene explained. "We complain about the same things. When we get together, our conversations are all about doctors and what restaurant to go to. And speaking of conversations, your mother and Daniel seem to be pretty cozy."

Watching the two of them together, I couldn't deny it.

"Dee Dee, I don't think I can wait until breakfast tomorrow," Daniel was saying to my mother, loud enough for me or anyone else in the room to hear.

Jeesh. My mother was getting more action than I was.

All the significant others were looking at Daniel and Dee Dee and nodding knowingly. Some were openly smirking.

I could take a hint. I was uncomfortable intruding on their intimacy. I walked over to my mother.

"Mom, I'm beat. I need to make some phone calls. I'll just go back to the condo with Jackson, and maybe Daniel, uh, Mr. Moore, can drive you—"

"I'll come with you," she interrupted nervously.

"Dee Dee?" Daniel questioned, his hand tightening around hers, looking like he was afraid if he let her go she'd disappear into thin air.

"Daniel, I'm sure you're exhausted after a long day, and you're going to pick me up early tomorrow, so maybe we'd better call it a night."

He was fervently stroking my mother's hand.

"I'm rushing you," he said. "I don't mean to, but when something is right, you just know it."

"Daniel, everybody is staring at us." Dee Dee frowned. "I'm going to get a reputation."

He laughed.

"At our age, I think that's considered a good thing."

"I just think—"

"Dee Dee," he said, breathing heavily. "Please come back to my place."

"You're right. I think we're moving too fast," she said. "Honey, take me home."

"Don't be angry with me," Daniel said, flashing my mother an endearing look.

“I’m not angry,” my mother assured Daniel, smiling. “I’m looking forward to our breakfast, to being with you, tomorrow.”

“Good, okay, well, then, I live right down the hall, so I’ll see myself out. Until tomorrow.” He had no interest in hanging around after my mother was gone.

“Goodbye, Daniel,” she said, pulling her hand out of his. “Honey, will you tell your aunt we’re leaving?”

“Okay. Goodbye, Mr. Moore,” I echoed, following my mother’s eyes as she watched him go.

“You like him, don’t you, Mom? More than like, from what I can see.”

“I do,” she admitted. “I liked him from the beginning. But I don’t want you to think that… I mean, that your father was—”

“I know Dad would want you to be happy,” I said. “You have nothing to be ashamed of.”

As we walked down the stairs and back to my mother’s unit, swinging Jackson between us, I brought up the unresolved issue of Palladino Properties.

“You haven’t asked about the business since I’ve gotten here,” I began cautiously. “Aren’t you interested in what’s been going on back in Atlanta?”

Dee Dee looked guilty. “Well, I—”

“I know it’s difficult to bounce back, and you’re still recovering from Dad’s death. But have you thought any more about not selling Palladino Properties but doing some kind of merger? I mean, you only have a few days left to decide.”

“That’s all I’ve been able to think about,” Dee Dee admitted anxiously. “I still have a lot of concerns about the contract. I’d really like it if Marc could look it over for me one more time. He was so helpful to me, doing all the paperwork after your father's death. Mergers and acquisitions are his specialty, aren't they?"

"Marc apparently has a lot of specialties," I said dryly. *Screwing secretaries is at the top of that list.* "I don't want him anywhere near that contract or in our business. In fact, I don't want him anywhere near me."

"Is something wrong between you, Honey? I haven't wanted to interfere, but I have been wondering."

"Where's Uncle Marc?" Jackson piped in.

"Uncle Marc is back in Atlanta," I said, not wanting to upset either one of them.

"It's nothing for you to worry about," I assured my mother. "Nothing I can't handle. Why don't you ask Barbara to take a look at the contract?"

"She's a divorce attorney."

Thank God. "But she's still an attorney. Maybe she can recommend someone else."

"She suggested Marc, said he was the best M&A attorney in Atlanta."

I sighed. Apparently, there was no end to my husband's fans…

"Are you going to sign?" I pressed.

"There's so much to consider," Dee Dee said. "I know your dad wouldn't have wanted me to sell the company outright. And I know you and Donny don't think it's the right thing to do. But it's a lot of money."

"More than you could spend in a lifetime," I countered.

"Honey, I'm not sure I want to run the company. I'm sorry."

"Mom, why not? You and Dad worked a lifetime for this."

"That's just it. I've worked a lifetime. I loved my career, working with your father and you and Donny. But I don't have the energy to start this new phase in my life. I think I'm ready to wind down."

"Now you're talking like an old lady, which you definitely are not," I said harshly. "You're the most dynamic woman I know. Look what you've accomplished. I've tried my whole life to be just like you. And you know you're Hannah's role model."

Dee Dee squeezed my hand. "That's sweet, but you know, sometimes I think it would be so great just to relax, do nothing, drop out. Take that cruise and sit on the deck and soak up the sun."

"Correct me if I'm wrong, but I think that's what you've been doing down here for the past year." That came out harsher than I meant it, and I could see that my mother took offense.

"It's just that you haven't really been involved in Palladino Properties for a long time," I said smoothly. "I think you need to get back in the saddle. Go into the office, go to luncheons, show houses, keep mentally active. It will give you a sense of purpose and an excuse to get out of the house. You don't have to work too hard, but you should stay affiliated. You've more than pulled your load in the past. Now it's my turn. Remember what Dad always said."

"I know, the Palladino persistence." My mother laughed.

"Do you think Dad would want you to give up?"

"Honey, I've spent my entire life with your father. I'm lost without him. If I was ever down, he'd be right there to pump me back up. But a lot of times I felt inadequate, not up to the task."

"That's ridiculous. You are the best broker associate in the city."

"No, Honey, you are. Watching you sell a house is a sight to behold. You're really the force behind Palladino Properties now."

"We're the best mother-daughter team," I compromised.

"Definitely," she agreed.

"If you hang it up, what would you do?" I asked.

"I don't know."

There was a slight chill in the air, so I dropped Jackson's hand, pulled off my sweater, and smoothed it over my mother's shoulders.

Jackson took the opportunity to run off.

"Jackson Palladino, you're a sneaky little devil. Now, get back here. It's dark outside. I don't want you to get lost or hurt."

Jackson giggled and walked back toward us, reaching out his hand.

"Does that mean you are going to sell?" I asked carefully, holding my breath, while I clutched Jackson's hand.

"I need to think about it some more."

"I understand, but don't underestimate yourself. An important man like Hammond Reddekker doesn't make frivolous offers. He thinks he can make money off us, and I think he's right. He knows Dad is no longer part of the equation and he still wants to buy our company."

"I want to do this for you and your brother and Hannah and most of all for your father, but it's so overwhelming, Honey, sometimes I don't think I can go on. I just want to curl up and die." My mother started crying, and I held her for a minute and composed myself before I realized we were passing the Jesus tree. The face on the tree was bathed in moonlight. Maybe the tree was trying to tell my mother something. But what?

"Don't ever say that again," I scolded lightly. My mother was scaring me and upsetting Jackson, and I didn't know how to handle it. "I couldn't take it if you left me too. I don't care if you sign this contract or not. I want you to do what's right for you, but I don't think you're in the frame of mind yet to make this decision."

"Don't cry, Grandma," Jackson implored. "I won't run off again. I promise."

Dee Dee caressed Jackson's cheek. Then she looked up at her vision in the branches.

"Tell me what to do. Just tell me what to do." I didn't know if she was talking to me or to my dad or...sending out a plea to someone else.

Then I noticed a red circular nailed to the center of the tree.

"What's this?" I asked, pulling it off.

"Oh, that's another flyer from the Seniors Against Sin group. They're a new faction here at Millennium Gardens."

"Aunt Helene told me about them."

"You see these flyers all over—in the clubhouse, nailed to trees. Taped on doors. Slid under doors. I've gotten a few of them already."

"What does this mean?" I asked, perusing the flyer. *"Stop Sinning Now."*

"Well, I guess they're some kind of religious fanatic fringe group. They're bothered by all the 'immoral behavior' they say is rampant around here. All the men and women living together without the benefit of marriage. They're traditionalists, and they believe in the sanctity of marriage."

"Well, so do you," I said. "You just lost your husband. Why would they pick on you, of all people?"

"Well, I guess they heard about Max and me and the cruise. Maybe one of them saw me at the dance with Daniel."

"You don't think they're dangerous, do you?" I asked.

"No, not really," my mother said, biting her bottom lip. "At least, I hope not. I just took the flyer off my door and threw it away. Then, in a few hours, it was back again. It's harmless. But bothersome."

"They're targeting you, Mom. Tormenting you. We've got to put a stop to it. I'm going to tell Donny."

"Don't tell your brother," Dee Dee pleaded, grabbing my arm. "He'll just blow it all out of proportion. He'll have me on the next plane out of here."

Well, that's the idea, isn't it, I thought.

"Anyway, I won't be here much longer," my mother reasoned. "The last thing I want to do is make waves. Aunt Helene still has to live here after I'm gone."

Chapter Ten: Love Letters

I feel it. That little lick of excitement in the pit of my stomach. That thrilling sensation. That frisson in my heart. I'm actually getting dressed and ready to be picked up for a date, *with a man I'm attracted to as more than a friend. Even if it is only breakfast. I don't think anything could possibly ruin the way I feel. All I can focus on right now is Daniel and how happy I am.*

When Daniel arrived, he was the model of decorum, looking handsome and muscular in a crisp white golf shirt, khaki pants, and brown deck shoes. But all sense of propriety deserted him when we entered his condo. Shutting the door behind us, he swept me up into his arms and began to nuzzle my neck.

"Daniel, it's only nine o'clock in the morning," I observed, giggling. For some reason I hadn't been able to stop laughing since he'd driven over to get me. My anxiety about the business had disappeared, at least for a while. "Okay, who cares what time it is?"

"Come over here," he motioned, resuming his seduction.

"I am here."

"Closer," he said, propelling me toward his bedroom.

"Aren't you going to give me a tour first?" I asked lightly.

"The tour starts in the bedroom," he answered,

kissing me.

"Daniel, please. We're hardly kids."

"Who cares how old we are? I feel like a schoolboy again, and I don't want this feeling to end. I think I'm falling in love with you, Dee Dee. I had all kinds of wicked thoughts about you last night."

"You dreamed about me?"

"I guess you could call them dreams."

"I thought you were going to make me an omelet."

He knitted his eyebrows.

"How can you think about food at a time like this?"

"You mean breakfast time?" I teased.

He gave me a long, warm, soul-stirring kiss and reluctantly steered me back to the kitchen.

"Okay, sustenance first, smooching later," he agreed. "You sit on this stool here. I don't want to let you out of my sight. I'm afraid you're a vision and you'll just disappear."

I laughed again and looked around the condo.

"You've done a wonderful job decorating."

"That's my wife's work, not mine," Daniel admitted. "I'm color blind, can't even match my socks or pick out a tie. She spent weeks getting this place exactly the way she wanted it. And she barely got time to enjoy it. She went so fast."

I didn't want him to dwell on unhappy thoughts, so I tried to get his mind off his pain. "Speaking of ties, you left this at my place the night before." I reached into my handbag and handed Daniel his bowtie.

"Thanks," he smiled, obviously remembering how he'd lost the tie in the first place. He took the tie from my hand and set it on the island in the kitchen.

When I looked around, I saw no sign of Christmas

anywhere in his condo.

"Do you have any plans for the holidays?" I asked.

"I'm afraid not. Without Natalie, this time of year is pretty bleak. I didn't have the heart to put up a tree. Natalie and I used to decorate it together, so—"

"What about your son?" I asked.

"Oh, he's expecting me to make an appearance on Christmas Day, exchange presents, the usual holiday stuff. I told him I wouldn't be coming this year. I didn't want to dampen his spirits. Then he said, 'Mom would have wanted us to be together.' Those are the magic words, so I guess I'll drop by with some presents for the grandchildren."

"Have you done your shopping yet?" I inquired.

"Well, no," he admitted.

We were quite a pair. Neither had I.

"Why don't we brave the malls together, then," I suggested. He cringed.

"Come on, don't be such a grinch. We'll go right after breakfast."

"Ho, ho, ho," Daniel shouted, suddenly seized with the Christmas spirit as he waltzed around the kitchen, grabbing things from the refrigerator and off the shelves, banging pots and pans together and making a big mess.

"I hope you have a maid," I commented dryly.

"Nope, I clean up after myself. I'm completely trainable."

"That's good to know." It was so easy being together with Daniel like this.

He brewed some coffee, cut up some shallots and mushrooms, and began frying them in butter. I watched him crack a few eggs, add milk, salt, and pepper, and beat them into a froth with a fork before pouring the mixture into the pan. Then he set the flame on low.

"Can I help? I feel so guilty doing nothing."

"You, my lovely woman, are my inspiration. Your job is to sit there and look beautiful, like a kitchen goddess. You make quite a picture."

"Well, I'll say one thing. You're good for my ego."

"I'm good for a lot of things. Stick around and you'll find that I'm very handy around the house."

"I'm sure," I smiled at the innuendo.

Before long, the omelet was bubbling, and Daniel folded in some shredded fancy sharp cheddar and covered the pan.

"It smells delicious," I said.

"So do you," he said, sniffing me. "Wait until you taste it. I can't wait until I taste you again."

"Daniel," I said, blushing.

Daniel set out the plates, cloth napkins, crystal, and flatware, and placed a bowl of cut-up fruit on the table. Then he divided the omelet and put half on each plate. He gave each of us two strips of bacon that he had microwaved a few minutes earlier. Then he poured orange juice from a pitcher into two goblets.

"We should have champagne. I feel like celebrating."

"Orange juice is fine," I said.

"I thought we could eat in the dining room. It overlooks the lake. There's a lot of sun this time of day."

"That would be lovely," I said, ready for some sunlight, just now realizing I had lived in the dark too long.

"I mostly eat in the kitchen, by myself, so this is a

real treat, being with someone—being with you, I mean."

"Thank you. It's a treat for me, too."

We ate, and drank our coffee and orange juice, and talked and laughed, and then just sat there in companionable silence. He reached for my hand.

"I can't seem to stop touching you," he said. "I was afraid that night at the dance, after the dance, was just a dream, that when I woke up you'd be gone. Like Cinderella at the stroke of midnight. And when you wouldn't come home with me last night, well, you have no idea how relieved I was when you answered your door this morning. And you don't know how good it feels just to do something as simple as share a cup of coffee and conversation with another human being over breakfast. This is my idea of heaven. I feel like I'm finally clawing my way out of the grave."

"I know the feeling," I whispered, choking a little on the lump that still knotted at the base of my throat whenever I thought about the past long, lonely, empty, miserable year following Stan's death and the fact that Stanley was buried so far in the ground that I could never get to him again. I wiped away a tear.

We walked into the living room. I stopped at each picture to ask questions about his wife, his son, his grandchildren. His wife had been lovely. Daniel hadn't said what she died of. And I didn't feel I should intrude on his grief by asking. Maybe a heart attack, like Stan, or cancer like so many others of my friends. His son was built like a linebacker, but Daniel had said he was a quarterback, a Heisman Trophy contender, in his day. He looked a lot like Donny. I guessed that was because they were both in their sports uniforms. And they had the same father.

"I'd rather talk about you," he said.

"Not much to talk about," I hedged. "My life's not very interesting."

"I'm interested in everything about you. Tell me about your job."

"Well, you know I'm a realtor."

"Sales," Daniel said.

"Well, sales is only part of the job. We provide a service. My husband, Stanley, used to say, 'Sales is just a piece of the pie.' What we're really doing is selling dreams."

"Do you like what you're doing?"

"Well, I haven't actually been doing anything to speak of since Stan died, as my daughter was quick to point out to me. Honey and her brother have been bearing the brunt of the work. It takes years to build up a business, a reputation. I passed on my experience to Honey, and she'll pass it on to her daughter, Hannah. But Honey and I treat the job differently. I love the job because of the flexibility it offers. I can be on my cell phone negotiating a contract and strolling my grandson. Technology has freed us, and I depend a lot on my fabulous team back at the office. Honey has all those resources available to her, but she doesn't take advantage of them. She won't ever let the job go. It's partly my fault, because I've been leaning on her so much lately, and I think it's starting to affect her marriage, although she'll never admit that to me. My son-in-law, Marc, was a rock after Stan died. But I think she's forgotten that. My daughter won't let go of the reins. She's single-minded like her dad and has to be in control all the time. His philosophy was 'If you're going to do something, do it right.' At the end of the day, Stan taught her to treat every client as if he or she is your only client."

"Stan sounds like a smart man."

"He was," I said. "He had a good head for business. He gave me a chance when I first moved to Atlanta with a new baby. He gave me a new life, actually."

"There must be disadvantages to the profession."

"Well, you have to be able to handle uncertainty and understand that nothing happens overnight. And now—"

"Last night, you said you had some important decisions to make," he prompted.

"Yes," I said. "About the family business. Apparently it's in vogue for corporations to acquire independent realty companies in different parts of the country. Well, as I told you, I've received a very generous offer from a wealthy investor, and I've made up my mind to accept it. I don't think I can handle the pace of running a real estate office any more. My son and daughter have really taken to it, though. When I accept this offer, I'd like to include a clause to keep them on. But it wouldn't be their company anymore. It wouldn't have my husband's name. That will be especially hard for Honey to take. Mr. Reddekker wants me to stay, but since Stan's death, I'm not sure I'm up to it."

"You seem fine."

"On the surface. You have no idea how far I've come. If you had seen me a year ago, well, I didn't even have the strength to get out of bed."

"Sort of like the night of the dance," he teased,

leaning over to kiss my nose.

"Daniel, I'm serious. I'm sure you remember how you felt right after your wife died."

"I haven't forgotten," he recalled. "It was pretty brutal. And damn bleak. I felt like someone had cut off a limb. A part of me died with her. I was completely disconnected and alone. I just sat around the condo staring at the four walls until I found myself talking to the furniture. Talking just to hear my own voice, to make sure I was still alive. I was just existing for the past few months—until you came along."

I shook my head.

"I can't be the antidote to your pain," I said. "I've learned you can't depend on others to get through the difficult times. Friends and family are a godsend, yes, but we each have to find our way back alone."

"I know what you're saying is true," Daniel countered. "But meeting you, being with you, the way we were that night at your place, finding that special connection, I can't help but feel hope that I've been given a reprieve from a life sentence of loneliness. I guess what I'm trying to say is you've already made a big difference in my world."

"Daniel, we just met," I said, turning away, uncomfortable with the lie. Then I faced him. "We don't know a thing about each other."

Daniel looked startled.

"What is it?"

"Well, that's the same sentiment, almost the same words I used, when I wrote to my sweetheart during the war. We'd only known each other for a few months, and that's how I started my first letter to her."

"Right, the woman you told me about last night.

And you said you still have the letters you wrote to her?"

"Yes."

"R-right here in the condo?" I faltered, trying hard to hide my excitement. "After all these years?"

"Yes."

I steadied myself as I leaned back against the wing chair.

"I took them out of the safe deposit box and brought them here after my wife died. The day she died, she asked me to forgive her. I couldn't imagine what she'd ever need forgiveness for. It turns out, all those years ago when she was helping me find my girl, she had located Dorothy after all, but she never told me because she was pregnant. She was frantic. She needed me. She knew it was wrong. She said she'd lived with the guilt a lifetime. I knew she was dying, so what could I say? How could I be mad at her? Right before she died, she took out a crumpled piece of paper with a name and an address on it and pressed it into my hand.

" 'Go find her.' That was the last thing she said to me. Of course I couldn't bring myself to look at that piece of paper. What kind of a husband would I be if I went looking for an old girlfriend so soon after my wife died? So I take out the letters every now and then and look at them and wonder what might have been. I wrestle with what to do. Sometimes I wonder if I should look her up again. I'm sure she's married. I don't even know if she's still alive. If she's not, I don't want to know. If she's with another man, I don't want to know that either. But that's selfish. Of course I hope she's happy. But I find myself fantasizing about finding her again. Sorry. I shouldn't be talking to you about this."

"Why don't I start on the dishes," I offered, afraid my face would betray the anguish I felt. He *had* looked for me. Still wanted to find me. If only he hadn't given up all those years ago. If only I had had faith in our love and gone to him before I married Stan, dared to defy my mother. All the "if onlys" in the world weren't going to change the outcome of lives that had veered off in two distinct directions.

"No, leave the dishes. Spending time with you is more important."

I had to get my hands on those letters.

"I'm in the mood for something sweet," I said. "Do you have any doughnuts?"

"No, but I can run out and get you some. There's a Krispy Kreme in the shopping center right around the corner from the complex. I won't be gone more than fifteen minutes. You'll be here when I get back, won't you? No vanishing, promise? No retreating? I'm an ex-cop and I'll just track you down."

"Are you a stalker?"

"Whatever it takes," he replied.

"I'm not going anywhere," I promised. He embraced me and gave me a long, slow kiss which I felt down to my toes. Then he gave me a naughty, speculative look.

"You sure you still want me to go all the way out to Krispy Kreme to get donuts? You taste pretty sweet. Delicious, in fact. I don't think we need anything else."

"Daniel, please," I said, my heart pounding as I placed my hand on his chest.

"Okay, your wish is my command. One dozen donuts coming up. Any special requests?"

"Surprise me."

The minute Daniel closed the door, I walked into his bedroom on unsteady legs. My hands were shaking. The letters had to be in this room somewhere. The closet was the most likely place. His unit was a two-bedroom, the same floor plan as mine. The master had a big walk-in closet. His wife's clothes and shoes were still hanging there, neat and untouched. I felt like an interloper. My sympathies went out to Daniel. I can relate to that, I thought, my heart constricting. All of Stan's things were still in our house in Atlanta. Even his glasses were still in their case on the nightstand where he'd left them. And his shoes, his wallet, all the dear little things that were constant reminders of the man I spent my life with. That's why I couldn't go back to that house. I didn't want to give the clothes away because that would be too final, but I couldn't bear to see them again, either.

Daniel's brown leather flight bomber jacket was still encased in plastic in the back of his closet, where it had probably been since he'd taken it to be dry cleaned right after the war. I smelled it and hugged it. The leather was still in amazing shape, just stiff and somewhat cracked with age, as I expected it would be after all these years.

The jacket was adorned with medals and insignia. I could imagine a younger Daniel, dressed in his uniform—looking big and powerful. That's how I'd remembered him, the way he looked when I last saw him. A tear slipped out of my eye and slid down my cheek.

What business did I have snooping around in the man's closet like an intruder? But I had to find those letters. See them for myself. They were not in the closet. Where could they be, then? I searched drawers and found old tax returns and business papers, and dusty boxes of loose family pictures. And a simple gold wedding band. He told me he'd just taken his off. I hadn't had the courage to do the same. I was avoiding what I knew would be a gut-wrenching experience.

Finally, in one of Daniel's drawers, I had my hands around a thick stack of letters, wrapped in a frayed blue ribbon. Could this be what I'd been searching for?

The pages were so yellowed and delicate, I was afraid they might dissolve right in front of my eyes, like a newly discovered Holy Scripture in an archaeological dig. My heart beat erratically. I felt a little like a common thief, except the letters were addressed to me in Daniel's familiar handwriting. So, by rights, they *were* my property.

He'd printed everything with small, perfectly formed, precise letters that looked as though they were written on lined paper. And there were some tags, documenting each of Daniel's bombing raids over towns whose names I'd never heard of—Ludwigshaven, Germany; Florennes, Belgium; and Nancy-Essey, Villacoublay, Tailleville, Melun, Lille, Toulouse, Rely, St. Omer, and Fismes in France. Then there were the well-known cities in Germany—Munich, Berlin, Frankfurt, Hamburg, Leipzig.

There was no time to read them all before Daniel got back from his donut run, but I was determined to take them with me. I did take time to sneak a peek at the first one. I slipped the top letter out from under the ribbon and started reading.

"My Dearest Dorothy,

As much in love as we are, we've only had a short time together. It suddenly occurs to me that we don't even know each other very well. So let me start by telling you a little something about myself, my darling."

As I read the first few lines, money slipped out of the envelope and a stream of tears slipped down my face. He hadn't lied. He *had* written, and more than one letter. He hadn't forgotten me. And he'd sent me money, like he'd promised. How wonderful it would have been to have received these letters during that long separation and to know that the man I loved, the father of my child, was still alive and that he still loved me. Why hadn't I received these letters back then?

"I make $21 a month and I'm sending $15 home in this letter. This is just a down payment on our future together."

Before I could finish reading the first letter, I heard Daniel's key in the door, so I stuffed the letters into my handbag and ran back into the living room. How was I going to explain away those damn tears?

"One dozen glazed, coming up," he said and placed one each on a dessert plate. "Minus one. I couldn't resist eating one in the car."

I wiped my eyes and bit into my doughnut. My tears were as hot and fresh as the glazed pastries. The doughnut was sinfully delicious and sweet, even mixed with my salty tears.

"It tastes wonderful." I smiled. "Thank you for going out and getting them for me."

"You haven't been crying, have you?" Daniel asked, frowning as he examined my face like it was a fresh crime scene.

"No," I lied. "Just got a little sentimental, I guess."

He squeezed my hand.

I wasn't ready to talk, so when I finished, I asked for another doughnut.

"I feel like a pig," I muttered.

"I like a woman with healthy appetites," he said, looking at me mischievously. "In the kitchen and in the bedroom."

Okay, now I was blushing again.

I ate the doughnut so fast that some leftover glaze remained on my lips. He came around and licked it off and inserted his tongue into my mouth. I responded. He caressed my cheek in his powerful hand.

"Oh, Dee Dee, come to bed with me. I want you so much. I need to be with you. I need to feel alive." He pressed up against me so I could feel just how much he wanted me, and I felt his breath, hot and heavy, on my face. I was tempted to stay.

"I've got to go," I protested weakly.

"But you just got here. I thought we were going Christmas shopping."

"I've hardly seen my daughter," I said, making excuses. "We haven't finished packing." Grabbing my bulging handbag, I broke away from him and walked toward the door. He was a former law enforcement officer. Surely he could tell I had stolen his letters. When he tracked me down, what would I tell him?

"At least let me drive you," he offered.

"I can walk. It's not that far."

"When can I see you again?"

"I…I don't know."

"Dee Dee, what's happened? If you think we're rushing things, we can slow it down. I know we got carried away the other night, but you have nothing to feel guilty about. I know you think it's too soon. But I won't apologize for the way I feel about you. You can't believe this doesn't mean anything to me. This is anything but a one-night stand. Dee Dee, I care for you a great deal."

"Please, Daniel, let me go. Just let me go."

I had to get out of there. Away from the confusion and disappointment I saw reflected in his eyes. I pushed past him and left him there without an explanation. It was unfair, but I just couldn't stay. I had to finish reading those letters. I ran all the way home. Winded, I got out my key and let myself into the condo.

I looked around. Then I heard Honey on the phone, her voice animated. She must be talking to a client. She was in her room with the door closed. Right now I had to find a quiet place to read. I needed to read those letters before Daniel started missing them. I'd read them and then find a way to apologize for running out and somehow put them back in his drawer before he knew they were gone. I ran past Honey's bedroom and locked the door to my room behind me. I picked up the letter I had been reading and resumed my foray into the past, to the strains of the music of the '40s—"Love Letters Straight from Your Heart."

Chapter Eleven: Flyboys

When we flew our plane over the Atlantic and reached England, we dipped down to 50 feet above the ocean, where we saw whales and sharks. I thought, My God, this plane could drop into the ocean and they'd never find us in this bottomless place. We're a daredevil bunch. We think we're going to live forever, that we're invincible. It's hard to explain. Some of the boys take life for granted. But my life means a lot more to me since you've come into it. I have one goal and that is to stay alive and come back home to you. But the Germans aren't going to make it easy for any of us.

I leaned against a pillow, settled under the covers, and, with the music of the past washing over me, continued reading about Daniel's missions—hardly believing they had happened a lifetime ago. Pausing, I pored over the letters, my hands touching each precious word as my eyes skipped over the reports about the missions themselves and focused on the personal words Daniel had written to me. I was almost glad to be reading these letters now, all these years later, now that I knew Daniel was safe.

IInd MISSION
BERLIN, GERMANY
MAY 7, 1944

We were not attacked by fighters on our first mission to Cherbourg, France, last night, but this time, the Germans knew we were coming. Anytime you go to Berlin, Frank Sinatra's voice is broadcast over a loudspeaker, singing, "There'll be a hot time in the town of Berlin." The Germans' idea of a joke, I guess.

Berlin is the worst target that ever existed. Ships around me blew up and went down. This time, we were attacked by fighters and my turret stopped as I was tracking them. I couldn't sleep that night thinking of how lucky I am and thinking of you.

**

VIth MISSION
LUDWIGSHAVEN, GERMANY
MAY 27, 1944

I saw about 10 German fighters shot down before they could get through to our formation. We ran low on gas coming back, but made it O.K. When I get back, and I have to believe that I will come back, I want to introduce you to all the guys. They feel like they already know you, the way I go on and on about how beautiful you are. None of them believe me. We call our ship the Honey, but the pin-up girl has nothing on you in the looks department. I've shown them a picture of you and they probably think I cut it out of a magazine. That I don't really know you. You're so glamorous and as lovely as any movie star. Sometimes I think I've dreamed you up, that all those months you existed only in my imagination. But I know you're real. I still feel the way we fit together on the dance floor and that last night with the rain coming down in sheets against the window. The desperate way you held me as if you knew it might be the very last time, the way you looked at me, the sweet way you loved me. Sometimes at night when I'm alone, I think I can still smell you, taste you. That's when I know it was no dream. And someday, soon I hope, I'll be coming home to my very own pin-up girl.

**

VIIth MISSION
FRANKFURT, GERMANY
MAY 28, 1944

Skimming over Daniel's words about the bombing raid, I went on to the more personal and puzzling part.

I haven't gotten a letter from you yet. Did you get the letter with my address? I'm anxious to hear all about what you're doing on the home front. How are things back in Pittsburgh? I hope you're having fun, but not too much fun without me. Is your mother still determined to keep us apart? Have you made any progress stating our case? Does the woman know how much I love you? If she did, she could never have any objections to our being together.

I wondered why Daniel hadn't received my letters and why I hadn't received any of his. I had written to him every day and handed the letters over to my mother to post. Poor Daniel. No one there to comfort him, to let him know they were thinking of him. All those newsreels I watched alone in a dark movie theater, worried sick. Not knowing if he was dead or alive. I imagined him fighting over there, but there was no way to reach him, to let him know how much I was praying for him. How desperately I was missing him. I went to his house but no one was home. I asked around and they said the Moore brothers were all off to war. Every one of them. How awful that must have been for Daniel's mother. How scared I was, but also how grateful I was to be carrying his child. If only I could have let him know.

**

VIIIth MISSION
FLORENNES, BELGIUM
MAY 31, 1944

Very uneventful; No flak, no fighters. Tonight I'll dream easier. I dream about you every night, you know. Waiting for word from you, my love. I hope it comes soon. Missing you is not getting easier. It's an ache that can't be washed away. But I know you're waiting for me and that's all that matters. I know what we're doing over here is important, but our love is all that's keeping me going. I'd rather be there with you than over here fighting. But then I realize you're the reason I'm fighting.

**

Skipping over the next two missions, I came to the letter dated June 6, the day that would go down in history as "D-Day," and continued to read with pride.

XIth MISSION
CAEN, FRANCE
JUNE 6, 1944

It was my 11th mission, on June 6, 1944, which also happens to be my birthday. You probably don't even know that.

They woke us at midnight, the earliest yet of any previous mission. We were told no abortions—no bombs in the channel. We flew straight across the channel and dropped our bombs about eight minutes before the first landing barge hit the coast in the Cherbourg Peninsula—formerly the worst flak area on the coast. We ran missions all day. Quite a lot happened. I got my personal message from General Eisenhower. It will be one of my most prized possessions. A letter from you would rank right up there, but so far I haven't heard from you. I'm sure there must be an explanation, some SNAFU. It would truly be history-making to get your letter.

They issued me a .45, which I'll carry on all future missions. I've killed from the anonymity of a top turret. I've watched Forts blow apart into a dozen flaming pieces hurtling toward the earth and ships go down in a flat spin and burst into a sheet of flame when they hit the ground. I've fought nausea and broken out in a cold sweat when I saw my first flak. Deprived of oxygen half the time, I've vomited in my leaking mask and all over the floor-plate of the turret during the really rough missions. The flak is as thick as the soup I flew in over 30,000 feet up. And it's accurate enough to really scare the hell out of us. Actually, I'm too sick to be scared. I sweated out this mission—as I always do.

I tell you this to let you know that I'm not particularly brave. The truth is I'm as scared as any of the guys. Of course, none of us will admit that to each other. We're all just putting on a front. But I want you to know me and everything about me.

I'm just a man. But I believe in what we're fighting for. And one of the things I'm fighting for is you and our future. I can see it so clearly in my head. I have a vision of you in our house, with lots of windows to let in the sunlight so I can see your beautiful face. You're holding our son—and we haven't talked about this, but I want a houseful of kids. Right now I don't know how we'll afford this life I'm dreaming of, but somehow we will, the two of us working side by side, building our new life together. I hope you're getting the money I'm sending and saving it. I can't wait to hold you in my arms again. I hope your mother isn't giving you too much trouble about us. But I will win her over. I swear I will.

I had to stop then because the tears were blinding me. Daniel would have loved a son, he would have loved Donny. He wanted children, our children. Oh, if only I had known then. If only I had been braver, stronger. If only I hadn't let my mother run my life.

I wiped my face on the sheet, picked up the letter, and continued reading.

I wasn't going to admit it, but over here you never know whether your next letter will be your last one. And so I want to have no secrets from you. I'll be honest. I couldn't dance at all right before I met you. All the soldiers were jitterbugging in the women's clubs where dances were held for the troops. I'd hardly ever talked to a girl in my life. I wasn't the social type at all. I'd never had a date in high school because I couldn't afford the clothes or the money to date. So there I was, just 20 years old, at a dance in the lower level Rec Room of St. Anne's Catholic Church. Some of the girls took pity on me and taught me how to dance. Don't be jealous, but without that experience, you probably wouldn't have given me the time of day. Something just clicked and I became a class jitterbugger and a smooth dancer.

Those lessons changed my life. I couldn't believe my luck when the prettiest girl in the club agreed to dance with me, talk with me, marry me. Could you tell how inexperienced I was? I was so hungry for you the night before I shipped out. I was fumbling around in your car like a clumsy schoolboy. But I was so in love that making love with you seemed natural, right. I can't wait until you're back in my arms again. Until our life together begins. It seems like I've already waited forever.

I remember you said I was the most handsome man you'd ever seen on or off the movie screen. Well, I don't know about that, but it sure made me feel good to hear it. Now it occurs to me that it must have been the uniform. In our uniforms we're highly revered, because the uniform represents the war effort, which is why I enlisted in the Army Air Corps. I wanted to be part of something important, something bigger than just me. I only have two stripes—but over here corporal is right under God because you can spend 30 years in the Army and never make corporal. Decked out in my bric-a-brac and braid and big gold wings left over from flying school (I washed out, I'm sorry to say), everybody salutes me. But they're not saluting me. They're paying their respects to America. And in my uniform, whenever I enter a restaurant or a pub, somebody offers to pick up the check because they're so happy to have us over here.

Okay, so if I am serious about this business of not keeping secrets, I have to tell you the whole truth. And you will probably agree with your mother that I am not worthy of you, that I have nothing to offer. But I happen to believe that we can overcome our backgrounds. So I will tell you my story.

Oh, Daniel, didn't you know I would have loved you no matter what you told me? How could you have doubted that?

I was born in Pittsburgh on Bedford Avenue in an area known as the Hill District, which was part of the inner city. My real father died when I was two weeks old. My stepfather was an average-sized man named Marty who drove a big Packard automobile, which was high class in those days. He convinced my mother that he would raise her little boy, so she married him and he formally adopted me. He turned out to be an abusive drunk who smoked several packs of Camels a day. He never smiled, but he managed to father six more children with my mother before the Depression. I was not permitted to see my real father's family. I wasn't really accepted. I had no father figure. I was just out of place. The guidance I needed that could have been provided by a father never came. And I've always wondered what it would have been like if my real father had lived.

That is why I promise you now that I will try to be the best father ever if we are lucky enough to have a child of our own.

I had to stop and cry again, for Daniel, for me, for our little boy who never knew his father.

Things were tough back in 1930. In those days our family moved constantly, never staying anywhere for more than a year because we couldn't pay the rent. I thought that was normal and that everybody moved each spring.

Is that honest enough for you? I want you to know what you're getting into if you still want to throw in your lot with me. I couldn't tell you this in person, but over here, now that I have a purpose in life—that is you—I feel I can tell you anything.

As kids, we kept the front door locked, because if somebody banged on the door, it was most likely a bill collector. And if we didn't answer, he assumed that we weren't home. We all hid behind the couch. I've never forgotten that. The Depression will probably stay with me forever.

For a period, we were on welfare. (Don't tell your mother.) And welfare meant wearing welfare shoes with a kind of a square point. When our shoes wore out, we just cut out some cardboard for soles. The winters were tough. In the welfare years, flour and sugar came in sacks. My mother cut out the neck and arms and added a shirttail hem and that was our upper underwear.

Being poor, in an area of affluence, was difficult. I felt out of place going to school in upper class Squirrel Hill. Growing up, my brothers and I interchanged clothing. In the early years, four of us slept in one bed in a house without a bathroom or heat. (Shades of military life to come.)

Being on welfare also meant that the family service organization in the Hill District handed out wicker food baskets with potatoes, carrots, a turnip, a loaf of bread, and about a pound of meat of some kind, wrapped in butcher's wrap. And we would walk home with our welfare baskets.

Marty was a gambler. When I wanted to take my mother down to Ludine's for a corned beef sandwich, we couldn't scrape up the $.15 price, because Marty drank or gambled everything away. Sometime, in around 1938, Marty gave me a dollar to go out and buy him some cigarettes. I came back with a loaf of bread and a quart of milk for my mother. Marty came at me, and I just stepped back and hit my stepfather square in the mouth and knocked him out. I took a shopping bag, gathered the few possessions I had, and left home.

I was in 11th grade; I had no money and I didn't know how I would finish high school. So I moved in with my grandmother. Every week, I prearranged to meet my brothers and sisters at the big Firestone station two blocks away from where they lived. The six of them would bring me up to date on what was going on, and then I'd catch a streetcar and they'd walk the couple of blocks back home. When I was with my brothers and sisters, I didn't feel like a stepchild. I felt a part of something bigger, like I do now.

So now you know—although you were always much too polite to ask—why I didn't have much money to take you out, why we always ended up at the USO dances and not on real dates, why I didn't have a car—why I never took you to my home. But, by some miracle, you fell in love with me anyway.

I can't wait to introduce you to my family. We're a motley crew, so I hope you're not too overwhelmed when you meet everybody. They're going to be shocked when they find out I got a classy lady like you to marry me. And they're going to love you. As for your mother, I plan to wear her down. I figure after this, being over here, doing what I'm doing, I will have earned her respect. It's not where you come from but what you do with your life that counts.

Oh, I loved him so much. I had then and I still did. Look what he'd overcome. I wish I'd had a chance then to tell him how proud I was of him. How proud I would have been to share his life.

Rubbing my eyes, I picked up the next letter. Donny was always asking about love letters, and I hadn't admitted there were none. But my son would give anything to read these letters from his real father, to find out, in his dad's own words, what he did during the war. He would treasure these words that made his father come alive. But what would he do if he found out his father *was* alive? How would he feel about me then?

**

XIIIth MISSION
BEAUMONT, FRANCE
JUNE 11, 1944

This was 12B, as Mission 13 is known. This was to be a short one to bomb an airfield in the invasion area. Coming back over the Cherbourg Peninsula—at about 9,000 feet—a perfect ducks-in-a-gallery formation—the Group after us caught a dozen bursts. Bursts that were intended for us. We were lucky. We came back across the channel at about 1,200 feet—pretty low for a big formation.

Still no word from you. It's hard when the other guys hear from their girls. But I'm not giving up. I have faith in us. I'm sure there's a reason you're not writing, but the waiting is hard. I imagine you're saving it all up and soon I'll get the biggest letter any soldier has ever seen. Or, better yet, a whole batch of letters that were lost in the mail will arrive. And all at once at mail call they'll dump them on me and I'll stay up the whole night reading them. And the rest of the night dreaming of you. Maybe there'll even be a picture. I've pretty much worn down the only one I have of us. It goes everywhere with me. I'm convinced you're my good luck charm.

**

Reading on, I rushed through Daniel's next three missions in Lille, Melun, and Bordeaux, France.

XVIIth MISSION
HAMBURG, GERMANY
JUNE 18, 1944

We just came back off a 24-hr. pass and the operations officer was waiting for us in our hut. No sleep that night. It was a little past midnight. The flak was very thick, but no enemy fighters. Still no letter from you. I miss you more and more each day. Sometimes I don't think I can stand not being with you. But I can dream, can't I? Remember the words to that song we used to dance to?

**

XVIIIth MISSION
BORDEAUX, FRANCE
JUNE 19, 1944

Hit this target four days ago. This time it was really rough. A few fellows I know went down. No one got out. We had trouble keeping up—Tail-End Charlie as usual, which is the best position, contrary to popular belief. Amazing that we came back. Flak thicker than ever before—flew through overcasts for hours. Very tired. But not too tired to dream of you again.

**

XIXth MISSION
HAMBURG, GERMANY
JUNE 20, 1944

Six missions this week alone! When I first got here, if you flew 25 missions, you could come back home. After Jimmy Doolittle came over to run the 8th Air Force, he raised the requirement to 30 missions. I just heard that we have to do 35 missions now. So, I guess I'm in for 35. It didn't help morale. They gave me credit for three under the new pro-rated plan. The more you have, the more you get. This was my first mission with another crew. I was pretty busy watching instruments most of the time. The pilot got hit in the face with flak—

the worst I'd ever seen—but it was really splintered glass. We destroyed Hamburg. It will burn for a week, I'm sure. No enemy fighters. No letters from you. I hope nothing has happened to you or your family. You have no idea what goes through my mind over here. Have you met someone else? If you have, I don't want to know. But I need to know. Not knowing is hell.

I skimmed over the next few missions. I couldn't afford to read them all. I would have to get these letters back to Daniel's condo as soon as possible before he discovered them missing.

**

XXVth MISSION (28TH)
TOURS, FRANCE
JULY 4, 1944

I just got back off a 48-hour pass. That just makes me lonelier for you because there's time to think. I went to a club. There was dancing, but all I could think of was you and how it felt to hold you in my arms. Sometimes I can hear snatches of the music playing that last night. But everything's so far away. I can see your face but then it's gone, and I can't dance with anyone else.

The weather was miserable and we felt sure that there would be no mission, but we got up about an hour after hitting the sack. We were after the same bridge. When we got there we couldn't see the target—it was no go. We brought the bombs back, but it counted as a mission.

My eyes were blurry but I continued to read.

**

XXVIIth MISSION (30th)
LEIPZIG, GERMANY

JULY 7, 1944

I got my "air medal" today. It's a beautiful gold-toothed emblem of an eagle. Can't wait to show it to you. Five missions to go. Got to make it. Got to get home to you and start our life together. That's all that's keeping me going now.

I wondered if that medal was still on his jacket. Wouldn't Donny love to see that?

**

XXVIIIth MISSION (31st)
RELY, FRANCE
JULY 8, 1944

We made a run over the target, but it was overcast, too hazy—I saw one Fort blow up from flak in the Group in front of us. Coming off the target, we ran into more flak. We got a few hits—one in the bomb bay. Since we couldn't find a target of opportunity, we returned to England with all the bombs. We were coming over our airfield at 3,500 feet, when it happened.

The ship on the right was thrown out of formation by prop wash. Our pilot put the ship into a vertical dive to miss the plane and saved us from certain death in a collision. But the big dive knocked several of our bombs loose and pinned the tail gunner to the bomb bay doors with a 250-pound bomb on his lap.

In the dive, the bombardier, navigator and radio operator were thrown to the top of the plane. The waist gunner also hit the top of the plane, and his gun hit him in the eye. I was hit in the back by my chain of bullets from the top turret. The control cables were strained, and the plane struggled to come out of the dive.

The ball turret gunner called me to the bomb bay

and hollered for me to do something for the tail gunner. When I got there, he was white as a sheet, pinned by the weight of a bomb, with another bomb loose and partially stuck in the slightly opened bomb bay door. I straddled the space above the open bomb bay door and lifted the 250-pound bomb off him so he could crawl out. My knees buckled a few times. I don't know where I got the strength. Then I crawled out and began to slowly crank the doors open to get rid of the bombs. I'm ready for the flak house. Four more missions to go.

We got a write-up about today's mission. They called it "Bomb Scare in the Air." The bombardier gave it to Public Relations. He made me out the hero. So, one day you can tell our son his dad was a hero.

I couldn't control the tears that were streaming down my face. I hadn't known a thing about this incident, but Donny had grown up thinking his dad was a hero and it turned out he really was. I wept softly for a while, with the covers pulled over my head so Honey wouldn't hear me.

**

Then I forced myself to continue reading. By now, though, I was desperate for Daniel's expressions of love and loneliness. Feelings that mirrored my own all those years ago. I began skipping over the rest of the missions—the 32nd over St. Omer, France, and the last two to Munich, Germany, and counting down, three missions to go, two to go, one to go and the final mission.

XXXIInd MISSION (35TH)
MUNICH, GERMANY
JULY 16, 1944

I'm happy to be writing this. I'm finished. I'm

trying to get a nine-day pass. Signing off and thanking all who prayed for me. I felt your prayers even though I haven't received a letter. I was lucky.

I'm in London now. I'm enclosing a picture of me in my uniform. Don't be shocked. Your "big bear" looks more like a ghost. I think I weigh 150 pounds. I'm absolutely worn out. How these people lived under the bombardment I don't know. But I did my missions, and now that I'm done, I'm kissing the ground because I'm alive and in one piece and, before you know it, I'll be coming home to you. I tried to keep my spirits up. I haven't heard from you in all this time. It was rough when all the other guys were getting letters from their wives and sweethearts, but we'll be together soon. I'm bringing home presents. I am coming to pick you up the minute I get home, but I don't know yet when that will be. So your mother better be prepared.

I'm sending this ring as a token of my commitment to you. It's not very big, but I promise you someday I'll get you a bigger one. I intend to marry you as soon as I get back. So start doing whatever it is women do to prepare for their weddings. We can talk about where we'll live. I'm partial to South Florida where I did my basic training. Florida's a place where you can walk along nice clean streets and reach out and grab an orange right off the tree. It really sounds like a nice place to live. No snow! But we'll make that decision together. I love you and can't wait to hold you in my arms again on the dance floor and off. It's been so long.

Chapter Twelve: Something's Wrong with Mom

The condo was entirely too quiet. I finished my phone conversation with my client and knocked on my mother's door.

"Mom, are you okay? How was breakfast?" I could hear her mumbling, but I could barely make out what she was saying.

"I'm lying down," I thought I heard her say. "I have a headache."

"Want some aspirin?"

"I've already taken some. I just need some sleep."

This wasn't a good sign. It was almost noon. She was regressing. Something must have happened with Mr. Moore. Something disappointing.

"Can I fix you something to eat?"

"Later," she snapped, then she was apologetic. "I'm sorry, Honey. Maybe later."

"Okay."

I wandered aimlessly around the living room. I didn't care what Donny said, I was going to let some light into this mausoleum. I pulled back the drapes and turned on every light in the room, overhead and lamps. Enough light to vaporize a vampire. I walked out onto the patio and looked down at the tree. Okay, this was insane. I could see Jesus now. I looked away. What was this world coming to? I decided to give my mother a little more alone time and then I was going into the bedroom to check on her. That's when I heard the sound of muffled crying, almost like a keening, and then I heard my mother screaming, "Noooooo!" And she wouldn't stop screaming.

"Mom, what is it?" I knocked on her door. "Open up or I'm going to bust the door down."

She was still screaming. I grabbed my cell phone and called Donny at the hotel.

"Get over to Mom's fast. Something's very wrong with her." I jiggled the lock to her bedroom door.

"Let me in, now," I insisted. The door was flimsy. I kicked it open. There was my mother, doubled over on the bed, surrounded by a pile of yellowing envelopes. She raised her head and turned her tear-stained face toward mine. She had finally calmed down. I think she was in a state of shock. I vaulted onto the bed and wrapped her in my arms.

"Mom, what's wrong? What are all these old letters?"

She hugged me back and wouldn't stop crying, but she wouldn't talk about the letters. She just sifted them with her hands and clutched them to her heart.

"Okay, what happened at breakfast?" Daniel Moore was the obvious culprit. She had left the condo a happy woman, walking on air, and now she was hysterical and depressed. She wouldn't tell me what was wrong, but I finally got her calmed down and settled under the comforter. I gathered up the pile of letters and turned off the light.

"Take care of my letters," she said softly.

"I will," I assured her, confused. "You go to sleep now." Sleep seemed to be my mother's life work.

When Donny arrived, he was frantic.

"What's wrong with her?" he demanded.

"She just started screaming and she wouldn't stop. I think she's having another episode, like when Dad died. She was reading these letters. I've never seen them before. They must be old letters from Dad."

"I thought she was getting better," Donny grunted.

"Me too. Obviously she's not. She went to breakfast with that new guy I told you about on the phone this morning, the one she met at the dance last night, Daniel Moore. And then she ran into the condo and locked herself in the bedroom."

"If he tried anything with her, I'll kill him," Donny ranted. "Can't he see how fragile she is?"

"I know. I can't imagine what else could have brought this on."

He grabbed the letters from my hand.

"What are these? Do you recognize the handwriting?"

"It's not Dad's," I said after examining them.

He opened one. And began reading. After a few minutes he looked over at me.

"Jesus, Honey. I think these letters must be from my real father," Donny said in disbelief.

Stunned, he collapsed on the couch.

"What would they be doing here?" I wondered.

"I'm going to read them," Donny announced.

"They're private. They're Mom's letters. Maybe you should ask her first."

"You said she was sleeping," he reasoned.

"Well, okay, maybe you can figure out what's going on, why they made her so upset."

I looked over at Donny, who was sagging on the couch. He was still reading his letters and tears were streaming down his face. As old as he was, he looked like a lost little boy. I had never seen him look like this—enthralled and defeated at the same time.

"Donny, what's wrong?" I walked over to the couch.

"She said she'd lost them," Donny said, looking up at me, looking lost himself.

"Lost what?"

"Their love letters." He kept reading, and every once in a while he'd make a comment.

"They weren't married. It says he was looking forward to their life together, to their marriage when he got back to Pittsburgh. Maybe that's why she never talked about him. She wasn't married when she had me. Maybe she was too embarrassed to tell me I'm illegitimate."

"You're not illegitimate," I argued. "Stanley Palladino adopted you. He was your legal father. And even if you were 'illegitimate,' it's just a word, Donny. It doesn't define the man you are."

"Look at the date on this one, Honey," he frowned. "This was written after my dad was supposed to have died. That's not possible. Could my father still be alive? I've got to wake Mom. I don't understand any of this."

I tensed at the knock on the door and left Donny reading his letters. When I opened it, Daniel Moore was standing there with a grim look on his face.

He acknowledged me but did a double take when he saw Donny. When I saw the two of them together I had to take a step back. They looked so much alike I thought I was seeing double.

"You must be Dee Dee's son, Donny Palladino," Daniel said, extending a hand. "I've followed your career."

"What the hell did you do to my mother?" Donny accused, springing from the couch and flexing his fists. Daniel lowered his hand. If I didn't interfere, Donny was going to throw a punch.

"Do? What do you mean?" Daniel was bewildered and just a little leery. Donny Palladino riled up was a frightening sight.

"My sister said my mother came home hysterical after she saw you. I want to know what the hell you did to her."

"Nothing," Daniel said. "We were having a nice breakfast and she just took off. I wanted to make sure she was all right. We had plans to go Christmas shopping. Where is she?"

"She's resting now," I said, trying to remain calm.

"I think you'd better leave," Donny glared. "You've done enough damage for one morning."

"I just want to make sure your mother is all right."

"My sister told you she was asleep," Donny said, barely able to control himself. "Just go before I do something we'll both regret."

"Mr. Moore, maybe you'd better—"

I followed his eyes to the letters on the couch and I could sense his agitation.

"My letters! My God, what are my letters doing here?"

Daniel went to the couch and started gathering up the letters as if they were precious gems.

Donny shoved him.

"These letters are from my father," he shouted. "Leave them alone."

"Your father? I don't understand. These letters

were in a dresser drawer in my bedroom. Dee Dee must have found them when I went out for donuts, and she took them. This doesn't make any sense. Why would she do something like that? Why would she go through my private things?"

Daniel picked up one of the letters and examined it.

"This is my handwriting. I wrote these to a girl I loved before I went off to Europe. I'd like them back. They mean a lot to me."

"These are addressed to our mother. Dorothy Lewis, in Pittsburgh. That's where she used to live."

Daniel paled. "What did you say her name was?"

"Dorothy Lewis."

"Dorothy. Dee Dee. Oh, my God. Oh, my God." He clutched his heart. He swayed, and I steadied his shoulders until he could regain his balance. He was so big I couldn't have supported him alone, and Donny definitely would have let him drop. Could this day get any worse?

"Mr. Moore, you'd better sit down," I said gently, leading him to the couch, not even beginning to understand what was going on.

"There must be some mistake," he said, close to tears. "Dorothy," he croaked. He couldn't catch his breath. He was still clutching his heart. Maybe I should summon one of the roving ambulances. "Dorothy is here?"

Daniel pulled out a crumpled piece of paper from his wallet.

"This address," he stammered. "Does it look familiar?"

I examined the piece of paper.

"Yes, this was our Grandmother Lewis' address in

Atlanta before she moved in with my parents. But that was so many years ago."

Then he pulled his wallet from his pants pocket and showed us a weathered picture. "Th-this, is this your mother?" he asked anxiously.

I looked at the picture. This was impossible. This couldn't be happening. How did Mr. Moore get this old picture of my mother?

"Do you have a picture of your mother when she was younger?" he asked, paling, needing to compare the two.

I grabbed my purse, pulled out my wallet, and produced my parents' wedding picture.

"Dorothy," he said, touching her face. "This is my Dorothy. Who is this man with her?"

"That's, that was, my dad, Donny's stepdad," I answered.

"Who was your real father?" Daniel asked Donny pointedly.

"He was a flyer. Killed in the war. World War II."

"Oh, Christ," Daniel said, his head in his hand, the truth beginning to become clear to everyone in the room but Donny.

"Dee Dee said that when her husband married her she already had a son..."

He stared into Donny's face. The face that looked so much like his own.

"Donny?" he extended his hand.

Donny pulled back.

"What's wrong with you, man?"

Mr. Moore couldn't quite bring himself to say what was on his mind.

"When were you born?" Daniel asked. Donny told

him.

"Your mother was Dorothy Lewis. She had a little sister." He paused. "Helene. Of course. I should have known."

"When did your mother meet your father, er, your stepfather?"

"In 1945. Right after the war was over."

"I don't know how this could have happened. I don't understand it, but she must have had a baby. Our baby. I wrote to her, but all my letters were returned, unopened. Her mother must have sent them back. I thought Dorothy didn't want me. I tried, but I couldn't find her after I got back. I've got to see her. I've got to know if she remembers me. If she knows who I am."

"Don't go in there," I warned. "She's distraught."

Daniel lowered his voice and rubbed his hands over his face. "I need some more information. I came back from the war and looked her up, but she'd disappeared."

"My grandmother moved the family to Atlanta when my mother was pregnant," I explained. "My mother got a job at a real estate firm and she ended up marrying the owner of the firm. That was my father."

"Was your grandmother a big woman, kind of gruff?" Daniel asked uncomfortably.

"My father used to call her a meddling, judgmental battle-ax," I answered. "And Dad never had an unkind word to say about anyone."

"Let me show you a picture of my son," Daniel continued slowly, fumbling with his wallet and handing Donny a photo of a big bruiser of a man.

I was the first to figure out what was happening here. And I didn't need a wallet photo to see the resemblance. It was so obvious. And suddenly it all fit together. Daniel was the missing piece that could complete Donny's life and soothe his longing for a father.

"Barry Moore," Daniel prompted. "He played for the Denver Bulls. Look at the two of you." He could have been Donny's twin.

Donny was a little slower on the uptake.

"What are you saying?" he asked.

After a few minutes of silence Daniel blurted it out.

"I th-think I might be your father," he faltered, still holding out the picture of his son.

Donny looked like he was going to be sick.

But suddenly the truth was there in plain view for him too.

And I could tell Donny was thinking, "My brother?"

"Th-this place," Daniel's arm swept the room. "It's..."

"I put it together as a tribute to my father's memory," Donny explained.

Daniel couldn't speak. "This is starting to make sense. She told you I was—that your father was dead?"

"Yes. Maybe she didn't know."

"Donny…" Daniel started moving shakily toward my brother, then stopped. I could almost feel him thinking, "Could you be my son?"

And Donny was obviously thinking, "You could be my father." Donny's face crumpled. He reached out a hand. He so desperately wanted to believe it. Both of them did. Two grown men trying to find a thread of connection.

But the knowledge was too tenuous, the

possibilities too monumental to contemplate, the disappointment too devastating to accept, without proof. Without confirmation from my mother.

The hope in the room was almost palpable. It was right there in Donny's eyes and on his tearful face, and it was written all over Daniel's, as well. He barely breathed the words, "My God, I could have another son. A son." He looked like he wanted to take Donny into his arms, but wouldn't that have been embarrassing if this was all just one big misunderstanding?

And I was thinking now that this Daniel Moore person had come into my mother's life and he thought he was Donny's father, wasn't this wonderful for Donny to finally have the father he'd been longing for, even if the man was screwing my mother. But how would my mother react? I thought it best to leave Daniel and Donny alone for a while to face off and work things out, to get to know each other, take each other's measure. I had a confrontation of my own to prepare for. Marc and Hannah would be here any minute. And I wasn't nearly ready.

Chapter Thirteen: The Confrontation

What should I wear to this confrontation? Maybe the teal power suit. I had a closet full of tailored suits at home. But the teal was too prissy. And this might be the most important meeting I'd ever have. I was so tired. I just wanted to be myself. So I picked one of my less wrinkled cotton shirts out of my suitcase, threw on a pair of jeans, combed out my hair, and waited for Marc to show his smarmy face.

Distracted by sounds in the hallway, I looked through the plantation shutters. Hannah and Marc were here, already. Seeing Marc just on the other side of the door was like a punch in the gut. All the feelings of betrayal welled up and I was beginning to feel nauseated. Straightening my shoulders, I tucked my shirt into my jeans, steeled myself to open the door, and pulled myself together. I didn't know how I would manage to function.

I tried to block out the sounds swirling in my head, imagining Marc and Trisha in bed. I heard murmuring, his and hers this time. Soft words, tender tones, sometimes no talk at all. That was even worse. I didn't want to think about what they were doing. What they had done afterward. Had they laughed at me when they were lying there in bed?

I didn't register how much time passed before I heard the knock on the door. Okay, I would get through this. But I would never again let him touch me or hurt me.

"Mom?" Hannah asked tentatively, peering around the door frame. She looked so young. "We're here."

When I opened the door all the way, Hannah bounded into my arms. We hugged until I almost crushed her, but she didn't seem to mind.

"I'm so sorry you had to see that," I whispered, still holding her and staring over her head into the lying eyes of my soon-to-be-ex-husband. "It must have been horrible."

To Marc I said coolly, "Thanks for bringing her," as I tried to shut the door in his two-timing face. "I can take it from here."

"Honey," he pleaded, holding open the door with his foot. "Please let me in. We have to talk."

This was one of those times I hated that my name was Honey. My legal name was Honey Palladino Bronstein, but I went by Honey Palladino for business purposes, and that would save me a lot of paperwork after the divorce, because I'd still be Honey Palladino. My life will go on without skipping a beat.

So I never knew if Marc was calling me Honey, as in my name, Honey, or lower case "honey" as in a term of endearment. That way he always got to slide by. That was the same way I felt on my birthday. Being born on Christmas Day, I inevitably got cheated because Hanukkah and Christmas often fall at the same time of year. So my presents were usually combination birthday-Christmas-Hanukkah presents. No one recognized the distinction.

Holidays around the Palladino household were always a hodgepodge because my dad celebrated

Christmas and my mom celebrated Hanukkah. "We have the best of both worlds," my dad used to say. This year there wasn't much to celebrate.

"You can talk to my divorce attorney," I replied. "I think you know her. Barbara Palladino."

"Jeez, that barracuda," Marc said, then noticed Donny in the background baring his teeth, so he shrugged his shoulders apologetically for maligning Donny's wife.

"I don't want a divorce," Marc said emphatically, moving away from Donny and closer to me. "We can work this out. You're taking this too far. Just give me a chance to explain."

"You can't explain this one away, you bastard," I said, covering Hannah's ears. "You were screwing your temp in *our* home in front of *our* daughter. Was she taking 'dick'tation?"

"Honey, you've got it all wrong. Are you going to let me in? I've gotta pee."

"Don't be waving that puny pecker of yours anywhere around me," I said, tightening my hold over my daughter's ears. "In my current mood, I might just be tempted to cut it off."

"Honey, please. Be reasonable."

"It's too late for that. You have this knack of always showing up at the wrong time and never being there when I really need you. You should have just dropped Hannah off. I don't want to look at your lying face. And I'm not talking to you. But I just want you to know that I'm going to take you for everything you have—including your precious Gold Wing. The wheels are already in motion."

"Not the Gold Wing!"

Well, at least I had my answer. If I was going to be jealous of anyone, it should be the Gold Wing. He obviously preferred the bike to Trisha.

"You're so pathetic. You and Trisha deserve each other."

"I'm going to fire her as soon as I get back," Marc promised.

"If you fire her for having sex with you, I'm not the only one who's going to be suing your ass. And you call yourself a lawyer?" At this point, I had to protect my assets.

"Who said anything about sex?" Marc said, managing to sound both sincere and surprised. "I came here to apologize, but not for that. I don't know where you got that idea. But I do have some things to apologize for. I don't know what got into me."

"Well, apparently the whole world knows that you got into Trisha." I couldn't resist.

I wanted to take Hannah into the spare room. She didn't need to be subjected to any more bickering or negativity. This was her Christmas break.

"Come in or stay out," I called over my shoulder to Marc. "I don't care."

"Everyone, look who's here, it's Hannah," I said with a false cheerfulness that bordered on hysteria. I introduced her to Daniel, who by now was openly crying. His eyes were fixed on my mother's bedroom door as if staring at it would make her materialize.

Still shell-shocked, Donny greeted his niece and gave his brother-in-law the cold shoulder after saying, "I'm going to beat the crap out of you, Bronstein." He whispered it fiercely into Marc's ear, and continued, "And that's a promise. I'm going to enjoy doing it, too.

And when I'm done, you're going to wish you were dead. You don't deserve my sister. You never did. Sorry, Hannah. Do we need to cover your ears again?"

"I'm almost twenty-one!" Hannah protested.

"Look, man, I said I was sorry," Marc said. "I just need to talk to my wife, *alone*."

I rolled my eyes. "Oh, now I'm your wife. You seem to have conveniently forgotten that you had one, earlier."

"Hannah Banana," Donny said, lifting his niece off the ground with ease and swinging her around, in an effort to deflect the tension in the room.

"Uncle Donny," she giggled. "Where are the cousins?"

"Barbara and the kids are at the hotel. I'll take you over to see them later. I hear you're shacking up at some frat house."

"Uncle Donny," Hannah protested. "They're enlarging our sorority house, so all the girls have moved into the Delta Sig house until the renovations are complete. The Delta Sigs got kicked off campus for a year for hazing. We're the only sorority on Fraternity Row."

"Pretty convenient," Donny drawled, drawing out the words. "I can put two and two together. I lived in one of those frat houses. I know what goes on there."

"Uncle Donny, nothing is going on."

Donny's eyes sparkled. "There'd better not be. Because if I ever find out anyone is messing with my niece, they'll have me to answer to. The Delta Sigs were pigs when I went to school there."

"Their House is still filthy," Hannah laughed. "They trashed it when they were kicked off campus. I found a dead bird in my room. And my room is one of the nicest ones. The first night I was sleeping on my mattress up in the loft and I heard these scratching noises. When I woke up I came face to face with a mouse. I started screaming and woke up the entire House. I think the mouse was more scared of me than I was of her, because she ran back into her hole."

I would have laid odds that Miss Mousey was really Mr. Rat, and I was also wondering whether the pink furry stuff my daughter had described to me earlier when she first moved into the House was insulation and if she was being exposed to asbestos and who knows what else. And all Hannah could talk about were the girls' frequent visits to "the neighbors," who it seems were the fraternity houses on either side of the Delta Sig House. When it comes to daughters, a mother's job is to worry about mice and men. And believe me, I was plenty worried.

"There's a cannon outside the house, and it's huge," Hannah continued, stretching her hands out in front of her as Donny continued to swirl her around the room. "And there are urinals in the bathroom. And someone painted a Confederate Flag across our ceiling."

"Wasn't that house founded by Robert E. Lee or something?" Donny asked. "You'll have to paint over it."

"The room used to belong to my roommate's ex-boyfriend. She wants to paint it pink so he'll be furious when he gets the room back next semester."

"Okay, Donny, put her down," I said impatiently, but I was glad Hannah had provided a diversion to take Donny's mind off his possible newfound father and her mind off what she had seen in Atlanta. "Hannah and I have important things to discuss."

Marc made a beeline for the bathroom and away from Donny, and I brought Hannah's suitcase into my bedroom and shut the door behind us.

"I'm so sorry you had to find out this way," I apologized as I led her over to the bed and she sat down next to me.

"You mean you knew?" Hannah asked, surprised.

"Yes, but being confronted with it in the flesh, so to speak, must have been horrible." I was giving her permission to make light of the situation, and she responded in kind.

"It *was* pretty gross," Hannah admitted. "Trisha has the biggest butt in the world. I'll bet she has to shop at the Big Ass Clothing Sale."

"You saw Trisha's butt?"

"It would be hard to miss." Hannah laughed. "And that's not all I saw."

"Breasts?" I asked, wrinkling my nose, trying to find some humor in this bizarre situation.

"Had to be fake. They were too perfect. And they were practically falling out of that skimpy bathing suit of hers."

"TMI," I said, putting my hand up. "Wait a minute, did you say bathing suit? She was wearing her bathing suit in the bedroom?"

"She wasn't in the bedroom, Mom."

"Tell me exactly what happened when you walked in on your father."

"Well, when I got there Trisha was sunbathing, practically in the nude, at the pool, stretching and well, posing, I guess you'd say, in plain view of Daddy. And then she took off her top."

"Where exactly was your father?"

"Daddy was in his bathrobe on the couch, watching *The Talk* and eating ice cream with a spoon out of the carton."

"They weren't together?"

"Not when I saw them, but come on, Mom. There's no telling what they had been doing before."

"Did he look at them—her, I mean?"

"No, I think he was really into his ice cream."

This whole episode was more than confusing. And the thing I found strangest about it was that Marc was home in his bathrobe, watching a talk show instead of working.

"Okay, we'll talk about this some more, but right now, let's go face the music. I need to get rid of your father, and I mean that literally."

"Mom, he swears he's sorry," she said hopefully. "I calmed down a little on the plane after he talked to me. Seriously, I think he means it. He says that bringing Trisha to our house was a mistake."

"Sorry, I can't give him a pass on this one, honey. It hurts too much. He violated my trust."

"Maybe it's a midlife crisis."

I choked. "Don't you think I'm going through my own midlife crisis? There are other ways to act out."

"Please don't divorce him," Hannah pleaded. "Ellie's parents are getting divorced. I know what Dad did was bad, really bad, but you still love each other, right?"

If there was any love left between us, Marc had squandered it. But I would make the effort for my daughter.

"I'll tell you what. I'll agree to talk to him, for your sake, but don't get your hopes up, sweetheart, okay?"

"Okay." She smiled. Hannah might have been approaching adulthood, but in many ways she was still a little girl, used to happy endings. Seeing her father with another woman, a practically naked woman, in our house must have been horrifying, but contemplating the breakup of her parents' marriage was apparently worse.

"Anything else we need to talk about? Doesn't that boy you're dating live in Boca?" I asked. "He's a Mormon, isn't he?"

"Yes."

"Don't they have more than one wife?"

"Mom, you're stereotyping. He told me they don't do that any more."

"Sure, that's what he *tells* you. Then after you're married, you'll discover he has two other families stashed away somewhere in Utah."

"Mom," Hannah complained. "It's not like I'm going to marry him or anything. I mean, I really like him, but he says we're too young to get serious. He says I could be the one, but he's not ready to start a relationship. He has his priorities. School—one; football, two; his friends—three; and then me."

"Well I already don't like him. You're almost twenty-one years old. Are you supposed to sit around and wait a few years until he's decided he *is* ready to get serious? And you should be number one on his priority list!"

"I know you're right, but I don't want to stop seeing him."

Hannah rubbed her hands together anxiously.

"Mom, how do you know you're in love with

someone?"

That was a difficult question. I had to think back—a long way back—to answer that one.

"Every second you're away from that person, you want to be with him, and you want to be with him every second."

"And how do you know he's the one?"

"He's the one person in the world who you love and who loves you back. The person you'd be lost without."

Hannah blew out a breath.

"Are you going to see him on this trip?"

"We're going out later tonight," Hannah confirmed.

"I'd like to meet him," I told my daughter.

"I already talked to him about that," Hannah reported. "He says he's not in the parent-meeting mood."

"Well, you tell him I'm in the boyfriend-meeting mood," I said dryly, wishing he were here now so I could give him a piece of my mind.

"He's not exactly my boyfriend. I mean, we hang out and everything, but on his Facebook, it still says he's single, not 'in a relationship.' "

"He's obviously not mature enough to handle a relationship," I counseled Hannah. "And you deserve better treatment than that."

"He just overthinks everything." Hannah said. "That doesn't change the way I feel about him."

"I think you should go right out and start dating someone else. See how he feels about that."

"I don't want to play games," she answered. "I can't."

I sighed. My poor baby. Maybe she knew a lot more about relationships than I did.

"I can show you his picture on Facebook," she offered. "He's really cute."

"He's probably afraid to face me," I said. "If he is truly interested in you, he should want to meet your mother. Didn't you say he was a vegetarian?"

"No, I said he was going to be a veterinarian. But actually, he is a vegetarian."

"A vegetarian veterinarian? No wonder he doesn't want to meet me." We laughed.

I have to admit, a future veterinarian is a step up from Hannah's last two boyfriends, whose names both started with a "B"—I thought for "bastard"—and who were both majoring in building construction. My nicknames for them were Building Construction Brad and Building Construction Bobby. Both of them had a fear of the "C" word—commitment. And both had left her to go back to their former girlfriends.

Mormons were big believers in family. Well, maybe multiple families, but families, just the same. Apparently they have the same hang-ups about commitment. These were the things I was storing up to tell Marc about our daughter. We used to laugh about Hannah's escapades at college, but there wasn't much time for laughter or confidences between us these days. I looked at my sweet, beautiful daughter. She was the image of my mother—her hair was long but she had the same color hair, almost silver blond, and ice-blue eyes. Thankfully Hannah hadn't inherited the Lewis hips or the Palladino nose.

"Ready?" I said, linking my hand with Hannah's. She nodded.

I got up from the bed and we opened the door, Hannah walking beside me, shielding me.

"Are you still here?" I asked Marc, who was coming out of the bathroom.

"Yes, and you're lucky we're here at all," Marc reported. "Atlanta is totally shut down because of the ice storm. They canceled our first two flights, and we got the last flight out before they closed the airport."

I knew all about the ice storm. Business was at a standstill, which was fortunate, since I wasn't going to be able to get home for a few days anyway.

"Well, you can just turn right around and get out of here," I seethed.

"I'm not going anywhere until we talk this out, privately."

"All right, let's go into the spare bedroom," I agreed reluctantly, leading the way.

He put out his hand, palm turned up.

"Hand them over."

"Hand what over?"

"Don't play dumb with me," Marc said, wiggling his fingers. "I want your BlackBerry and your cell."

I squirmed but gave them up under protest, and he handed them to Hannah. Then I followed him into the guest bedroom and Marc locked the door.

Anything to get this over with. I could see Marc wasn't going to budge, and the only way I was going to get rid of him was to listen to what he had to say.

Chapter Fourteen: Facing the Music

At first Marc didn't say anything. Then he started the battle with a snide remark.

"Wait, listen," he urged, cocking his head slightly. "Do you hear it?"

I listened and heard nothing.

"There it is again."

"I don't hear anything."

"Exactly."

"Exactly what do you hear?" I asked, frustrated, seconds from walking out on him.

"Silence. Blessed silence. No cell. No raspberries. No distractions. I finally have your undivided attention."

I scowled. I didn't like to be without my two lifelines. And I was uncomfortable being out of touch. In my business, communication is key.

He sat me down on the bed.

"Okay, you wanted to talk, so talk," I said.

"What I really want to do is this," he said, trying to kiss my lips while invading my space with his slithering tongue. I shoved him back.

"You don't get to do that anymore," I said, uncomfortable with his sudden need for intimacy.

"Honey, you've got to believe how sorry I am," he said, putting his arms around me.

"And I don't have to believe anything you say," I

said pushing him away.

"Can't we forget this ever happened?" Marc pleaded.

"Forget? How do you expect me to forget something like this?"

"Honey, I know it looked bad to Hannah, but I can explain."

"Okay, I'd like to hear your so-called explanation."

He hesitated.

"You can't be serious about a divorce. You know I love you. Please don't do this to us." He seemed contrite.

"Marc, I'm not the one who did this to us," I pointed out in a reasonable tone. "And I don't know that you love me. How would I know that?"

At that moment, I was tired of being reasonable, tired of the bantering, the verbal fancy footwork. Lashing out, I started pummeling him with my arms, trying to land a punch. He blocked the blows and tried to grab my arms to keep me from hitting him, but his moves were defensive.

"Okay, why?" I shouted. "I want to know why. Wasn't I attractive enough? Sexy enough? Did you get tired of me? Why, Marc?"

"Honey, no. It's none of those things. And nothing really happened. I promise you."

"I know you and Trisha take long lunches every afternoon."

"How do you know that?"

"I just do."

"There's a reason for that."

"I'd like to hear it."

Marc hesitated again.

"Are you just making this all up as you go along?" I accused.

"No."

"Well, why then? What's wrong with me?"

"There's nothing wrong with you," he said quietly. "It's me. Honey, I said I was sorry for bringing that woman into our house."

"But why, Marc? I really want to know." Okay, so I wasn't the best cook in the world or the best housekeeper. I didn't use fabric softener, all my steaks had freezer burn, and all my perishables were way past their expiration dates. And I had my first eyebrow wax when I was forty-five. But there had to be more.

"I don't know what to say," Marc said thoughtfully. "It's just that you never have time for me anymore. You're always in a hurry. I know that's no excuse for what I've done. But you don't really need me. You're the number one sales associate in your office, you're in the Hundred Percent Club, the top one percent, you're in this Circle of Excellence and that Elite Club, and you've won this award and that award, and you're in the Atlanta Board of Realtors' Top Twenty, but where do I fit in?"

"Marc," I said, taking a deep breath, "It's my job."

"Well, you spend way too much time doing it," he pouted. "And you go about a million miles a minute. You never give the rest of us a chance to catch up. You left me behind a long time ago."

"That's ridiculous, and you know it," I argued. "And for your information, my goal is not just to earn a living. The key is to be of value. And my value is not just putting people in the car and unlocking the door to show a house. I'm an advocate for that property and for my clients. They're not just buying a house, they're buying a lifestyle and we're fulfilling their dreams. My clients are looking for my opinion and my expertise. I have to be available 24/7. I have to stay in touch. If you're going to do something, do it right."

"Now you sound like your father."

"What's wrong with that?" I bristled.

"Ever since your dad died, it's like you have to prove yourself to everyone. You don't always have to be in control."

"No, Marc, you don't understand. I'm not in control of anything. I'm barely holding it together. You know I've had to pick up the slack since Dad died and my mother fell apart. I'm trying to keep this business going and keep my mother from selling it. And you are encouraging her to do just that. I needed you to back me up and you stabbed me in the back."

"All you had to do was ask for help."

"You were preoccupied."

"There is nothing going on between Trisha and me," Marc said. Then he added, "Okay, she thinks I'm a big deal. She doesn't know any better, but at least she looks up to me. You know, the way you used to."

I had to admit that I hadn't felt that way about my husband in a long time. I was self-sufficient. I really didn't think I needed anybody. I frankly didn't have time for anybody, but I hadn't realized, until now, that it even bothered my husband, who I thought was just as independent-minded as I was.

I looked up at him. He really did look sorry for what he'd done. Not that I would ever forgive him.

"You know, every time I call you you're not in the office," I accused. "Have you been with Trisha all those times?"

Marc turned away. But he looked more nervous than guilty.

"Marc, what's wrong? You used to be able to tell me anything. Is there something else you're not saying?" *Oh God, please don't let Trisha be pregnant. Anything but that.*

"It's embarrassing," Marc started.

"More embarrassing than being caught with your pants down in front of our daughter?"

"That's not what happened," Marc insisted.

"Well, tell me, please, what did happen?"

"It's about work."

"What about work?" I said, annoyed.

"You have no idea how much pressure I'm under," Marc began.

"You're a partner in the firm. You shouldn't have to be working hard at this point in your career."

"I'm still responsible for 2,200 billable hours a year."

"That's no different than it's always been," I said.

"The firm's M&A activity has dried up," Marc said. "There's nothing for me to do. They're keeping me on, but I just go into the office and sit there. It's humiliating not to be productive. It's driving me crazy. They're going to vote me out at the next partners' meeting."

I was stunned. This came directly out of left field.

"Are you sure?"

"Grant wasn't supposed to tell me, but he's a good friend, so he gave me a heads-up."

That was why Vicky wouldn't say anything to me.

"When is the vote?"

"Right after Christmas," Marc replied.

"Is there anything you can do?"

"Not really. There's going to be an incentive for me to leave quietly. When I turn sixty-two, I get insurance and a pension—an annuity."

"Well, I guess you could retire," I suggested.

"And do what?"

"Watch 'The Talk' and eat ice cream in your bathrobe?"

"Very funny."

"What can I say? I'm a funny girl."

But this situation demanded a serious response. "Why didn't you come to me before?"

"And tell my super-successful, high-powered wife and her dynamic family that her husband is a failure? You'd just be ashamed of me."

"What?" I said, completely baffled.

"You won't even use my name. Honey Palladino. That's what you call yourself. But you're Honey Palladino *Bronstein.*"

"I didn't know that bothered you," I said sincerely. "Now let's get back to your problems at work."

"I thought about changing firms, maybe moving out of Atlanta, but I know you're tied to Palladino Properties and you can't leave. I've tried to tell you a million times, but then the phone would always ring and it would be the office or a client or the bank or something about the funeral or your mother. You never have any time for me, for us. And you never listen."

Was he right? I hated to admit it, but some of what he was saying made sense. Was that why he was encouraging my mother to sell Palladino Properties? Because then I'd have more time for him? Or was the reason more sinister? Even I could put two and two together. And the more I thought about it, the more his actions added up. I was starting to get a sick feeling in the pit of my stomach.

"Marc, why did you really encourage my mother to sell the company?"

Marc didn't hesitate.

"Because she doesn't want to run the business anymore."

"*She's* not running it," I said, and I could feel the resentment creeping into my voice. Had it been there all along? "Why didn't she tell me that herself? Why did she have to come to you?"

"Because she's told you a hundred different times in a hundred different ways, but you weren't listening. Didn't have time to listen."

I took a deep breath. I didn't like what I was about to accuse my husband of, but I had to know.

"I have a question for you, and I want an honest answer. Did promoting the sale have anything to do with your problems at work? A nice fat, juicy deal would go a long way toward cementing your position at the firm."

Marc's eyes opened wide and his mouth dropped. I think he was truly blindsided.

"Honey, I would never do that. I can't even believe you'd think that I would take advantage of you and your family that way. I was just trying to help your mother."

I blew out a breath. Okay, I was way out of line. But I was still mad.

"Then tell me why you lied about your business trip to New York. Did it have something to do with the sale?"

"How did you know about that?"

"I'm asking the questions here."

"I went there for a job interview," Marc admitted. "And I got an offer, a good one. I wouldn't be a partner. I'd have to work my way back up. I'd be what they call Of Counsel until I could prove myself, again."

"A job offer?"

"That's one of the reasons I was encouraging your mother to sell the company. I figured if it was a done deal, you'd have no choice but to go to New York with me."

"So you lied when you told me you were going to your firm retreat?"

"Yeah. I couldn't tell you the real reason."

"Did you take Trisha?"

"On a job interview?"

"Well, I thought, I mean, when I called the office they said Trisha was out too."

"You were checking up on me?"

"Well, after I saw this," I said defensively, handing him the 4X6 of Naked Trisha I had just taken out of my purse.

"Christ, Honey. Where did you get this?"

"It was mixed in with our family Thanksgiving pictures. Look familiar?"

Marc looked truly surprised. "I loaned Trisha my camera so her boyfriend could take pictures of her. Then I forgot about it."

"If there's nothing going on between you and Trisha, then why was she at our house, prancing around half naked?"

"She was typing my resume and cover letters to

send out to prospective employers. I didn't want her doing it at work."

"Hannah said she was topless at our pool. There's no computer out there."

"She said she wanted to work on her tan. I didn't even notice. Honey, I went to New York alone, I promise you. Since I was going to be gone, I gave Trisha the day off."

"Are you telling me the truth? There's nothing going on between you and Trisha?"

"I'll be honest. She did come on to me, but I set her straight."

I blew out a long breath. You can get a lot of exercise jumping to conclusions. So my husband didn't go to New York with another woman. If I could take him at his word.

"Marc, I'm sorry about your job, really," I said and meant it. "But I wish you had come to me. We could have worked something out. You're an adult. You need to act like one. I was drowning, I still am, and your answer is to slap me in the face by bringing your temp home in the middle of the day? And why were you wearing your bathrobe?"

"Honey, I didn't even go into the office that day. I was so depressed, I just stayed home. I didn't think you would find out."

"Oh, now there's an original answer. That's right up there with the ever-popular, 'Everybody does it.' "

"I have to admit, having someone her age interested in me made me feel good, young again. For God's sake, I'm almost sixty."

"You're not almost sixty. You're fifty-five, and I'm right there behind you. I know getting old is the pits. But it's much worse for a woman, and I really believed you were sleeping with her. Vicky and Grant and who knows how many other people at the firm knew about your little luncheon rendezvous, but I didn't. It's humiliating. And you let them think you were sleeping with her, didn't you? Why? Because it was good for your reputation?"

Marc hung his head. Apparently he had no answers. At least not the right ones.

"I'm supposed to be able to depend on you and trust you. You're my husband. How can I ever do that again? I don't even know what I ever saw in you."

"You said you were attracted to my big brain," Marc teased.

"I was. Until you stopped thinking with it."

"Honey," he said, reaching out to stroke my hand. I shivered involuntarily. He could still get to me, and that's because I was still in love with the bastard, but I wasn't going to let him know that, so I pulled my hand away.

"I told you nothing was going on between Trisha and me."

"I work hard to lose weight and then you hook up with some lard ass," I whined indignantly.

"She does have a big butt," Marc admitted, looking at the photo again. "And a pretty small brain. I mean, how smart can she be if she's hanging out with an old loser like me? She probably doesn't even know I'm on the way out of the firm. I guess the gossip hasn't reached her yet. Otherwise, she wouldn't be wasting her time."

"And what does that say about me? I married you."

"I'm glad you did, and I prefer your butt," Marc

said, smoothing his hands around my ass, trying to get on my good side.

“Cut it out,” I spit, pushing him away. “And we’re not done here. Are you telling me that with the least bit of encouragement you would have jumped on the opportunity—or her?”

“She made herself available,” Marc admitted, “but I wasn’t biting.”

“Sounds like a fish story, the one that got away.”

“Honey, you can’t see it, but you’re totally stressed out,” Marc said. “You’ve got to stop internalizing everybody’s angst. You have enough angst of your own.”

“I think I have a right to my angst, after what you did. And in case you don’t know, selling a house is one of the most stressful situations that exist. I admit it. I worry about my listings. I care. It bothers me if a deal falls through. I worry about my people.”

“You see, there, you worry more about your people than you do about your own family. Sometimes you stress out about things in the business you have no control over. You’ve paid your dues. And you’re still taking calls at midnight. You’ve got to draw the line. Your mother doesn’t let the job run her life.”

“Right now my mother isn’t *doing* the job. And my mother has her own style of doing things. I feel I need to be accessible at all times.”

“Maybe you need a bigger team,” Marc suggested. “Hire another personal assistant. You certainly have the volume to support that expansion.”

“We’re getting squeezed out by all the mega-firms,” I said.

“A merger could change all that,” Marc sulked.

"But there isn't going to be any merger, thanks to you. My mother is just going to sell the business and Donny and I will be out of a job. And there will be no more Palladino Properties. All my father's hard work—gone."

"I told you I thought if she sold you'd be free to come to New York with me. It was selfish, I know. I'm sorry. I was only thinking of us, of myself."

Marc grabbed my hands.

"Come on, baby," he coaxed. "Give me another chance."

"I've already moved on," I said stubbornly.

"What do you mean?"

"While you were off meeting your temp, I met my significant other."

"Your what?"

"I met someone. We're going on a Christmas cruise."

"Unbelievable. Honey, you can't be serious. You just got here. What's his name?"

"Max," I said stubbornly.

Marc rubbed his hand over his face. "He lives in Boca?"

"Right here in Millennium Gardens, down the hall, as a matter of fact. It's very convenient."

"Oh, so he's an old geezer."

"He has all his working parts," I argued, trying to keep a straight face. "And he thinks my butt is perfect."

"Okay, that's it. We're going home, right now. Pack your bags. I'm getting you and Hannah out of here. We need some alone time to work things out."

"You can't give me orders any more. Barbara said—"

"Barbara is a barracuda. She thrives on other people's misery. I don't give a damn what she said. The only lawyer you need to listen to is me. You and Hannah are coming home with me. You're my wife, dammit."

"I don't know if I still want to be," I whispered, and suddenly it was all too much and I broke down.

"Oh, Honey, sweetheart, please don't cry," he said, and took me into his arms, kissing the tears away from my face. "I'll do anything, anything you say, if you'll just forgive me and take me back. I know I lied to you, but I didn't do anything wrong. I know what it looks like, and it's unforgivable what I put you through. But I'll make it up to you, somehow, I swear."

"Words, Marc," I sniffled. "They're just words."

"I won't give up," Marc insisted. "A wise man once said, 'persistence pays.' "

I squared my shoulders at that reference to my father and continued, "I have something else in mind. I want you to transfer half of your portfolio to me, now. Barbara will handle the transaction. Think of it as a trial separation—of assets."

"I never heard of that."

"I just made it up."

"You're just about to sell your family business for millions. What about that?"

"That's mine," I asserted. "What's mine is mine. And half of what's yours is mine. I hope Trisha was worth it. Maybe when I'm completely financially and emotionally independent, I can think about whether to forgive you and judge your sincerity. And, there's one more thing. I was serious about wanting temporary custody of the Gold Wing."

"But you don't even know how to ride a motorcycle," Marc sputtered.

"Well, then I'll have to learn or you'll have to teach me."

Marc exhaled and then looked resigned.

"Agreed, to everything you say. Honey, I said I love you, and I mean that. I never stopped loving you. You know that, don't you? We just got off track. I am going to get rid of Trisha, find her another job with another firm, something. I don't ever want to see her again. God, when Hannah walked in, I felt so low that she had to see me that way. What a loser I am. You should have seen the way she looked at me. She hates me."

"She doesn't hate you," I said. One thing I did trust about Marc was his fitness as a father, and I knew neither of us wanted our problems to impact Hannah. I was mad at him, but I didn't want to put our daughter in the middle. "She's upset now, but she'll get over it. She wants to see us back together."

"That's what I want too, more than anything," Marc said, "if you would just give me another chance. I was your first, Honey. I want to be your only."

I was still locked in his arms, but I couldn't look at him. Tears were streaming down my face. He wiped them away.

"Marc, since I've been here at Millennium Gardens, I've seen how sweet it is to be in love. Age doesn't matter with people here. What they have together is so special. That's what I want. Someone to grow old with."

"Growing old sucks," Marc muttered.

"Well, yes, it does. But it's going to happen, is

happening. Don't you want someone to grow old together with?"

"I guess if I have to, you're the one I want to grow old with," Marc said. "It's true. I won't mind it as much if we're together. Whatever you want me to do. I can change. I'll be whatever you want me to be."

"I want you to be the man I thought you were," I said stubbornly. I fidgeted with the comforter and tried to shift out of his arms. "I just want you to love me, again, like I'm the only woman in the world who matters to you," I continued, my bottom lip quivering. "That's all, Marc. I just want you to love me."

"Oh, God, I do love you." Marc was close to tears. He was kissing me, first gently, then desperately like he couldn't get enough of me. "Forgive me, please forgive me."

I bit my lip. My body was responding to his, he was saying all the right words, touching me in all the right places. It had been a long time since the two of us had wanted each other like that, desperately, passionately—at least at the same time.

"Marc," I said softly. "We can't do this. Everyone's right out there. I don't want to do this right now." But I was lying to myself and to him.

"I know, Honey, it's just that I want you so much." And I could feel how much he wanted me. I was shaking.

"Honey, I'm sorry. So sorry." We were both breathing heavily. "Tell me what I can do to make this right."

"Sssh," I said. "It's okay. I want to believe you mean that."

"I do," he said, kissing my lips and holding me.

"Do you really think I have a puny pecker?" he said, trying to make me laugh.

"Well, the evidence indicates otherwise," I smiled and got a devilish twinkle in my eyes. "Will you take me for a ride on *my* new Gold Wing?"

"As soon as we get home," he promised. "Now you've got to get me out of here in one piece. Maybe stand between me and your brother."

I laughed. "I should let him take you apart. He's dying to. And you deserve it."

"I know," he said. "Donny never really liked me."

"He has good instincts about people," I replied. "I guess I should be grateful you didn't go after my personal assistant."

"Your personal assistant is a guy."

"Exactly."

"That's very funny," Marc said dryly. "And talking about guys, do I have to be worried about this Max guy?"

"No, actually he's interested in my mother. Oh, Marc, there's so much going on you don't know about. I think Donny's found his father, his real father. It's that big bulk of a man in the living room. I don't really understand it yet. My mother will have to explain it to us. And I know you're against it, but I could really use your help negotiating this merger. I don't want my mother to sell the company. It's the wrong thing to do. And we have to give Mr. Reddekker our answer tomorrow."

"Whatever I can do, I want to help," Marc said sincerely, folding me into his arms. "I want to be there for you, to make it up to you."

"I haven't said I'm forgiving you."

"I know. I have to win back your trust and I'm prepared to do that. To grovel if I have to."

"Groveling is a good first step. What about your job offer in New York?"

"We can talk about that later, at dinner."

"You know I can't go with you, to New York, I mean."

"I know," he said, looking disappointed but resigned.

"And knowing that, you'll still help me negotiate a merger?"

"Yes," Marc agreed.

Trying to meet him halfway, I said, "We'll make it work somehow. I'll visit often. You can fly home. I'll find the time. I promise."

"I need you now, Honey, I need you with me."

"I know, and I haven't been there. But all that will change."

"How can it change if we're living apart?" he sulked.

"I will find a way," I promised. "I'm very persistent."

We strode out of the bedroom hand in hand. A big smile lit up Hannah's face. Donny looked disgusted and disappointed that he wasn't going to be able to rearrange Marc's face.

"You caved," he mouthed. I shrugged.

Right now, Donny had a lot to deal with, and I thought it would be best to leave my brother alone with Daniel, and with my mother, to work things out. Donny was sprawled in a chair and Daniel was sitting on the couch opposite him. Both were brooding and agitated, facing each other warily like sullen bookends. There was still no sign of my mother.

"How about if I steal my two best girls for a fancy dinner?" Marc said, reaching for Hannah's hand, trying to break the tension.

Hannah looked at me and then back at Marc.

"It's okay, honey," I assured her. "It's all okay."

I waited for the inevitable round of negotiations. Hannah and Marc love Mexican food, and when the three of us go out together they always insist on Mexican even though they know how much I hate it.

"How about Italian?" Marc suggested.

"Sounds great, Daddy," Hannah replied sweetly, as if they had already rehearsed the conversation.

Maybe a leopard could change its spots.

"Hannah, what did you do with your Mom's communications toys?"

"Marc, they're not toys," I insisted.

"They're in my purse," Hannah replied, handing them to Marc.

"Now be a good girl and go in and get your dad a nice big glass of something, a soft drink, water, whatever."

Hannah sprinted into the kitchen.

Marc was definitely up to something. He could scarcely contain his smile.

Hannah came back with a tall glass of Diet Coke.

Marc held the BlackBerry gingerly with two fingers and with a gleam in his eye, balanced it over the glass.

"Marc, no!" I screamed, when I realized what he had in mind. "You wouldn't dare drown my BlackBerry." I grabbed it from his hands.

"That's one way to get rid of it. Do you think you

can leave it home for one night?" Marc asked.

I frowned and agreed, managing to look mildly repentant while he confiscated the device.

"And hey, Honey, why don't you go and change. Put on something flashy!"

Surprised, I walked into my room to find the mildew dress. No time like the present to see how much my husband had really changed. When I returned to the living room, Marc whistled.

"You look great in that dress," he said. "Why haven't you ever worn that before?"

I rolled my eyes.

Hannah took Marc's hand and Marc took mine. We walked out the door, our little family intact, at least for the time being.

Chapter Fifteen: Reunions

Donny and I were arguing in whispers about the advisability of barging into the bedroom to talk to his mother when she finally opened the door. Her face was tear-stained, her eyes swollen, her pallor ashen. I noticed she was wearing a tiny diamond chip on a gold band on her wedding-ring finger. That was a milestone, I knew, parting with her husband's ring. I took a closer look at the ring she was wearing. It was the promise ring I had sent her while I was overseas. She was wearing my ring. That must mean something. It was a reason to hope.

"Daniel," she said, looking up at me, blinking away the tears. Something was definitely wrong. "I've got something to tell you." Then she noticed Donny. "And you too, Donny."

"Dorothy," I said, calling her by the name I used to know her by. She looked surprised.

"I took your letters," she said.

"They're *your* letters."

"Then you know?"

"When did you first know?"

"When I saw you walking toward me at the dance," Dee Dee said. "You really haven't changed much. And I thought you'd figure it out when we danced together, and then when we...but you didn't."

"I knew there was something special about you," I

said. "I was drawn to you from the beginning."

"Mom?" Donny asked, concerned. "Are you okay?"

"Oh, Donny," she sighed. "I'm sorry if I worried you and your sister."

He held out the sheaf of letters.

"You read the letters?" she asked.

"Are these my father's letters?" he asked, turning to me. "Is this man my father?"

Dee Dee looked at her son and her face seemed like her heart would break. She couldn't say the words, but she nodded. Her tears wouldn't stop flowing.

Donny's eyes remained locked on mine. Neither of us knew what to do next.

Then I reached out and embraced my son.

"Donny," I said, tears pooling in my eyes. "My son, oh, my son. Are you really my son?"

"D-Dad?" Donny managed, choking on the words he'd been holding back, words he'd wanted to say for so long.

Neither of us could speak for a long time after that. We just hung on to each other, tried to grasp the miracle.

"I want to hear all about your life," I began. "I can fill in the blanks for you about mine. I have so much to tell you, but I don't know what to say, how to start. I'm so sorry I wasn't there for you. I'm so happy to have you now. This place, this tribute you assembled, it's pretty special. We've got a lot of catching up to do, son."

****

I watched the two of them begin to bond, get to know each other for the first time, poring over those infernal World War II books. They were so much alike. Like carbon copies. Of course I had seen that over the years, watching Donny grow up. But now, to see the two of them together, in the same room… Well, it was amazing, sort of like those pictures they show on the sports channel, of famous people who have an uncanny resemblance in the "Separated at Birth" segments. It was like I knew all along something was missing from my life but I never knew what that something was and suddenly, when I had it, all the pieces fit. And all my questions were answered.

But of course this was just the beginning of Donny's questions and his wonder at finding his real father. Not that Stan wasn't the best father in the world to Donny. He had proved that in so many ways. That was why I married him, although it was clear now that Daniel was back in my life that the love I'd felt for Stan was a different kind of love. And for Donny, Daniel was salve on all that bottled-up raw longing, the salve that would finally start the healing process. The two of them had so much to catch up on, so much time to make up for.

Donny wasn't thinking straight now, but he would come to resent me for not telling him about Daniel. Especially when I told them that I knew Daniel was looking for me. I knew he was alive the night before my marriage to Stan. And I did nothing. And I was prepared to face up to that. But when I did, it would be the end of this beautiful dream.

I was determined to return to Atlanta and see the merger through. I couldn't disappoint Honey and Donny. I just couldn't. I knew that. As for Daniel and me, what did we really have? A memory so many years ago. Was that enough to light a spark and reignite a full-blown relationship? I wasn't sure about anything. Did I love Daniel for what he was and what he once meant to me or for the man he'd become? Or did I love him because I was drowning in loneliness? Maybe a little of both. We were two different people now, who had gone off on two different paths. We'd always be connected by Donny, but I knew I was fooling myself if I thought there could be anything more between us. If he would even want there to be. And Daniel's ties were here. His dream was to start his own detective agency right here in Millennium Gardens. And the people here needed him. He could do so much good. So why would he want to follow me to Atlanta?

It had been a trying day for all of us. A lifetime of questions was not going to be resolved in one afternoon. I was exhausted and weak and I couldn't face any more conflict right now. It took some convincing for Daniel to leave. He agreed under one condition. I had to promise to meet with him and Donny together later tonight after I was rested, to sort things out and decide where we would go from there. The whole situation was a big, complicated mess.

Daniel walked out the door, followed by Donny, muttering something about wanting his son to see his uniform.

I needed to get out of there, too. I grabbed a light sweater, ran a brush through my hair, rinsed my face, and put on some lipstick. I was sure my eyes were still bloodshot from all the crying. But since I'd met Daniel, I'd actually started to pay attention to my appearance again. I was finally back among the living. And it felt good. Although I didn't know how Daniel and Donny would feel toward me after we had our talk. Both would blame all those wasted years on me, years that Donny could have known his real father. But I didn't see them as a waste. I was very happy with Stanley, and he was a wonderful father to my son. And if it weren't for Stan, I wouldn't have had Honey. She was the light of my life.

I wanted to wish Max a Bon Voyage. He had been so sweet and shy when he'd withdrawn his invitation to the cruise. It sounded like he'd memorized a script when he called me on the phone. Yes, he'd definitely been practicing. He hadn't wanted to hurt my feelings, I knew. I had been expecting it and I had pretty much decided not to go with him anyway. I was delighted when Birdie came along to take my place.

I opened my front door, and when I turned around to lock it, I noticed a fresh red Seniors Against Sin flyer taped to the outside. Irritated, I tore it off the door, balled it up in my fist, and stuffed it into the pocket of my slacks. I'd discard it in the trash on my way back home from Max's. I walked down the breezeway to the end of the hall. I got to Max's apartment and knocked on the door. There was another red flyer taped to his door. Would these people ever stop? Were they kooks or were they dangerous? I was almost glad I wasn't going to stay in Millennium Gardens long enough to find out. Max would be troubled by the flyer, so I removed it and stuffed it into my other pocket.

It took Max a long time to answer the door.

"Dee Dee," he exclaimed. "What a wonderful surprise." He hugged me.

"Are you all packed?" I asked.

"Yes, my bags are in the spare bedroom. Birdie and I are so excited." Max hesitated. "I mean I'm sure you and I would have had a wonderful time together on the cruise."

"Max, don't be silly. I'm glad you're going with Birdie. She's a lovely woman. And I hear the Caribbean is beautiful this time of year. Well, that's all I came to say. Have a wonderful time, and, well, I won't be here when you get back, so I wanted to say goodbye and thank you for being such a wonderful friend to me."

"No, thank you for being there when I needed you," Max said.

"I guess we kept each other company," I agreed.

"Dee Dee, it was so wonderful knowing you. I hope you'll come back to visit."

"I plan to, and it makes me happy to know you're in good hands."

Max smiled and hugged me again and walked me to the door.

Chapter Sixteen: My Son Has a Million Questions

"Daniel, uh, Dad, thanks for letting me take these albums, and for letting me see your bomber jacket," Donny said, opening the door to his mother's condo. "I want to see all your pictures. I want to know everything about you for all those years we were separated. This will be a great start. I want to know the whole story about you and my mom, from the beginning. Anything you can tell me. Everything you can tell me."

Donny rambled on, "Oh, and I want you to meet my wife. Barbara's great, and my kids..." He hesitated. "Your grandchildren. You've got three beautiful grandchildren."

I beamed. "I've already met your son. He's the image of you. He's great. I can't wait to meet the rest of your family."

"And Dad, hey, you don't mind if I call you Dad, do you?"

"Mind? Of course not," I said, then hesitated, testing the waters. "Son."

Donny looked at me and we both broke out in the biggest smiles. Then, tears threatened again as I looked at my boy. Well, not a boy anymore. A man.

"I've got these books, about the war. Well, I guess you don't need any books. You lived it. It must have been, well, tell me, how was it?"

I smiled at my son. He had a million questions. I

had missed that phase of his life, that part of his growing up, all the questions, but I thought his mother and I should answer them together.

"Do you think we can disturb Dorothy—I mean, Dee Dee—I mean, your mother—and ask her to come out and join us?" I asked. "She could help me tell the story."

"Sure," Donny said. "Let me go get her."

"Mom," Donny whispered, rapping lightly on the partially unhinged door. "Mom, it's Donny. Are you awake? Daniel's here again. We're both here. Could you come out?

"Mom?" Donny called again.

"She must be dead to the world." Donny laughed. "She sleeps a lot, you know, since Dad, I mean since, well, you know."

"I spent a lot of time in my room too, after my wife died," I explained. "And it's okay to call him Dad around me. He was your father for all those years. I'll always be grateful that he was there for you and your mother."

"I'm glad you understand," Donny said, turning on the light. "Because Stanley Palladino was a hell of a father. A hell of a man."

"Mom," Donny called out again, then peeked into the bedroom and found an empty, unmade bed. Puzzled, he turned back to Daniel. "She must be in the bathroom. She's not in the bed."

Donny checked the bathroom, came out, and went straight into Honey's room.

"Bathroom's empty. She's not in Honey's room either. That's strange. She knew we were coming back to talk to her. Let me try calling some of her friends, or my aunt. She may be at Aunt Helene's."

Donny went through his mother's address book and after several phone calls still couldn't locate her.

"She's disappeared," Donny said sullenly.

"You don't think she left to avoid talking to us, do you?" I speculated.

"Well, now that you mention it, I guess I wouldn't want to face the two of us either. Maybe she just went for a walk to, you know, think about things. She spends a lot of time down by that tree. She calls it her Jesus tree. Maybe we should take a look down there."

I hadn't heard anything about a tree, but I was willing to try anything. I desperately needed to find her.

"I'm kind of worried about her. We've both been getting these flyers from some group known as Seniors Against Sin. They're targeting me, your mother, and some other people in the complex."

"Why is this the first I've heard of it?" Donny snarled, turning to me.

I reached into my pocket and handed the nearly destroyed flyer I'd retrieved from my door earlier that morning.

Donny smoothed out the red sheet, read it and scowled.

"What kind of crap is this? Who are these Seniors Against Sin? And what do they want with my mother? My mother is the most decent woman I know."

"I'm looking into it. But I think there might be reason to worry," I said. "There was an elderly couple found dead in their bed right in your mother's building the other day. An elderly couple, 'living in sin.' Now that may just be a coincidence. But I've sent one of these flyers over to a friend of mine at the Sheriff's

Office to dust for prints. It's a long shot. Let's not waste time speculating about that now. We need to find your mother."

We walked out of the condo together and took the elevator to the first floor. By now, it was dark outside. I was beginning to get a bad feeling, and I always trusted my hunches.

"It's this way," Donny motioned.

I followed, then sprinted past my son.

"Mom?" Donny called out.

"Dee Dee? Are you out here?" I echoed.

No answer.

"It's so damn dark out here," I brooded. "You can't see a thing."

"Watch that you don't trip," Donny warned. "There are a lot of dead palm fronds and tree branches left over from the storm."

"Dee Dee?" I called out again.

Suddenly, I saw a crumpled form lying on the ground under a tree. As I got closer, I realized it was Dorothy.

"Dorothy!" Not daring to breathe, I pointed. "She must have tripped and fallen. She was all alone out here. We should never have left her."

"Mom?" Donny cried and ran to his mother. He started to lift her.

"Don't move her," I cautioned. "Is she breathing?"

"I don't know," Donny said.

I swiftly moved him aside, lifted Dorothy's hand, and felt for a pulse.

"Barely," I confirmed. "I think she's lost consciousness. Who knows how long she's been out here. She could have a concussion."

I cradled Dee Dee's head in my lap and pulled out my cell phone. As I moved her I realized there was blood on my pants where her head had rested.

"This is Detective Daniel Moore," I said, shaking. "I need an ambulance at Millennium Gardens. I have an emergency here. Zinnia, Building G. Someone will be there to direct you."

"The police are on their way," I told Donny. "Could you wait in front of the building and bring them back here?"

Donny nodded.

Dee Dee looked so pale in the moonlight, so beautiful. So frail. What if…?

I looked at my son to steady myself. Usually cool and collected, I was about to lose control.

"I can't lose her, not now," I said, choking back the tears. "Not again." I leaned over, smoothed her hair out of her face, and kissed her on the lips, but she didn't respond.

"It's okay, Dad, it will be okay," Donny said, looking on helplessly. He turned toward the building and walked away to direct the ambulance.

Dee Dee still hadn't regained consciousness when the ambulance team took her vital signs and lifted her onto the stretcher.

"I'll go with your mother," I said to Donny. "You find Honey and meet me at the hospital."

Chapter Seventeen: I'm No Prince Charming

"You can go in now, Detective Moore," the nurse said. "The doctor will have her discharge papers ready in a few minutes."

Dee Dee stirred in the hospital bed.

"Detective Moore?" she said, narrowing her eyes.

"I guess you're awake then," I replied sheepishly.

"Are you supposed to be flashing that badge of yours around like that? I thought you were retired."

"I only impersonate an officer when I want to throw my weight around," I pointed out. "When I need to interrogate suspects."

"Is it time for our talk?" she whispered, frowning, looking up at me. "Are you going to interrogate me? I don't think this is a good time. My head, Daniel. It hurts so much. Can you get me some aspirin?"

I reached over to the side table, poured her a glass of water, untwisted the cap, and handed her two pills. "The doctor said you could have these for the pain if you needed it." She looked so damn vulnerable. "I'm not going to question you, for heaven's sake. You're in the hospital."

Dee Dee looked around the room. "What am I doing in a hospital? Did something happen to me?"

"Do you remember anything about last night?" I asked.

Dee Dee pressed her hand to the back of her head

and winced. "I remember saying goodbye to Max, and then I walked outside, over to my tree and—well, the part after that is just a blur. I must have tripped on a branch in the dark and hit the back of my head on a tree root. I guess everyone at Millennium Gardens is talking about this. The silly old woman wandering about in the dark, tripping over dead tree branches."

"They're hardly saying that," I corrected. "And you didn't trip, Dee Dee. You were knocked out. The doctor thinks someone hit you over the head with a flashlight or some other blunt object."

"Who would want to do that?"

"The police are investigating, and I'm helping them. You've been getting those Seniors Against Sin flyers. I'm afraid your 'accident' might have something to do with that group. Did you notice anyone following you last night?"

"Well, I might have heard some leaves rustling, but I didn't think anything of it. I thought it might be a stray cat."

"Hmmph," I groused. "There, uh, was a lot of blood and, well, you were unconscious for we don't know how long."

Dee Dee sat up, alarmed. "Unconscious?"

I pressed her forehead down and eased her head back onto the pillow.

"No sudden movements," I cautioned. "You're fine now, but Donny and I were a little shaken when we first saw you. If we hadn't come along, who knows what would have happened."

When my cell phone rang, I turned to Dee Dee. "Do you mind? I've been expecting this call." Dee Dee shook her head.

I stayed on for several minutes, grunting throughout the conversation.

"Just as I suspected," I said, pocketing my cell phone and taking Dee Dee's hands. "We got the results of the print I found on that flyer on your door. It's a match to Charlotte Simms, or Cher, as you call her. Only her name isn't Charlotte Simms. That's an alias. She has a list of priors a mile long. The woman is not only a vamp. She's a con artist. Those flyers started appearing when she came back in town. The police are going to bring her in for questioning."

"Oh, my, Daniel. I don't like that woman, but I never thought she could do something like that."

"Oh, she's capable of that and a lot worse," I assured her. "In fact, the police think she might have been involved in that couple's death in your building last week. Some kind of love triangle gone wrong. But don't worry. I'm not going to let you out of my sight until we have enough proof to charge her."

I rubbed Dee Dee's hands. "But enough about that. I'm here to take you home. Your kids were here all night, and I finally met Barbara. She's quite a woman. She really had the doctor running scared. The first thing she did was announce that she was an attorney and that nothing better happen to her mother-in-law while she was under his care."

"But Barbara's a divorce attorney," Dee Dee said.

"Doesn't mean she couldn't separate him from his assets. I'm just grateful she was here. You got the best of care, let me tell you. And your son-in-law Marc, he was a big help too. When I convinced the family you were okay, they went back to the apartment to start packing your things. They want to take you back to

Atlanta today. The doctor said it would be okay for you to travel. Hannah wanted to come, but she stayed at the hotel with the kids—my grandkids." I couldn't help beaming. "Our son, he was ordering everyone around, making sure you had everything you needed. I think he would have carried you to the hospital himself if I'd let him. He's very single-minded. I wonder who he takes after?"

"His father, no doubt," Dee Dee said, her eyes twinkling. "Daniel, I know we have to talk about—"

"That can wait till I get you out of this place. You had us all pretty worried. They did X-rays, all kinds of tests. You had to have some stitches. You've got a bandage up here." I touched the affected spot on her head gingerly, but she drew back in pain. "We'll have to keep a close eye on you. You have a lot of friends at the complex who are worried about you. Your sister was here most of the night. I had to forcibly remove her from the room and send her home to get some rest. She called this morning, and apparently we're the big topic of conversation over the breakfast tables and in the clubhouse."

"There's probably going to be a big spread about us in the *Millennium Gardens Gazette*," Dee Dee joked.

"It's already slated for the front page." I grinned.

"I'm just glad I'll be gone by then. I don't think I like being in the spotlight."

I looked at her.

"Did you mean what you just said? You'll be glad to be gone? What about me, us?"

"Daniel, I—"

I sighed.

"Do you remember me kissing you last night?" I

asked softly. "When you passed out, I did everything I could think of to try and wake you up."

"You mean like Sleeping Beauty?"

"I guess I'm no Prince Charming."

Dee Dee took my hand and tears glistened in her eyes.

"You're my hero," she said softly.

That wasn't a commitment, but it was something. Now was not the time to pressure her, but time was running out for us. I could see it in her eyes.

Chapter Eighteen: Second Chances

"I wanted you to see my tree, in the daylight," I said, "before all the leaves start growing back. Somehow I think this tree had something to do with bringing you back to me." The morning light streamed over the golf course and illuminated the live oak tree.

Daniel examined the tree, which was still bare where the face was exposed. He didn't laugh or question my sanity. He just nodded. It was exactly the right reaction.

"But we're not all the way back, are we?" he asked, bringing my hand to his lips and holding it there. "Have you definitely made up your mind to go to Atlanta? Is there anything I can do to change it?"

"I appreciate you finding me and getting me to the hospital. I'll always be grateful."

Daniel swung my hand down but continued to hold it.

"I don't want your gratitude, I want your love," Daniel said sullenly, then he shrugged. "Thank God Donny and I got to you in time."

"You know, I'm just so happy to be alive and here with you," I said.

Daniel looked at me nervously.

"We never did get to have our talk," he remarked.

"I know," I said softly, loving the feel of his fingers twined around mine. "Last night everything was so fuzzy, and I just couldn't focus on anything else. I was so tired."

"Donny and I stayed up all night talking while you were asleep," Daniel said.

"Did you resolve anything?"

"No. We both have more questions. But we were so grateful you are okay, and we were so happy to have found each other that it overshadowed everything. We don't blame you, you know. We love you too much for that."

"You'd have every right to," I said. "I should have had more faith in our love. I should have stood my ground and stayed in Pittsburgh, no matter what my mother said."

"You didn't even know I was alive."

"About that, I did finally know, the night before my wedding," I admitted, biting my bottom lip.

Daniel looked at me with an inscrutable expression.

"My friend came to the wedding, from Pittsburgh, and she said you were looking for me, but it was too late by then," I rushed to explain. "And when my friend told me about the other woman who was with you, I figured you and she were—"

"Natalie was already pregnant by then," Daniel acknowledged, guilt etched in his eyes, "only I didn't know it. I'm sorry. I was at fault for letting that happen. But I had given up hope too. And I wouldn't have left her after she told me. But you have no idea how much I wished it were your child, our child."

"You never knew I had our child. That wasn't fair to you or to Donny. And I wouldn't blame either of you for hating me. For cheating you out of your life together."

"You did the only thing you could have. Your mother was the only one at fault here. But Stanley Palladino gave you and Donny a good life. I'm grateful to him for raising my boy. He did a fine job."

"He did. He was a decent man, and I couldn't do that to him, run away the night before our wedding. And I didn't know if you still wanted me. I wish you had known Stan. He had the biggest heart. He welcomed us into his life and swept us all up in the force of his excitement and love. The Palladino brand of persistence was hard to resist. Once Stan made a decision, there was no stopping him. I'm not sure he would have let me walk away."

Daniel turned serious.

"I never stopped loving you, you know," Daniel whispered.

"And I never stopped loving you," I echoed. "Circumstances kept us apart."

"Hush. You mustn't worry about it. I don't want to waste our last precious minutes alone together."

Last minutes. Oh, dear. How can I let this happen? How can I let him get away again? But there's the business and my children to consider. It was at that very moment that I knew I had made the right decision.

"I don't think they'll go through with the deal without me. I can't destroy my children's legacy. I have to go back to Atlanta."

"I'm not going to let you get away again," Daniel said. "I lost you once and I'm not going to lose you again. If you truly decide to stay in Atlanta, I'm going to follow you. Don't you understand that's what being in love means? It means I can't live without you. I don't want to."

"That's a beautiful sentiment, Daniel," I said. "But your life and your home are here. Your son and his family are here."

"My other son, you mean," Daniel said. "Dee Dee, don't you know that you're my life now, my family? My home is where you are. I have nothing left here but memories. We can make a new life, new memories, together. I want to be near my first son and my grandson, Jackson, and the twins."

"Hayden and Taylor," I said. "The girls are adorable. Jackson is a bruiser. He's going to take after his father and his grandfather."

"I can't wait to meet the girls this afternoon when we all have lunch at my son's house. And then I'm afraid Honey and Donny are going to insist that you get on the road."

"How did Barry react when you told him you have a son by another woman? What must he think of me?"

"I explained the whole story and he can't wait to meet his new family. All of you. And he'll welcome you because he'll see how happy you've made me."

"What about your dream of opening a detective agency at Millennium Gardens?"

"Dreams can change."

"But you told me you have a project," I protested.

"Yes, remember Hank Adams, the man we met at your sister's party, the Vice President of the Millennium Gardens Boca Raton Community Center? He's responsible for security, and he hired me to look into those Seniors Against Sin flyers. I'm very excited about it, even if it doesn't pay much. Normally they'd have had their security contractor look into it, but they wanted to keep it quiet. That kind of thing isn't good for sales. We may have gotten to the bottom of that little problem, but I'm hoping it will lead to more work around here."

"Yes, Millennium Gardens is just a hotbed of crime and sin." I blushed.

"The pheromones are running rampant around here, that's for sure," Daniel agreed, waggling his eyebrows. "Everyone is either having sex or thinking about having sex or wishing they were able to have sex. Present company included. In fact, I think I feel my pheromones beginning to kick up."

"The biological clocks are certainly ticking," I said. "People just want to find love and happiness for whatever amount of time they have left in life."

"That's exactly my point, Dorothy. I want to spend forever, or what's left of the rest of my life, with you."

I sighed. It was hard to think in terms of forever anymore. At Millennium Gardens, forever was a relative term. My son tended to see life in sports metaphors. As Donny might have said, I was at the bottom of the ninth or at best, in the seventh-inning stretch, heading for that big dugout in the sky. I didn't know what was waiting for me out there, but I did know that at that very minute I was right where I wanted to be.

"This is so much to process," I said, clasping and unclasping my hands nervously. "There are so many complications. We've only just met again. And things are moving so quickly. How do we know we can build a life together? How can you be so sure?"

"How can you be so sure we can't? It's Christmas. I believe in miracles, and I think this is our miracle.

Maybe it's fate, but I think maybe God had a plan for us. I don't know how it happened or why it happened or how we found our way back to each other, but are you willing to squander this gift?"

I looked at my tree. Tiny leaves were already beginning to hide the face. By next spring it would no longer be visible. I was afraid I'd never see it again. Afraid I might forget it. My memory wasn't what it used to be. But I remembered Daniel and all the feelings he stirred up inside of me. I searched my heart, and I couldn't hide from the love that was there.

"There's so much to do," I explained. "Stan is still living in my house—I mean, his things. I haven't removed them."

"You must have been in my closet when you looked for the letters. So you've seen that Natalie's things are still there, too. I don't want to betray her memory, either."

"She gave you permission," I pointed out. "Permission to find me."

Daniel touched the trunk of the tree.

"I think this is a strong sign that we have to move forward, not forget or erase the past and the wonderful memories we've shared with others, but to build a new future on the memories we started so long ago. The way I see it, we're lucky. How many people get this kind of chance to start over?"

"You'd be taking on a lot," I said. "Are you prepared for that?"

"Dee Dee, I just can't imagine my life without you in it. I've never felt so sure about anything before. I'm a pretty persistent fellow too. I'm prepared to fight for you, do whatever it takes for us to be together."

"As your significant other?"

Daniel laughed.

"No, there'll be no sneaking around back and forth to each other's condos. If we're going to be together, then we're going to be together all the way. I won't settle for anything less than you as my wife."

I looked down at the ring I had retrieved from Daniel's last letter. It was still on my finger. He wrapped his hand around mine.

"I guess we're already engaged." I laughed.

"Well, as soon as we get to Atlanta, I'm going to buy you a diamond that's worthy of you."

"I want to keep this one," I protested, unable to stem the tears of regret. "The one I should have had. I want the life I should have had with you."

"I know," Daniel said softly. "I can't bring back that life, that time again. And we wouldn't want to. You wouldn't have Honey and I wouldn't have Barry. But we're together now, and I'm ready to start a new life with you. I really don't care where we live. By the way, I got you a Christmas, uh, Hanukkah present," he said, smiling. Daniel reached into his jacket pocket and handed me an envelope.

"You didn't have to do that. I didn't have time to get you anything."

"You're my Christmas present," he said solemnly.

I tore open the envelope eagerly. "Daniel, these are cruise tickets."

"I know," he said, his green eyes twinkling again. "A two-week New Year's cruise to the Caribbean. But don't expect to see too much scenery. We won't be leaving our cabin."

"But I can't leave now. The merger, there's so

much to do. Two weeks away is too long in my business."

"This is going to be our honeymoon cruise. Our needs have to take precedence. And we have a lot of time to make up for. The business will wait. I have a feeling everything will work out. I've already cleared it with your kids. You were going to go on a cruise with Max, weren't you?"

"I don't think I really intended to go through with that."

"That's because Max is not the love of your life."

I turned to Daniel, and he took me into his arms and kissed me with familiar tenderness. I didn't want to live my life without this man. That was one thing I *was* sure about.

"Okay, I'll go," I agreed. "But what about your new job? You have a lot to investigate."

"The police are handling that," Daniel said. "That can wait, but we can't. Let's tell the kids. We have a lot to celebrate this year."

Chapter Nineteen: The Most Important Things

It was Christmas Day, my birthday. But as usual, no one had acknowledged it. Hannah and I were lying on the couch at Mom's condo, our heads resting on the armrest at either end, our feet touching, nestled under a warm cashmere throw, reading our respective novels. It felt so good not to be on the phone or working. I couldn't remember the last time I had actually read a book. My brain had truly been on overload. Now that I was not moving at warp speed, I could see how hard I'd been pushing myself.

How often had I just relaxed like this? All my problems and pressures were receding, literally seeping out of my head. The absence of deadlines was glorious. I felt bone lazy and languorous, and it felt wonderful. I was truly enjoying the slower pace of life here. Millennium Gardens had worked its magical spell on me.

We were all packed. Donny and Barbara were going to swing by later and load everything into their rented SUV. I had been expecting Marc to stop by and at least wish me Happy Birthday, but he hadn't. Maybe he had reconsidered wanting to reconcile. Maybe I was just too much work. Or maybe I just worked too much. What Marc did was wrong, lying to me about his job and bringing Trisha into our home, but I realized with a sudden clarity that I had all but ignored him since my father's death—and way before that. I was all consumed with Palladino Properties and hadn't saved enough time for my own husband. Last night, we'd had a nice family dinner, and when Donny called to tell me Mom was in the hospital, he was a godsend. At the end of the night, however, at my insistence, Marc had gone back to his hotel room. Hannah and I stayed at my Mom's condo.

"Mom?" Hannah asked. "You awake?"

"Hmmm?" I murmured, barely able to muster enough energy to respond.

"I wonder if I could ask you a few questions about the business. I know I have to make a decision about my future, and I'm wondering what it will be like to work at Palladino Properties. I think I want to work there after college, but maybe there are other opportunities out there I'd like better. I don't even know if I have what it takes to be successful, like you and Grandma have been. But I want us to have that closeness you had, to work together. I want that very much."

I smiled and reached for her hand.

"That's very sweet. I want that too."

"And there's no doubt in my mind you'll be a success at anything you do," I said, slipping off my reading glasses and placing my book on the coffee table. This time I paid attention to my daughter, really paid attention.

"You're persistent, and persistence pays." Hannah laughed, no doubt remembering her Grandpa Stanley's mantra.

"But in our business you also need to be aggressive, and you need to be flexible. You need to be able to change gears at a moment's notice. And you're always in demand. Clients are like kids, needy little children. They hang on you, and if you care about them, it's easy to become emotionally vested. They need to know what's going on all the time. You have to tend to them. You can rarely go on vacations because you have to work.

"Grandma's more selfish about her time. She doesn't take every client who comes along. She's more selective. I'm more chained to the job," I admitted. "The biggest downside to the business is that your time is not your own. Let's say a couple comes in from Ft. Lauderdale who is thinking of moving to Atlanta. You have a nice family weekend planned, but they're coming in on a Thursday and they want to look at everything, right through to Monday. People love to sightsee. You're expected to drop what you're doing and give up your weekends and holidays. Until this one, there hasn't been one Christmas where I haven't had a major deal going. But most people aren't even sure about what they want. Grandpa Stanley always used to say, 'Buyers are liars.' And what he meant was that buyers don't know what they want until they see it. They tell you they want a one-story and then they buy a split-level. They tell you they want a house with a basement and then they buy on a slab. It's an emotional decision.

"The pro to this business is that you do have freedom, mobility. You can be outside. To some extent, you're the manager of your own time, the master of your destiny. It's a fabulous career, and you can earn a lot of money if you work hard and you have good contacts. You can control your own schedule.

Especially if you have your mother pinch-hitting for you."

"Will I be able to support myself when I first start out?" Hannah asked.

"Well, you have no predictor of income," I said. "The market is always fluctuating. You could have four good months and then go six months with no income. I used to worry about those dry spells. The times when I didn't have a call in two weeks or a sale in six months. You've got to have another source of income, especially the first three years. It takes a minimum of three years to build up your business. You can't eat or even pay your fees if you don't have another means to support yourself or another income. But you won't have to worry about that. You'll come in with a built-in business. That's why Hammond Reddekker is interested in us. He's anxious to strengthen his company's presence in the Southeast. He's impressed with our prestigious portfolio, our quality real estate products and services, and Grandma and Grandpa's experience, vision, and leadership track record."

"But I don't want any special favors just because I'm your daughter," Hannah said.

"And I wouldn't give them," I answered. "You'll earn your own way. If you work all the time and you have a number of assistants, you can be very successful. But you have to be a real dynamo."

"Then I'd have to work too hard," Hannah said.

"I was a workaholic when I first established myself," I admitted.

Hannah shook her head. "Mom, you're still a workaholic."

I frowned because this wasn't the first time I'd

heard that accusation. Hearing the truth from my husband was one thing, but to have it confirmed by my daughter really brought it home. I think my mother was trying to tell me the same thing for years, but I hadn't been listening.

"Why did you decide to go into the business?" Hannah wanted to know.

"Well, I'd seen how good Grandma was at it. I had done the nine-to-five thing before and I was successful, but I wanted to be in command of my own job, wanted to run my own business."

"Didn't you ever worry about working so closely with Grandma?" I knew she was really asking whether she and I could work together.

"Well, at the beginning I did worry that I couldn't do it. That it would be too much mother-daughter togetherness. That I could never do things the way she wanted. Originally, she wanted an assistant. I knew I could never please her, that I'd never be able to do it right. I knew I had to be a realtor, have my own business in my own right, before I felt secure enough emotionally to be able to take criticism from my mother. I didn't want my success to be predicated on hers."

"Exactly," Hannah said. "You do understand."

"Yes, but that's not the way it was at all. She got me started. At first, we co-listed some properties, not everything. She had her own business going. I brought a few clients of my own to the table. So while we teamed listings in the beginning, eventually she put me on my own listings. By and large, we each had our own buyers, but typically when we list a house, we'll work it together."

"What if we team up and I get married and my husband doesn't like that arrangement?"

"Well, that depends on how my future son-in-law will feel about me. I'm not so sure about the Mormon."

"Mom, I'm not marrying the Mormon. We're not even dating, officially."

"Okay, well, if your husband's not supportive or has any issues with me, that's another story. A man can be jealous, and he might not like the time his wife spends with her mother. He'll say she expects too much, calls too often. There was a point where Daddy felt that way about Grandma."

"How could anybody not love Grandma?"

"It's not that he didn't love her; he was jealous of all the time I spent with her, away from him." *Why didn't I see that before?*

But Marc was a dangerous topic that the two of us had agreed to avoid for now.

"Did you ever have arguments with Grandma?"

"We never had an argument. That's the uniqueness of a mother-daughter team. We're not driven by money and who gets what and what is fair. We're a family."

"What about working with Uncle Donny? How is that?"

"Donny is a natural at residential real estate," I answered. "Right now, the Atlanta housing market is starting to recover. We're experiencing strong, steady growth and we're not as subject to the volatility experienced in other markets. But Donny's ability to reduce inventory, even in a softening market, during a slowdown of new housing starts, or a 'housing bubble,' is nothing short of miraculous. Donny is very believable, and he's a man of his word. But I think it has more to do with Donny's looks and magnetic personality than the fact that Atlanta is a desirable place to live and has one of the best housing values in the nation."

"Yeah, Uncle Donny is hot," Hannah agreed.

"Hot or not, Donny and I make a terrific team. My mother and I also make a great mother-daughter team. And so will we, sweetheart."

Hannah put down her book. "What's the secret of your success?"

I put down my book, too, closed my eyes, and started talking. "The average homeowner will move every three to seven years. And I have the ability to match my clients with the perfect house: whether they want a bigger house—new construction or a resale; a second home; have to move for their jobs; want a different school district; or are retiring and need to downsize to a condo. And I can usually do it within a month, sometimes a week, but that's rare. Luck has a lot to do with it.

"That mystique is just part of the reason our firm is so successful. And now I feel like I've been reborn because I'm getting all these first-time homebuyers, children of my original clients who want to buy condos. Or my clients have come full-circle and have to move out of their homes because they get sick and must move into condos or assisted living facilities. I don't want to turn them down when it's personal like that, even though some of the properties they're interested in are pretty low-end. I'm busy enough with high-end business, the luxury market, but every client is important to me.

"In the end, as Grandpa Stanley used to say, 'this

business is all about selling dreams.' "

"One more thing," Hannah asked. "Will I have to use a BlackBerry? I'm kind of fond of my iPhone."

"Well, you'll need a computer and a mobile phone. Realtors who are very successful, are selling all the time and have great business skills, will generally want some kind of palm pilot. Most of us are just technologically adequate, not necessarily very skilled. We can do it, but if you're busy selling and you're in the car, or taking a class, you're not at your computer seven hours a day. You can pay assistants to do that. The really successful realtors don't pull listings from a computer. They're connected; they have great referral sources. I'd say ninety percent of realtors operate out of a daytimer. They write it down. That works fine. That's what Grandma does. That's what I used to do until Vicky got hold of me and dragged me into the twenty-first century. She's trying to convince me to upgrade our computer system. But forty percent of realtors use palm pilots. They can be incorporated into your lockbox key. So you can have one tool that lets you in doors and has all your data. This merger, if it goes through, will give us access to the latest technology."

"I think this is the first time I've ever seen you really relax," Hannah observed, continuing, "What about time? Will there be enough time for children?"

"Well, of course there will be time. I had you, didn't I?"

Hannah paused before she spoke.

"Mom, don't take this the wrong way, but I want to be the kind of mother who will be there for her children. And I want more than one. And I want them to know that they're the most important things in my life...more important than work."

Tears welled in my eyes, threatening to spill over.

"Is that the way you felt?" I levered myself up and stared straight into my daughter's eyes.

"I always knew you loved me," Hannah said. "But I always got the feeling that your work came first."

I swiped at the tears with the back of my hand.

"Nothing is more important to me than you, sweetheart. I thought you knew that."

"Don't cry," Hannah said. "I didn't mean it as a criticism. Grandma was there for me when you couldn't be. But all those times, I wanted you."

I sat up all the way and hugged my daughter across what seemed like an impassable gulf.

"Oh, God, Hannah, I never knew you felt that way."

"And maybe Dad did too," Hannah answered.

I didn't know what to say. I was blindsided. All of a sudden the image of myself as the strong, super career woman shattered into a million pieces. I had been so caught up in that life that I'd let the precious years with my daughter slip away. I slumped back on the couch, full of doubts and regrets.

And maybe Hannah was right about how I had shut Marc out. Maybe, now, I understood how he felt.

After we stopped talking, I closed my eyes. Just a little nap. That's what I needed.

Chapter Twenty: The Gift

I felt a tug on my throw and I pulled it back up to my chin. I didn't want to leave my cocoon. I felt something warm and wet on my nose and my lips.

"What?" I said, sitting up, still drowsy.

"Happy Birthday, sweetheart," Marc whispered in my ear.

"Where's Hannah?" I asked.

"She's over saying goodbye to your aunt," Marc said.

"And Mom?"

"I guess she's saying goodbye to Daniel."

"Oh," I said, thinking what a shame that she and Daniel were not going to get their happy ending. Donny had gotten his Hanukkah present—a father. But my mother was determined to go back to Atlanta and see the merger through. I knew she was doing it for our sakes. She deserved a rest after all these years. She deserved to be happy. But she was a Palladino, and Palladinos were persistent. She didn't want to spoil this opportunity for Donny and me. And it was my fault. I'd pressured her into it.

"I have your birthday present," Marc said, grinning from ear to ear. "I hope you're going to like it."

"You didn't have to get me a present, Marc."

"I wanted to." He sat down beside me on the couch.

"Here, let me show you."

He handed me a festively wrapped package.

"All I could find was Christmas wrap," he apologized.

"That's fine," I smiled. "You know I love Christmas."

I untied the ribbon and tore open the wrapping. When I peeled back the tissue paper, I didn't recognize what I was looking at.

"It's an electric coat liner and gloves," Marc explained. "It's sort of like an electric blanket. You wear that under a heavy outer jacket and plug this wire into the connection on the bike. Then the thermostat regulates the heat."

"Oh, it's for the Gold Wing," I said, suddenly understanding. "Thank you."

"Well, that's just part of it."

"Now here's your Hanukkah present. That goes with it."

I opened the second gift and was touched to see Marc had bought me my own helmet with my name, *Honey Palladino Bronstein*, engraved on it.

"Oh, this is so nice," I said, tears springing to my eyes.

"But that's not the best part," Marc said. "There's another gift."

He handed me a flat package, which I hurriedly opened.

"A map?" I asked as I pulled the paper out of the box.

"Not just any map," Marc said, smoothing it out on the coffee table. "Look, I've marked the route of the trip we're going to take, at least I hope you'll agree to take it with me."

"What kind of trip?" I asked.

"Okay, see here, we're going to take a trip across the Western United States and into Canada. We'll start off in Atlanta, then ride to Blue Springs, Missouri, then on to Boulder, Colorado, then to Frisco, Colorado, then Leadville," he said tracing the path with his fingers. "Then we're going to take the Million Dollar Highway through the Rocky Mountains, to Black Canyon, then go to Durango and over to Ouray. Then we'll make overnight stops in Moab and Cedar City, Utah. Next, we'll head to the Grand Canyon, through the desert to the Pacific Coast Highway, Monterrey, and on to San Francisco, then to Lake Tahoe, Napa, Sacramento, and Portland. We'll do all the touristy things, eat crab and stare at the sea lions at Fisherman's Wharf, sample wine in Sonoma, see the redwood trees. All the things we never had time to do."

"I'm sure the pioneers would have loved to have had a Honda Gold Wing on their journey across the country." I laughed.

"I'm not through," Marc said seriously. "We're going to take the ferry to Victoria Island and then, and you'll love this, we go to Canada, to Jasper and Banff and through Banff National Park, then on to Waterton, in the Canadian Rockies, where I've got us a reservation at the Prince of Wales Hotel. Then we travel to Glacier National Park and Butte and Red Lodge, Montana. Then it's on to Yellowstone National Park and to Grand Teton National Park. We'll travel on Going-to-the-Sun Road to Wyoming and down the Beartooth Highway. It has an elevation of about 13,000 feet. We'll return to Atlanta on Highway 90 through

Nebraska, Iowa, and Kentucky. We're going to criss-cross the entire country."

I looked up at Marc. He had hardly paused to take a breath, he was so caught up in his plans. I didn't think I'd ever seen him so excited.

"Marc, this sounds like a long trip."

"I figure maybe about a month."

"A month!" I exclaimed, then bit my lip when his face crumpled.

"The Gold Wing is perfect for long-distance riding," Marc argued. "I know it's a long time to take off. But we won't be leaving till mid-May. By then you'll have smoothed out the kinks in this investor deal, and maybe Donny can take up the slack. Your mother will be there too. And if it works out that Vicky is appointed CEO, like you suggested, she'll be a big help to you. And I figure we need this trip, this time alone. It will be just you and me together, roughing it. It'll be raining and cold sometimes, but the scenery is going to be so spectacular. It will be an unbelievable adventure. Maybe we'll even see a whale or a gray timber wolf or a herd of buffalo. We'll cram our iPod full of music and take audio books. And that electric liner will keep you nice and warm. And I'll keep you warm, baby. Please say you'll come with me."

He looked so hopeful. How could I disappoint him? I thought of all my commitments, all the hard work ahead. A month was a lifetime to be away in the real estate business. So many things could change. So many sales lost. So many missed opportunities. And all of a sudden, just like that, I could see what was important. And it wasn't the job or the money or even the merger. What was important was sitting right here next to me on the couch.

"Marc," I whispered. "I'd love to go with you. We'll make it work somehow."

He gathered me into his arms and held me, like I was his most precious possession, and then he looked into my eyes and bent down to kiss me gently on the lips.

"Thank you, Honey," he smiled. "Thank you."

"Marc, could you take another look at the merger contract? We were so dazzled we couldn't see beyond the offering price."

"Are you currently being represented by a law firm?" Marc asked.

"Well, no, but maybe you could represent us through your firm. It would be a big piece of business."

Marc took my hand.

"You trust me to handle this for you...after what I put you through?" Marc asked.

I hesitated, but answered honestly, "I do."

"Somehow I doubt that Donny wants me on board," Marc said dryly.

"Well, I'll admit he was hesitant at first, but when I told him we were trying to work things out and that I love you, he—"

"You love me?" Marc asked hopefully.

I nodded.

"Oh, Honey, I know I'm still on trial with you, but I want us to work, and I'm going to be the kind of husband you can be proud of. I really do love you." He embraced me and kissed me, the kind of kiss he used to give me when we first fell in love.

"I think it would help if you made an overture to Donny," I suggested. "Meet him halfway. Possibly ask if you could go to a Braves game with him, let him give you a play-by-play."

"You know I hate sports," Marc said flatly.

"What I don't know is why? What do you have against baseball?"

"Ron Rafferty," Marc answered.

"Huh?"

"Your brother reminds me of Ron Rafferty."

"Who is Ron Rafferty?"

"He was this kid I went to school with. Well, actually he was more than a kid. He looked like Arnold Schwarzenegger on steroids. He was the biggest jock and the biggest jerk and the biggest pain in my ass. He was also the biggest..." Marc hesitated.

"Bully?" I guessed.

"Sounds like you knew him," Marc said.

"Every school has a Ron Rafferty, or a female version, who picks on your imperfections and insecurities and makes you feel bad about yourself," I said. Having Donny Palladino as a brother had been a blessing for a girl whose hips were too wide and nose was too large. He saved me from a world of grief. If anyone even looked at me cross-eyed, they had to answer to my big brother.

"Ron Rafferty made sure I never fit in, that I never got picked for the team, any team," Marc said. "Or if I did, I was always picked last. No one ever chose me. I was always too uncoordinated, and Ron never passed up an opportunity to remind me of my weaknesses. And if he did pick me for his team, it was just to trample all over me. I never got to play. I was always too small. So I had to be smarter. But it's not something you ever forget."

"I chose you," I said quietly.

Marc pulled me into his arms and held on tight.

"I know, and that's one of the reasons I love you. You could have had anyone, and you chose me. And I'm going to make you glad you did."

Marc released me and asked, "Do you have a copy of the proposed contract with you?"

"Yes, it's in my briefcase," I said, and pulled out a copy for him to review.

Marc spent the next half hour reviewing the contract, making notes in the margins.

"You finished the contract already?"

"I've been over it with a fine tin fork," Marc said.

"Toothed comb," I replied.

"Huh?"

"It's a fine-toothed comb."

Marc was grinning. He was starting to sound more and more like my father.

"What are you smiling about?" I wanted to know.

"It's a good thing you pulled me in on this before you signed."

"What's wrong?"

"Nothing major, but I know I could get you more money, and more control, and a greater share of future profits, to start with," Marc began, "if I have permission to negotiate for you."

"You do," I said. "I've already cleared it with my mother."

"Okay, then, I'm going to make a few phone calls, call in some favors, do a little digging before I give Mr. Hammond Reddekker a call. Do you have his home number?"

"Yes, but are you really going to bother him on

Christmas Day?"

"Why not? The contract deadline is today, so I think he would expect to be bothered," Marc said. "Is your Fax set up?"

"Yes, it's right over there," I said. "Thank you for handling this. But one thing—since you'll be replacing Trisha, I get to screen your new secretary."

Marc laughed.

"She'll have to be at least sixty-five, as flat as a board, and as blind as a bat so she can't see how luscious her new boss looks. I'm going to have to keep a closer eye on you from now on, like Barbara does on Donny."

"Please don't even mention that woman's name," said Marc. "No more talk of divorce. I'm going to give you a reason to come home early," Marc promised. "No more working late. And no more BlackBerry when you get home. You've formed more of an attachment to that thing than you have to me. You're the only thing I want vibrating in our bedroom. And the only person I want you to keep in touch with 24/7 is your husband. From now on, we put each other first."

As if on cue, my cell phone rang and I automatically picked it up.

"Honey Palladino—"

Marc grabbed the phone and finished off my sentence.

"Is unavailable at the moment. Please try your call again later—much later. And it's Honey Bronstein!"

"Marc, did you just hang up on someone?"

"Yep. It's Christmas. If I have to fight for us to have time together, I will."

He put his arm around me, and I nestled my head

against his shoulder.

"I really miss my little Honey Bunny," he said, and I snuggled closer.

"You haven't called me that since we first started dating," I marveled.

"Well, that's how I feel, like we're starting over."

After a while we walked out onto the patio and looked down at the Jesus tree. I saw my mother and Daniel underneath the tree, arms linked, looking like they never wanted to let each other go.

"Marc, what can we do about them?" I wondered. "They are so clearly meant for each other. And now some miracle has brought them back together. It would be a shame to lose something that precious. My mother thinks she needs to be tied to the business, but she's given her life to it and now she deserves a life of her own. I understand that now.

"My God, when I think how close we all came to losing her last night!" I sighed. "If Daniel and Donny hadn't thought to look outside under the tree, and if they hadn't gotten to her in time, I don't know what would have happened. We're all so grateful to Daniel. He stayed with Mom all night. And he displayed the Palladino brand of persistence.

"And of course Daniel is now Donny's hero all over again." I smiled. "You can see how in love Daniel is with my mother. I want so much for things to work out for them. But I don't see how they can."

"Let me see what I can do," Marc said. Then, after he had made and received several phone calls, he advised, "Sit back and watch the master at work."

Marc dialed the phone and reached Hammond Reddekker on the first ring. I could only hear Marc's side of the conversation. Marc's reputation as a top-notch attorney was well deserved. He certainly didn't sound like he lacked confidence.

"Yes, Mr. Reddekker, this is Marc Bronstein with Ludlam, Powell and Bronstein in Atlanta. I'm head of the firm's M&A section. First, let me wish you a Merry Christmas. I'm representing Palladino Properties in the buyout.... Since today, as a matter of fact," Marc answered. "My connection with the Palladinos? My wife is Honey Palladino Bronstein.... That's right.... Yes, Honey Palladino is a very impressive woman. In fact, she and her brother have been running the firm for the past year, while Dee Dee Palladino has been busy establishing the Boca Raton branch of Palladino Properties to take advantage of the booming market in waterfront properties.... Yes, I've reviewed the contract. Your initial offer is very attractive. It's a very good starting point."

I waved my hands and made a face, imploring Marc to be cautious or Mr. Reddekker and his millions were going to walk away from the table. He was clearly ignoring my urgent signals.

He continued, "My clients were inclined to accept, but we'd like to make some minor adjustments to the language and the terms. If you'd be kind enough to give me your Fax number, I'll shoot the revised contract right over with my recommended changes. I just wondered if you were aware that there are other offers on the table. And that we've been approached by an investment bank about an IPO that has some merit. We're weighing all our options. We'd like to get this wrapped up before the end of the day.... Yes, you can reach me at this number for the rest of the day.... Great.

Well, I'll look forward to hearing from you, sir."

Marc hung up the phone. I jumped on him and started pounding.

"Are you crazy? The offer he made us was more than generous. And the part about the Boca branch? We don't have a Boca branch."

"Well, then, I suggest you get busy picking up some waterfront listings. That way your mother can spend as much time as she wants here with Daniel."

"And what you said about the other offers, that's not true."

"No, but it could be if I pursued it, and besides, Hammond Reddekker was only offering you a fraction of what your firm is worth, and he knows it. I'm just asking for more capital to help your company expand and negotiating a little more flexibility to ensure that your family will continue to have local control of the company's day-to-day operations. Don't worry. He's not going to back away. I thought I was being extremely reasonable."

"Marc Bronstein!"

"Honey, you said you trusted me. Do you?"

Now there was a question. I used to think I could trust my husband implicitly, but he'd let me down. What I realized was that, even though he'd lied to me, what I told him a few minutes ago was true. I still trusted him.

"Yes," I answered, "but all this uncertainty is making me crazy. And what was that comment about Donny and me running the firm? My mother and father built this firm. My mother's role in this company is essential."

"I was just setting the stage," Marc explained.

"You said your mother doesn't really want to work so hard anymore. She needs the flexibility to be able to control her own destiny, and so do you and your brother. The way I'm setting this deal up, you'll be holding all the cards. Your mother can be as free as a bird or she can work as hard as she wants. This deal isn't based on her commitment to stay on as CEO or in any other capacity for a certain number of years. And this contract will be ironclad. Reddekker will never be able to make a move without you and Donny. But it's still your mother's deal. She signs on the dotted line and she gets the proceeds of the deal."

"I just hope he doesn't decide this whole thing is not worth it," I fretted. "We had so many plans."

"Do I look worried?" Marc replied. "You have to have nerves of steel in this business. And you can't be the first to blink. I thought I'd lost it, but I'm still on top of my game. Come on, that Fax machine is going to go off in no time with Reddekker's counteroffer. And then we can finalize this deal and get on with our lives. In the meantime, I have an idea about how to work off some of this tension you're feeling. All this wheeling and dealing is really getting my blood flowing. And as long as we're in the bedroom..."

"Marc!"

"Get that trim little butt of yours over here, Honey Bunny," Marc ordered.

About a half hour later, when I was lying in Marc's arms and he was kissing my face, I thought I heard a noise. "Is that my BlackBerry?"

"It better not be," Marc said, frowning. "It's the Fax. Let me go get it."

When he came back to bed, he was carrying a sheaf

of loose papers and smiling smugly.

"Give me those," I insisted.

He handed me the loose sheets.

"Oh, my God," was all I could say after I'd skimmed the sections with changes. "He's doubled his offer. And he's agreed to all your terms. And look, he's even agreed not to change our company name. Now my father's name will become a household word. Thank you, Marc!"

"I knew that would mean a lot to you," he answered, assuring me, "Reddekker wants this deal so bad he can taste it. Let me just give him a quick call and tell him to Fax over a clean copy so your mom can review and sign it. And I saved the best for last. Do you know what he said to me at the end of that last call? He said, 'Bronstein, you drive a hard bargain. I could use a man with your talents. How would you like to come to work for me?' When I told him I couldn't leave Atlanta, he said he'd throw some business my way. Even having a fraction of Hammond Reddekker's business would be a windfall for our firm."

"Oh, Marc, that's wonderful," I said. "Now you won't have to take the job in New York. This is a wonderful birthday/Hanukkah/Christmas present!" I wrapped my arms around my husband. "I don't know how to thank you."

"Oh, I can think of a way," Marc said softly and took me into his arms. "Reddekker can wait. But I can't."

A word about the author...

Marilyn Baron is a public relations consultant in Atlanta. She's a PRO member of Romance Writers of America (RWA) and Georgia Romance Writers (GRW) and winner of the GRW 2009 Chapter Service Award.

She writes humorous women's fiction, romantic suspense, historical romance, and paranormal. She graduated from The University of Florida in Gainesville, Florida, with a Bachelor of Science degree in Journalism and a minor in Creative Writing.

Born in Miami, Florida, Marilyn lives in Roswell, Georgia, with her husband, and they have two daughters. She loves to travel. Her favorite place to visit is Italy, where she studied for six months in her junior year of college.

Read Marilyn's other books published by The Wild Rose Press, Inc.: Her historical (romantic thriller) *Under the Moon Gate*, and its prequel, a historical, *Destiny: A Bermuda Love Story*. She also has a suspense series at The Wild Rose Press, beginning with *Sixth Sense* and *Homecoming Homicides*, with others to follow.

Author e-mail:

marilyn@marilynbaron.com

Petit Fours and Hot Tamales blog:

www.petitfoursandhottamales.com

To find out more about Marilyn and her books, visit her Web site at:

www.marilynbaron.com

Also available from The Wild Rose Press, Inc.

Under the Moon Gate by Marilyn Baron
http://amzn.com/B00CGDQ1S4

Letters and Lace (The Ronan's Harbor Series) by M. Kate Quinn
http://amzn.com/B00C1K5JYY